Miles
From
Nowhere

Miles From Nowhere

A Novel
by
GEORGE A. HOPKINS

MILL CITY PRESS

Mill City Press, Inc.
2301 Lucien Way #415
Maitland, FL 32751
407.339.4217
www.millcitypress.net

Paperback ISBN-13: 978-1-6628-3918-4
Dust Jacket ISBN-13: 978-1-6628-4521-5
Ebook ISBN-13: 978-1-6628-3920-7

For Mitch and Beau
I'm sorry for the times I failed.
I'm so proud of both of you.

TFMMDCT

People are not stupid because they can't write novels,
but because they can't conceal them when they do.

—**Anton Chekhov**

When the summer's ceased its gleaming
When the corn is past its prime
When adventure's lost its meaning
I'll be homeward bound in time
Bind me not to the pasture
Chain me not to the plow
Set me free to find my calling
And I'll return to you somehow

—**Marta Keen Thompson**

Prologue

When I was young, I wondered why my parents never smiled. With time, I watched as my siblings developed the same disposition. In America, they say that your dreams will take you as far as your talents will allow. That's not really true.

Sumner Plaine was the only home I knew. My parents carried me across the border when I was two years of age so technically, S.P. was not my first home. Zacatecas still holds that ultimate moniker for Mama and Papa. That's where they smile, I'm told. To them, Sumner Plaine is a consequence. It holds no place in their collective hearts. My siblings, who are much older, and my parents believe that I should feel the same. That I should somehow long for a land I do not remember. To my family, S.P is a long way from nowhere. It would never be home.

Home. It's the first thread laid and the last strand broken. It is the substance of all unbreakable relationships. Any relationship without a common community can never be as strong. Your hometown itself becomes a parent, and all good guardians thrive in our company yet want us to go. They revel in our independence because they know they will endure within us despite the fact that we pull away. Their essence remains even when their presence isn't felt. Home is our entrance into a world that we long to be part of.

Sumner Plaine is the seat of Sumner County. Halfway between somewhere and nowhere, offering something and nothing, existing at one time or another. Close enough to the Rockies to feel their effect, too far to enjoy their benefit. Here clouds are rare. Rain is rarer. Most outsiders assume ag products are our principal invention but all who live here know that our primary commodity is wind, and like all assets in excess supply where there is no demand, it is impossible to get rid of, even when it's free. The dust on the horizon absorbs any blue it comes in contact with. Late in the day, the fusion leaves behind a hue within a color scheme that can't possibly exist, something like a brown paper towel that has cleaned up spilled Blue Raspberry Kool-Aid. Yet nearly every evening, after the shrouded horizon has given up its identity, the disengaged image becomes a veiled scape of fine dust particles trying to escape their earthly confines and subtly altered wavelengths inversely attempting to find a place away from their heavenly source. As the day concludes and the solar orb finds its evening home, a new realm is created; one that you'd swear could only exist in the imagination of God. Like receiving an unexpected gift, sunsets here can leave you speechless.

Sumner Plaine, known to the faithful as S.P., is a quiet prosperous ag-based community claiming few noteworthy personal identifiers. To our east, there was a world-famous athlete who broke the four-minute mile as a high school student. The world witnessed that young man's hope for Olympic Gold dashed as he finished second in the '68 Mexico City Games. The whole world talked about that. Here, we've had no such athlete. To our north, a wounded WWII veteran methodically came to political prominence and ended his career only one election shy of the presidency. The whole country witnessed that. Here we've had no such politician. To our west, a murder occurred that was infamous enough to spawn a book (and subsequent movie) written by an out-of-place New Yorker who decided to change the literary landscape of his time. The entire nation read about that. In our wholesome county, we have yet to experience our first murder, so there's nothing like that to talk about.

To the world around us, it's not that we don't exist, it's that we exist without purpose. Like brown M&Ms or ear hair, no one knows why we are here. This is fly-over country. I once told a woman I met in a Kansas City coffee shop where I lived. She said she hadn't heard of it but was pretty sure they fly over us on their spring break skiing trips to Aspen. We make jokes about our home too. The difference is, we don't believe the jests. Sumner Plaine is at the core of each one of us, yet it is much more than that. It is the warmth that incubates our birth. It is the caul of our inspiration; a perpetual embryonic membrane that not only shelters us but keeps our dreams from desiccating with time. It is the invisible nutrient of our growth and the conspicuous comfort in our demise.

I would like to think that I was somehow part of what makes this portion of southwest Kansas important. I wish I somehow played a role in its character. Immigrants are vital to the region. It was on our backs that the agriculture industry was able to sprout during that period in history when the bulk of the region, those which were unwilling to open their doors to such an influx, struggled to find their own economic root system. But that's immigration as a whole. An individual immigrant, like myself, is of limited value in the eyes of most. Too many times each one of us have been looked down upon, insulted, violated, and worst of all, ignored. All of these have happened to my family enough to chase them back to their place of comfort. They came because they searched for money. They returned because they lost their dignity. I stayed because I had hope. And because I had an uncle with a restaurant and a green card.

My life struggles were similar to my parents'; though even in the midst of personal difficulty there were moments of acceptance, accomplishment, even joy. But as I am dying and look back on my life, I realize that it was the potential of acceptance and accomplishment that gave me the perception of happiness, not true joy. And I did have potential. I was smart. I was pretty. I was fluent. I played by the rules. Yet I realized early on that it was my pedigree that restricted my capabilities, not my talent. I even tried to re-create a more direct connection to my new home. I looked for relationships with people who were born into the life I wanted. I tried to attach my hope for change to their connection with the status quo. Other than Papa, I loved only two men in my life. Both were Anglo. Both were bona fide. In the end, they brought me only heartache. In the end, nothing that I dreamed of ever emerged.

Death is inevitable, an understatement. I suppose it is unique to all though I don't know how that can be determined. For me, hearing was the first to go. I could see what was being done with my lifeless body. It made me sad, an emotion that quickly faded. My sense of touch was gone for I didn't feel any of my movements. The dryness to my mouth had no taste. My sense of smell was next yet the memory of the aroma remained. I remember that final sense of musty field crops with the ever-present hint of cattle drifting on the breeze, migrating much like the inhabitants of Sumner Plaine. And just after my sight grew too dim to recognize, the last bit of cognition clenched to my existence. I went from "what just happened" to "what's happening," from "not knowing" to "knowing everything," from "why" to "now I understand," all in an instant. My final thoughts on this earth were that of wonder. I wondered why I didn't listen to my parents. I wondered if my love was misplaced. I wondered if anyone would miss me. If nothing else, S.P. now has something to talk about.

ONE

Reunion

(Summer 1981)

Jackson and Bo made their way to the old square table in the back, immediately grabbing the nearest drink coaster and slipping it under the left front leg. It was the convenience of the location that made it their perpetual backdrop, for it was the nearest in proximity to the shuffleboard game. It was an underutilized distraction for the most part as was the imbalanced table. Ted's Tavern, the bar of their youth and misery, on the other hand was not. Seemingly always busy, it was a popular place after a hard day's work and Saturday night. Located just a block off the main drag, its paneled walls and linoleum floors offered up comfort and companionship to all ages. The majority of Ted's patrons were blue collared and young. After the first round, most were fixated on Ms. Pac Man and Galaga, video games located in the opposite corner of the bar. Popularity aside, those video games would never do for Jackson or Bo or any of their friends. It was shuffleboard that offered the best opportunity for individual or team competition, for which these two were always searching. When these two paired up, few could compete.

It was the Thursday night prior to the five-year class reunion of Jackson and Bo's class of 1976. Sumner Plaine High School huddled its graduates every five years. It was during this and other such community gatherings that Whiskey and Wright (as they were often called) would gather together their core group of friends for a red beer (Budweiser and tomato juice) at their favorite bar. Whiskey and Wright were nicknames hatched by Coach Bolin for his most prominent middle infielders, Jackson Daniel Stillwell and William Beauregard (Bo) Wright. For a time, the two even batted one and two in the line-up which aided in the novelty. Even the public address announcer at the ballpark used the moniker when announcing the starting line-up. Eventually the entire community participated as the two were as inseparable as they were well-known. The lore of Jackson and Bo, however, has never been a subject of discussion between these two former high school standouts. Clearly there were drunken times where the regalia of past triumphs flowed like active waters over polished rocks. And if Slim and Five were there, the well-worn stories would go on all night.

Jackson and Bo were most known for their accolades on the diamond but in fact they played every kind of sport offered. Jackson was considered one of if not the best all-around athletes to wear a Sumner Plaine Bison uniform and Bo's dad, William Bedford Wright, who used to be a teacher and coach before changing careers to law enforcement and eventually being elected Sumner County sheriff, had Bo involved in every sport imaginable since the age of five. It was sports that first introduced the two boys. They played on the same YMCA basketball and city rec flag football teams from third through sixth grade. There was also swimming, golf, tennis, track and field; but the only sport that truly captured their attention and enthusiasm was baseball. It consumed their summers. Nothing was more important to them. In those days, it was baseball before boobs. Of course, that didn't last long. But when the subject of baseball came up, you would think that they were discussing the doctrine of salvation as focused and delighted as they became. And all of their friends played too. Good friends. Close friends. Their parents recognized this as well. No one could ever remember a closer group of young men. Even as they aged, they all would remain tight. To this day and surely for years in the future, each one could tell you every name and every position of that championship team where Five, Whiskey, Wright, and Slim made up the infield.

In elementary and middle school, they played against each other season after season. However, when that great glorious day arrived, the first day as sophomores at Sumner Plaine Senior High School, the venue of their predestination, the source of their confirmation and justification, redemption was offered and deliverance was granted. Everything changed; as if they were lifted out of their old form and born anew to be baptized into a new faith. And for S.P., the community, and the school, all things were as they should be, for the singers were now a choir, their voices assembled in triumphant jubilation, offering joy unto the congregation within their diamond-shaped celestial cathedral christened Lewis Field. Say hallelujah!

When Five and Slim showed up, preparations for the night's competition were set. They were well into their third round when the noise level was elevated with the arrival of Ben and Bugs. They were less rambunctious than in the past, but only slightly. Janice, the head barkeep and the wife of the owner, was good to them. She had always simply looked the other way when offered a clearly inaccurate identification. Now she easily overlooked the occasional spilt drink and frequent loud outbursts. She knew how to intervene when things were just about to cross a line. And always interceded when the next drink would be too much. It was a maternal characteristic that she as well as the entire community would take on safeguarding these young men. Something that carried on long past its requirement.

"How's law school?" Slim asked of Bo. He could as easily have asked the same of Jackson but didn't dare interrupt his concentration when the disc was in his hand. Jackson would just as soon rap someone in the mouth, even a close friend, as let them get away with messing with his competitive edge.

"Fine," Bo replied as he walked to the other end of the table for his turn at the game. "I have some catching up to do but it's going all right. How about you? You have a job yet?"

"I've got a job!" Slim barked. "Jobs actually! I'm doing well."

"I know you are. Just asking. You're the entrepreneur of the group. You'll be swimming in money before I'll make my first dime." This was another reason why Slim and the others would rather converse with Bo instead of Jackson. Whiskey's cocky arrogance was always on display and had been since anyone could remember. Slim avoided it. Five ignored it. Ben and the rest ran from it. Bo, on the other hand, embraced it. He never took personal Jackson's frequent rants, always finding the positive in his friend's demeanor. Some thought Bo to be a suck-up in the beginning but had come to respect him for his ability to be unaffected by their boisterous friend. Even if it would be years before Bo would actually stand up to Jackson.

"Are you still working at the sporting goods store downtown?" Bo inquired of his close friend Five. Instead of answering, Five shook his head yes, as was his manner. No words but always a response.

Slim, as he frequently did, answered for Five. "He's the inventory manager now. I think he really likes it. Not required to speak much."

Slim and Five had become increasingly close. They were the only ones from the team who remained in Sumner Plaine since graduation. All the rest had gone off to college or started a career in a nearby community. They all supported one another as needed but Five and Slim's relationship rivaled that of Jackson and Bo's bond. In school, the four were always to be found in the same proximity. Now, not so much. Jackson and Bo because they went to different law schools in different cities. Slim and Five because they were more reclusive by nature. But all that was thrown to the wind when they were together at Ted's.

As the night went on, people would drop by the table and back-slap their way around the gang. Most everyone wanted to be seen with the group or at least be collegial. Soon other members of the class of '76 arrived, socially preparing for the primary gathering on Friday and Saturday nights. Even a few girls showed up. Ted's was, for the most part, a male dominated dive but on occasion a pretty face would walk through the door. That night Bo received a sharp elbow in the side when Valeria walked in. Most of the gang glanced then ignored her. She knew, or at least thought she knew what they all were thinking. It bothered her but didn't interfere with her intentions. Jackson looked her up and down and up again before giving her a wink and returning to his turn at the table. Only Bo raised a hand to wave hello. Yet he, like the rest, chose not to stop at her table of friends as the night progressed. Jackson kept prodding Bo to make a move, even yelling "there he goes" as Bo eventually moved in Valeria's general direction. He stopped short, however, and sat at the end of the bar to say hi to Willy.

Willy, another member of the class, more an acquaintance than a friend, was sitting alone at the bar trying to have a conversation with Janice. Bo asked if he wanted to come join the crew but Willy said he had to work tomorrow.

"Will we see you tomorrow night?" Bo asked in a friendly way.

"No, I didn't see her last night."

Fully understanding Willy's disability, Bo smiled. He looked Willy directly in the face so he could read his lips and said, "Good to see you again, Willy."

"Good to see you too, Bo. Maybe I'll see you tomorrow night at the reunion."

"I'll be there, buddy," Bo loudly claimed as he firmly pulled Willy toward himself for a short manly hug.

And with that Bo returned to his friends. Willy left for the night. As Bo turned away from the bar, he glanced over to where Valeria had been sitting and noticed that she was no longer there. Bo scanned the bar for several moments with no success. He blushed as he noticed that Jackson saw him looking for Valeria. When he walked back to the table, Jackson gave him another sharp elbow. "You still want some of that, don't you?" Bo smirked and tilted his head at the jest. Pretty soon they were all giving Bo a hard time about Valeria. They, like she, thought they knew something about what Bo was thinking. They were mostly wrong but Bo didn't let on one way or another. Few were aware that Bo had a steady girl in Topeka where he was going to law school. Jackson of course knew but did not think that should ever stop the attempt for another conquest.

The comments about Valeria did however allow the conversation to drift back toward the old fabled stories of SPHS. Most of those gathered around the shuffleboard game were members of the baseball team so, as always, each outing of their senior year was brought up in succession, culminating in the enthusiastic retelling of the championship game. It was the only story that didn't require any aggrandizing. As the stories were relived, most everyone in the bar eventually listened in. Sumner Plaine loved its baseball and the 1976 Bisons were thought to be the best in ages.

The evening ended as it began, with Jackson and Bo closing down their favorite table in their favorite bar in their favorite place on earth.

"I heard that your brother is dating Cindy," Bo commented while eyeballing his drunken companion.

"Careful, that's touchy stuff." After a brief pause for Jackson to realize that he didn't have any wisecracks to say about one of Bo's former girlfriends, he said. "I almost forgot. Mom wants you to come over tomorrow. She made tamales for you to take home."

The next day was spent primarily with their families though if truth be known, all wanted to spend the afternoon at Five's house. At least for this trip home, they were good boys and gave the appropriate amount of effort on the home front. A gesture that their moms appreciated but their fathers hardly noticed. Jackson's dad was gone again for the weekend and Bo's dad was, well, Bo's dad.

The reunion went off without a hitch, as they say. Most agreed that no one had changed all that much. Many classmates were still in school and those who weren't hadn't altered much with time. That night, Jackson kept close to his clique while Bo enjoyed the time catching up with people not normally associated with the baseball team. All truly enjoyed Bo's company. Even the few teachers that found their way to the Friday night gathering searched out Bo for a quick hello. It became more evident as the night extended into the late hours that each different walk of life existing within the class of '76 had two things in common. They all thought Bo was as pleasant as always and that Jackson was still a jerk.

As the Friday night social came to a close, the only disappointment rendered by the two friends was that Valeria was nowhere to be found. Jackson vocalized his misfortune to Bo and Five of, and (although it was obvious to most) his desire to get laid. It was commonplace for Jackson to express his most derogatory and disgusting thoughts to Bo and Five. There was never a risk for reprisals. Bo, because he took it all in stride and Five, because of his reticence with the human language. Bo, oppositely, kept his feelings to himself. He would have liked to see Valeria but for completely different reasons.

Saturday night was, as Jackson put it, about as lame as it comes so the two hung around for the food then sneaked out when someone suggested that they all sing the alma mater before the awards were given to the most changed, largest brood of children, most hair loss, etc. Bo didn't scream out "Alma maters are for fags," as they were sneaking away— Jackson did that—but Bo too thought it was somewhat juvenile. Announcements were made. A few classmates had died. About a dozen were serving in the military. The date for this fall's football homecoming was provided for those who were interested. Jackson and Bo missed all that. Bo tagged along with Jackson as he spent the entire night, without any luck, looking for Valeria.

TWO

The Easter Egg

(Spring 1983)

I t was a perfect plan! Perfect if (and there is always an if) he could pull it off.

Bo hadn't dated much in high school. He'd hit the standards, prom, homecoming, etc., but not much outside of that. He'd wanted to have a girlfriend, but had high expectations. She had to be someone he was attracted to who hadn't gone out with Jackson or Five. Both criteria were of equal consequence. So, it wasn't until Bo got to college that he would find girls that met both standards. Nancy and Bo first met in the fall of '77. They sat across the room from each other in COMS 322. It was a required oral communication class given during the first semester of their sophomore year, requisite for both accounting (Nancy) and political science (Bo) majors. Interesting that in an oral communications class, they noticed each other but never spoke a word until the last month of the class when they were paired together for a mock political debate presenting opposing views of the trickle-down theory of economics.

Their first "date" was to prepare for that presentation, and they'd had a standing weekend date night ever since. Their attraction was not very plausible. Of course, since they were twenty years old, most anything with different anatomical parts was engaging. But they were in different courses of study. They had differing sensibilities. Their views on the future were not quite in sync. However, since they started slowly, first as acquaintances, then as friends, then as willing participants in their first attempt at love, they slowly became fused at the heart, not simply attached at the hips. It was as if they were growing up together.

Outsiders would have claimed that they were both more mature than most their age. It was their immaturity as individuals however, their unfledged exposure to romantic relationships, that laid bare their unpredictable future. As a couple, they had a ways to go. The fact that they were willing to learn from and teach each other suited their patient demeanors. Each step was considerate. Each stride was exciting. They concerned themselves with the needs of the other before satisfying the desires of themselves. It was this behavior that kept the relationship moving forward.

When they graduated in 1980, plans were made based on William's (as Nancy first knew him and insisted on calling on him) being accepted into law school somewhere and Nancy finding a job nearby. When the acceptance letters failed to arrive, Nancy gave up a good offer in St. Louis to stay in Lawrence with Bo while he figured out what he would do next. Bo was more dejected than anyone could tell. Even Bo was surprised when he couldn't escape the doldrum he was in. The decision was made to stay at KU and work on a master's degree. Possibly he could teach. Nancy assumed that this was but a small delay and that Bo would reapply to law school in a year or two. She encouraged him and doted on him and loved him. She chose to maintain enough hope for the both of them. However life was going to present itself, it would do so simultaneously to both of them. She was convinced that Bo was her man. In his depressed state, Bo wasn't sure of anything except that life was much more tolerable in Nancy's presence. With her, he even found himself forgetting painful memories from his past; the ones that used to permeate his daily thoughts became transparent when they were together.

Marriage had never been the center of any specific conversation as Bo and Nancy dated, but they had talked around the subject enough to know that it was a distinct and pleasing possibility. With the disruption of Bo's plan of going to law school, each, without saying so, knew that any consideration of marriage would need to be put off until his future direction was more established. The fall semester lingered with indifference. To Nancy, it was just a normal wrinkle in the fabric of tomorrow, a defect that could easily and quickly be smoothed out with patience. To Bo, his disappointment made the temporary wrinkle feel much more like a permanent defect. One incapable of being mended. But he kept his head up for the most part and didn't let on how much of a failure this rejection had made him feel. When the call from Washburn came in late November, Nancy was elated. It was validation of her faith in their future. Bo was glad also, but found it difficult to overcome the anguish he felt during the last six months; a feeling that was compounded when a counselor at the enrollment office let on that Johnathon Stillwell had highly recommended him. Bo had not asked Jackson's dad for a letter of recommendation during the initial application process. Plus, there wouldn't have been a need for an endorsement after he was denied entrance that fall. He knew that the generosity of the Stillwell family was somehow responsible for his fate. Serendipity only goes so far. Bo accepted the help and made the best of the opportunity though it galled the proud young man. He chose not to let anyone know of his awareness. He kept his feelings deep inside.

All turned out as hoped and less than three years later Bo, doing well with his final exams, graduated law school in May of 1983. Nancy had stayed by him with a dedication that rivaled Bo's mother. Bo loved Nancy for it. More importantly, he felt she deserved exactly what she had been wishing for. When Bo had to move to Topeka for law school, Nancy again quit a good job and pulled up roots. She moved to Topeka in order to be of any help necessary for Bo's accelerated law school schedule. In addition to being a study partner, Nancy worked fulltime as a bookkeeper for a family practice medical clinic and each weekend volunteered at the First United Methodist Church as a kindergarten Sunday School teacher. For the last two years, Nancy had organized an Easter Egg Hunt on the west lawn of the church property. She would purchase the eggs. (They were the plastic kind, able of being separated into two halves.) She would fill each egg with candy, nickels, and a tiny folded copy of Matthew 19:14. There would be enough for each child to find three or four of them. It was quite a task because Nancy took on the preparations and the expense herself. Each year, due to Bo's harsh schedule, he would study while she spent the Saturday night prior to Easter Sunday getting each egg ready. She was determined to provide the same experience this year as well.

On April 3, 1983, Bo joined Nancy at church. He hid the treasures for her while she completed the Sunday school lesson with the children. Shortly after, the doors flew open and a screaming surge of six-year-old humanity overwhelmed the grassy courtyard. That year there were more adults than usual to experience the children's joy and marvel at the work Nancy had done. One little girl found an egg which was difficult to open and brought it to her teacher. Others looked on while Nancy struggled herself to open the pesky ovum. She didn't notice that the egg was somewhat off color and slightly larger than the others she had filled. The adhesive residue around the perimeter of overlapping rims didn't concern her as she easily scraped it away so she could wedge her fingernails into the margins. Once it popped open, Nancy instinctively handed it to the little girl but was amused at her reaction. Upon closer inspection, the egg contained a ring, a diamond ring, a diamond ring with a note that posed a question. WILL YOU MARRY ME?

Everyone but the kids were in on the act. The pastor and his wife, the office staff and their families, all of the children's ministry team of volunteers had slowly proceeded to the lawn and had inconspicuously appeared just outside the building. There were even a few passersby who smelled out that something big was about to happen. Once Nancy looked up at Bo, biting her lip to keep from crying, and shook her head yes, the entire church family erupted in applause. It was perfect. Bo had pulled it off.

Spring graduation came quickly and while Bo was waiting for bar results, he was sending out resumes to any law firm he could think of. Law school had left him and his future wife in a financial hole that needed a swift shovel full of cash. Bo's parents were unable to help much and so debt was incurred to pay most expenses. Bo did have an occasional part-time job throughout his schooling, but never enough to overcome the unrelenting onslaught of tuition and fees. Nancy had money and was willing to share, but Bo would have none of it. Her money could be used when the time was right to set up a future home or perhaps a down payment on a house but not for his debts. Bo wouldn't allow it. Getting married at a time when he had less assets than his bride was a source of consternation similarly to his feelings about the assistance he'd received from the Stillwells. But again, no one would recognize these internal issues. Bo wouldn't allow it.

The wedding was set for early fall when the St. Louis humidity could be tolerated and the risk for adverse weather would be limited. Nancy desperately wanted an outdoor wedding. A ten-thirty a.m. ceremony on the fourth Saturday in September would be the chosen time and date. Much needed to be done. Bo was consumed with the application process of finding employment. Interviews, phone calls, follow-up contacts. Without any luck, Bo was beginning to question his choice and abilities. He had been reminded by several firms that though they had no openings, there were a couple of positions with the Shawnee County Public Defender's office. It didn't sound appealing. Prosecutorial work was much more in his skill set but no positions were available there either. The husband-to-be was beginning to worry about not having income lined up in preparation for his wedding and new family responsibilities. Bo never thought of his dad as a good father, but he knew him to be a good fiscal provider for his family. He refused to be less of a man than his dad. Bo ultimately gave in and accepted an initial interview with the county's human resources department. It was used to verify Bo's qualifications and to institute the required background check and drug testing. This was simply to test for history of felonies and determine whether an applicant was coked out of their mind at the time of the interview. In later years, when Bo would be accepted as a county prosecutor, the testing would be much more extensive, including *any* evidence of drugs in the system and a DNA profile to be logged into the national data bank. The HR person noticed Bo's lack of enthusiasm during his entrance interview. She encouraged him to complete the process even though he might feel unemotional toward the prospects of being a public defender. She reminded him that even a short stint as a defense attorney is very helpful in improving one's legal skills and is always a beneficial addition to one's resume. He took her advice. When offered the job, Bo resigned himself to the obvious.

Nancy felt sorry for Bo as he struggled with the lack of prospects and the acceptance of what he considered an inferior position. She was so proud of him. She felt being a defense attorney was the most honorable of callings, but when Bo gauged his accomplishments against what Jackson had accomplished in his life, Bo lacked such satisfaction, unimpressed with his own status. Nancy was relieved and content. She prepared something special to celebrate Bo's new job. She planned for the two of them to go to Kansas City for an elaborate dinner. A suitable restaurant was chosen where they could relax, talk, and dream of their future. After the meal, Nancy suggested that they shop for tuxedos tomorrow and since the clothier was located near the Plaza, she thought it would be a shame for them to drive home to Topeka and back again in the morning. Nancy had reserved a hotel suite and was suggesting they spend the night in Kansas City. It was a bold move for the bride-to-be. As a couple, they had decided months ago that they would rather wait until after marriage before committing to a physical relationship. "Much has changed," she stated as she drew closer to Bo and whispered. "I think we are ready."

The setting was perfect and the timing was right. The moment was emotional because this was to be the first time for both. The romantic evening had slowly peaked. The intimacy was wistful and the love-making was passionate, but as newcomers to the act, the sex was clumsy and brief. It didn't matter, for not only did they love each other, they trusted each other completely. It was the blissful hour after that they spent holding each other in the first bed of their oneness that legitimized their union. Nancy had always been happy and serene. Bo, though always displaying control, had been lacking a level of confidence and security he had always seen in his best friend, Jackson. After that night, Bo began feeling better about his place, more comfortable in his own skin. The next morning, as you might expect, they were both confident in the fact that practice makes, if not perfect, better. The a.m. sex was much better but nothing would ever top the feeling they shared the night before. Nothing. The entire weekend was just what Bo needed. His wife had discovered just how important she was to Bo's psyche. This would not be the last time that she would be able to bring him from dark places into the dawn.

Bo had completed two major cases and was starting to understand the process of public defense when their wedding day arrived. He was excited, but just as much, was ready to have it over. Nancy had gone on and on. Since she was a small girl, Nancy had romanticized Forest

Park in every celebration imaginable. From birthdays to end-of-life memorials, she saw this beautiful location in the heart of St. Louis as the perfect venue. Having a wedding there was a dream and a forgone conclusion. She and her mother were fully engaged in the plans. Bo felt involved also, even though he didn't do anything. When you hear every detail and concern regurgitated ad nauseum, night after night, you either get sick or you mutate to become immune to the pathogen. For Bo, it was all a bit much. The experience was agonizing for the former high school athlete. Being coached in anything outside of sports was tedious at best. But he took the directions in stride and became the most dutiful of spouses. He knew how important this was to Nancy, and as he was slowly understanding, it would be important to him as well.

A morning wedding was chosen specifically to avoid the assault of late day humidity. This abuse would have been guaranteed since the previous afternoon provided two inches of rain and the high on that Saturday was predicted to be above ninety degrees. What they didn't plan, because it occurred with such infrequency, was late morning fog. Thick as peanut butter. Bo jokingly suggested to his best man that it was thick enough that Nancy wouldn't be able to tell if they pulled a switch during the ceremony. Jackson suggested they also try it for the wedding night. As you might hope for the perfect couple planning the perfect wedding, the fog lifted on cue and shards of assorted filtered wavelengths sprinkled their presence throughout the park. The pavilion behind the seated guests became a golden and regal backdrop to the ceremony. The fountain, positioned as the center piece to the gathering, twinkled with multicolored points of light altering in time with the synchronicity of an orchestra. And as they were gathered together in the "presence of God and these witnesses," as if Noah himself was one of the guests, an uninterrupted rainbow emerged above the tree-scaped horizon to the west. Throughout her life, other than Bo's unique proposal, the only story that Nancy was more delighted to recount was that of her wedding ceremony.

The first years of their marriage were much like their storybook start. Bo, showing more talent than even he expected, was promoted to lead defense attorney which included a nice raise in salary. Nancy got a job with a prominent accounting firm that allowed her time during work to study for the CPA exams. She passed them on only the second attempt. With thirty-year fixed rates above ten percent, they had chosen not to purchase a home but were able to rent a nice cottage only fifteen minutes from downtown Topeka. They started to put money aside. They worked hard, played much, and loved like there was no tomorrow. Time passed quickly.

In the spring of 1986, Bo received a call from Jackson. He stated that he just wanted to talk about the upcoming backpacking trip, which surprised Bo somewhat. Jackson never called just to talk. Bo thought that perhaps the subject of backpacking would be enough to legitimately instigate a phone call from Jackson but this still seemed odd.

"Well, Jackson Daniel Stillwell. This is a surprise. What's up?"

"Nothing really. I just wanted to make sure I had the date right for the trip to Colorado. When are we planning to go?" Jackson asked in a tone that sounded to Bo like there was something being held back.

"The Sunday after the ten-year reunion. Can you have everything ready for us by then?"

"Not a problem. I'm looking forward to it."

"Ten years is too long. We should do this more often." Bo exclaimed as he sat down on the couch, a notable difference since a Whiskey and Wright phone conversation was usually so short that it could be performed while standing on their heads. "How are things in Southern California?"

"I love it out here! You and Nancy have to come for a visit."

"What all have you been doing?"

"A little bit of partying but mostly working and learning to surf. It's actually not too difficult." Which, coming from Jackson, was code for harder than hell to perfect. "And you, how's married life?"

"So far so good." Which, coming from Bo, was code for awesome. Jackson was retaining an added bit of information for the very end of the call but wanted to drag Bo along as long as he could. Eventually Bo cut to the chase. "OK. So, why did you call?"

"I just got married."

"I knew there was something else! When?"

"Yesterday!"

"Holy mackerel!"

They spent another ten minutes hashing over the details of this new addition. The two had become four which added greatly to the joy that Bo felt in his own life. His existence, while at times painful and insecure, had matured like elegant wine, offered in a chalice that never ran dry.

For the next two months, the approaching class reunion and subsequent bromance trip (a snarky reference that Nancy frequently used to describe their gatherings) was all Bo could talk about. It had been ten years since their inaugural hike in the Rockies, occurring just after their high school graduation. Bo must have packed and repacked a dozen times and each time he did he would review his actions by recalling multiple memories of that first trip to the mountains. Nancy now fully understood Bo's patience while she was planning her wedding.

Recently, Bo had reconnected with some of the other friends from his high school class and had mentioned the trip to Carlos and to Willy. Both had accepted the invitation. The group would now be six instead of the original four of Jackson, Bo, Five, and Slim.

Just before Bo was to head west for the reunion, Jackson called again. To Bo, Jackson's tone seemed both sad and angry. The fact that he was drunk again heightened his emotions. He was clearly upset about something. Jackson started with his disapproval of the inclusion of Carlos and Willy to the guest list. He knew that Carlos would not be ready when it was time to go and thought that Willy would just slow them down. "Willy has no equipment and won't be in shape for the altitude," Jackson whined into the phone. Bo thought it was rude not to invite them once they were aware of the trip. "Well then, you shouldn't have mentioned it!" This type of disagreement with some friendships might carry forward for several days. But like other arguments in their past, it was never mentioned again. Friction between these two dispersed into imperceptible fragments that would disappear with the sunrise of a new day. An enviable art that neither could re-create in any of their other relationships. "I thought you wanted to be a judge?" Jackson questioned as their phone conversation continued long after its normal duration. "You can't be a judge unless you have prosecutier… prosecutori… the experience of a prosecutor, you know that," Jackson blurted, now heavily slurring his words.

"I don't know," Bo objected. "There's nothing in the statute that states you must have prosecutorial experience. Besides, there haven't been any openings in the DA's office for some time. They've got a bunch of lifers up there."

Bo was correct; his big break would not come for several years. An open position did become available sometime after they returned from their backpacking trip. Bo applied but didn't get the nod. He had his foot in the door though; such that his chances were better the next time around. Nancy, who was proud of the work Bo did with indigent defendants, liked the idea of this career progression. She always thought Bo would be the best of judges. Everyone did. Bo had become a respected lawyer and admired human being. His self-esteem was changing. His place in life had become more to his liking. His potential seemed unlimited and he was truly happy.

THREE

We Had a Deal.

(Spring 1985)

I f you travel south out of Sumner Plaine, take a right at Amarillo, then turn left at Barstow you approach *la ciudad de angeles*. They say approach because you never completely arrive. You can never catch a setting sun. The evolution of L.A. is constant. Like a mirage, it has an unachievable allure. Los Angeles may be home for angels and Dodgers but not everyone. Jackson Daniel Stillwell was raised in the rural Midwest, competed in the Big 8, and was educated on the East Coast. With that pedigree, you would hardly think that L.A. would agree with this young attorney from Kansas. It didn't take long though for this city to absorb this phenom. Los Angeles is the real estate version of Jackson Daniel himself. L.A. is lean, brown, smooth, athletic, and exciting. She's cloaked in American spirit without concealing her Mexican soul. Her coastline is powerful and elegant. Her foothills are appealing and precarious. At times champagne. At times tequila. Black tie and cutoffs. Always balanced. Usually in control. They were meant for each other even though the union could not have been foreseen by either.

Jackson dove in head-first yet never assumed he would adapt as readily to or be so quickly consumed by the California lifestyle. Commuting from the Upper West Side to Morningside Heights was the enviable situation that Jackson found himself in while living in New York City. If you have money, NYC offers every distraction you can imagine. Every distraction. A person could hide there or be exposed completely and in either instance no one would notice. Or if they did, no one could tell because the city's expression never changes. And while the habits of the city could get you into trouble; they also can present opportunity and connections unavailable in most other settings.

Jackson took full advantage of the city. As an undergrad collegiate athlete, Jackson had to develop time management skills in order to succeed adequately to a level that might interest an Ivy League law school while keeping himself securely off the bench of the Jayhawks baseball team. The former was a goal of his dad's. The latter, more so a goal of his own. Being a Division One athlete is not an easy assignment—if you actually have to go to class. To Jackson's benefit, KU took this cocksure, audacious high school student and created an efficient, focused university scholar. To Jackson's detriment, it took a steady dose of amphetamines to aid in the crusade. His family and friends never noticed. His coaches encouraged it. In fact, there were two Igloo coolers present in the dugout for every game, one with water and one with "the Kool-Aid." As all addictions, popping *Diablos*, as they are referred to within the cultural diversity of S.P., became a habit that was considered the answer, not the problem. It became the bridge connecting reefer and Coors to cocaine and Crown Royal. All of the vice not withstanding, what was created at Columbia University was a mind whose potential was exclusively acknowledged and praised by the elite of the legal and business academia. To the business world, he was becoming the golden child turned blue-chipper turned rock star. Of course, Sumner Plaine always knew it. Whiskey and Wright called it their James Bond connection. The difference was that one wanted to be Sean Connery and the other actually was 007.

New York City celebrated the mental capabilities of Jackson Daniel, but this unathletic urban turf did not jibe with Jackson's natural physicality. New York was clammy. New York was cold and flabby. For him, it was a soft life veiled by sooted windows shuttering out hidden horizons. It was a weak existence shadowed by skyscrapers of doubt. It wasn't Jackson Daniel Stillwell at his natural core. The essence of his personality did not fit this place. A choice was always inevitable; for in the city, you either acquiesce or you rebel. There is no middle ground. When the chance to go west was offered, there was never any doubt of what Jackson's next move would be. Over the next decade, this legally accomplished, taxation proficient, savvy manipulator would become a business machine. Jackson's success would have been restricted in the compressed metropolitan environment of New York City. He needed a place to provide the energy that would maximize his unlimited potential. California was that place. California would become the spinach that this Popeye would need.

Jackson quickly chose a place to reside. He probably should have researched it a little more, but after feeling shut up in the city, he wanted to start living as soon as possible. He should have researched his apartment location because the proximity to the beach eventually didn't compensate for the fifty-minute commute to work five days a week. But the siren call of the gold coast was impossible to ignore. The glow of those gilded shores would, for a while, blind him to all else. The Stillwell family of Sumner Plaine was an outdoors family. The ocean however, was not their typical location of choice. Living on the High Plains of Kansas, the closest site for leisure and recreation was the Rocky Mountains of Colorado. Skiing, hiking, stream fishing, all were activities that the family lived for. Once the ice was off the ponds and the snow was off the trails, the backpacking trips were set. Once the snow was on the trails and the ice was on the pond, the ski trips were on. They would vacation in Colorado at least three times each year. They, even for a time, owned a cabin in Summit County, but found that it limited them to fewer locations and stifled their passion of new venues. They sold the place after only two ski seasons.

The point is, before 1984, Jackson had been to the beach once in his life and had never surfed. As he stood on Huntington Beach Pier and viewed the players on the ocean waves, his competitive nature overwhelmed him. He bought a board that day, which made him a memorable character at the nearby surf shop. Not only because the purchase was of the most expensive surfboard in the shop; Jackson also purchased a half dozen lessons on the technique of hanging ten. Actually, he took two instructions and was able to out surf his teacher on the third outing. So, he became accomplished with ease—as was common with all athletic endeavors throughout his life. That first summer Huntington Beach was his home away from home. He hated the crowds but loved the competition. Similarly, Jackson was committed to his first job at Williams, Brown, and Fairfield. He dedicated every last minute to perfecting his skills on the waves and in the boardroom. He sacrificed everything to achieve perfection in both. It was Bo's dad, as Jackson and Bo's Little League coach, who first introduced Jackson to the concept that striving for the unattainable goal of perfection makes excellence that much easier.

After the first season of traveling an hour and a half from home, each way, to Huntington Beach, Jackson wanted to try a new surfing venue that people were talking about at work. Surfrider at Malibu Beach had a reputation of being one of the first epic locations for talented surfers. It was less crowded and closer to his apartment, located just north of downtown Santa Monica. March is always the best month for surfing because it merges the warmth of the spring with the waves of winter. Jackson made his way to Surfrider on March 9, 1985. It was a Saturday. He remembers it easily for two reasons. One, it was on his second wave of the day that Jackson was slammed to the base of a swell in a fashion he had never experienced. He was turned every way but inside out and was nearly down for the count. It took all of his athletic abilities to find the surface. It was the first time he had been beaten. That day, he gained a new respect for his adversary. And two, it was the first time he laid eyes on Crystal. Jackson had never seen a body like hers. Even amongst the scholarship women athletes at KU, there wasn't one close. Crystal Evans, whose name Jackson would quickly determine, was a tall blonde with South Beach legs and Malibu Beach breasts. There wouldn't have been room enough for the thought of a dime between the tightly fitted wet suit and her smooth contours. Contrasting with the second wave, this time Jackson was down for the count.

She actually approached him after seeing his near demise on the ocean. He assured her that he was fine and wanted to get right back on the horse, a phrase she had not heard before. That was his in. For the next two days, they surfed and got to know each other. Their likes were the same. Their dislikes were the same. Their competitive natures, though coming from diverse upbringings, were the same. And their sexual desires were clearly of the same vein, for it was not the wipeout that gave Crystal the initial motivation to advance toward Jackson. In her eyes, he was Adonis incarnate. Since their apartments were less than five miles apart, nothing stopped them from their obvious passion.

They were all over each other, but it wasn't only the physical attraction. Jackson never smiled as much in a lifetime as he did the first two weeks of their romance. Crystal couldn't remember a man she felt more confident in or comfortable with as the man with whom she now shared her bed. In a way, it was too fast. In a way though, there was no stopping it and so they both acknowledged the warning signs, accepted the high surf, and let the wave take them down.

There was only one true difference between the two. Crystal was relatively uneducated. After high school she worked as a secretary at an elementary school. After a few months turned into a few years, she became bored and enrolled in a two-semester medical assistant curriculum from a local community college and was now working as a post-op technician in an outpatient surgical clinic. It was part of the UCLA Health System, offering diversified surgeries from a number of surgeons. She enjoyed the fact that, though she was not specifically expert in one medical field, she became very knowledgeable in many and as such, indispensable to her employer. The patient interaction was natural for her. She was loved by people who would only know her for a very short period of time. Perhaps it was that Midwest temperament that first attracted Jackson to her. Perhaps not.

Crystal was very independent and was proud of her ability to support herself on a meager salary in the expensive city she loved. She, like Jackson, loved her parents, but also didn't feel close to them. Her mother had recently died, and though Crystal didn't mind looking in on her dad from time to time, she didn't relish it either. He still lived in the same house she was raised in, not far from the beach in Santa Monica. Quickly Jackson and Crystal found themselves talking about the future. Not necessarily theirs as a couple, but their view of how they might fit into each other's portrait of their future, where each saw themselves in the next few years. Jackson wanted to continue experiencing the SoCal lifestyle that Crystal had enjoyed all her life. She wanted to continue to surf and be a part of the surf scene. They both appreciated money and the freedom it provided. They enjoyed the finer things that wealth could provide but not to the point of sacrificing the lifestyle uniquely available in Los Angeles California. They wanted to travel. They wanted to party. They both revered their childhood but not parenting as an occupation.

So, it became obvious that children were out of the question, at least for the foreseeable future. They were both adamant about that.

They worked hard each week and played hard every weekend. For twelve straight months they were together almost continuously. They would even on occasion show up at each other's work place. They were in love. It was easy to understand. One late evening in April of 1986, while they were watching the sun set off the Santa Monica Pier, Jackson asked Crystal if she would like to get married. It was a question as opposed to a proposal. It showed his lack of certainty yet it was matched by her desire to postpone her answer while she thought about it for a day or so. They finished their beers and made their way back to her apartment. They walked separately at first. Jackson eventually reached for her hand. Soon she was on his arm with her head on his shoulder. Before they reached the door, she stopped their movement and faced her lover. "I would like to marry you." A subtle smile came to both their lips as if they were acknowledging the inevitable.

They chose not to wait. Neither were sentimentalists. Both were pragmatic. The wedding/elopement took place the following week at the L.A. County courthouse. No family, no friends, no fuss. Their apartment leases weren't up until the end of the year so they alternated apartments based on convenience. They were happy. Nontraditional perhaps, but happy. Nothing actually changed with the new arrangement. No one could tell the difference. No one knew, except one. The day after the civil ceremony, Jackson called Bo. They were both excited at the prospect of each being married. It was another similarity they both enjoyed. It made Bo feel special that he was the only one to know. He wasn't to tell a soul until Jackson and Crystal figured out a way of breaking the news to everyone. It was an announcement that would never happen.

They had been married only three weeks when Crystal determined she was pregnant. She was afraid and Jackson was angry. She promised that she was on the pill, but she might have been a bit off schedule. She was crying. She felt ashamed for some reason. Jackson's behavior didn't help. The only way out, as was agreed upon by both, was an abortion. The thought of the procedure frightened her as much as raising a child. But she knew it had to be done. If not, there would be no marriage. The next day, Crystal set up the appointment with the doctor who would make the referral. Jackson didn't see her for three straight days. He wondered what was happening to them. When Crystal showed up on his doorstep, he was relieved. She seemed resigned to the act and they tried to start over. It didn't take long for them to realize returning to normality would be difficult. Eventually, Crystal told Jackson that though she went through with the abortion, she now regretted it. She now knew that she eventually wanted to be a mom. She also knew that each time she looked at Jackson, she would never be able to erase that image or forgive herself for what she did. They filed for divorce the next day. Jackson spent that evening on the beach where they first met. As the sun reached toward its resting place and signified the end of a long brutal day, Jackson felt like crying but couldn't. When the sun disappeared behind the clouds on the horizon, a conclusion to the day came, and to Jackson's loving temperament as well. "Fuck her. We had a deal." He left for home and immediately started drinking. Bo didn't find out about the divorce until Jackson came home for their tenth class reunion. It was never mentioned during the drunken phone call Bo received that night though as he later thought about it, the divorce surely was the reason behind Jackson's demeanor, not the guest list for the backpacking trip.

***

On the Sunday following the reunion festivities, Jackson, Bo, Slim, Five, Carlos, and Willy left for the mountains. This was a five-day backpacking trip that had been in the making for over a year. Jackson didn't quite feel up to it, but wouldn't have let his friends down, even if it was to be his last days on earth. They all learned of Jackson's short-term marriage on the way out to Long Lake, high in the mountains just south of Rocky Mountain National Park. It was the place they all remembered well. It was the exact same location as their first trip shortly after their high school graduation. This time however, they would struggle to find the same path and ended up reaching their familiar campsite nearly an hour later than normal. By the time they arrived, Jackson was feeling better. In this company there were no fears or regrets. There was no pain or worry. It was as if this group of friends, when together, forged a barrier protecting them all from the foes of the world. They were invincible. They were unbreakable. They were one.

It didn't take long before things were completely back to normal. Jackson could tell this because his three-week marriage was the butt of all jokes. So much so that no one remembered to ask if Jackson brought the Judge, at least, not until Slim broached the subject. That story clearly changed each time it was retold. The basis of the fable lies in the fact that Jackson's father was an avid hunter and owned several guns. When their family went hunting, they would bring the shotguns and the Judge. It was a pistol-sized 4–10 shotgun that someone would carry in case the group stumbled upon a rattlesnake. It was much easier and safer to use when shooting at someone's feet than with a long, break action 12-gauge shotgun. When backpacking in the Rockies however, the *snake* Judge would only piss off a bear so Jackson's dad always carried a different Judge. The *bear* Judge. This six-shooter was an original 1955 snub nose Colt Python. It could clearly do more damage to a bear than piss him off. The biggest joke was that no matter how many times any of them had been backpacking in the mountains, none had seen a bear. Yet Jackson's dad always told him to take it with them for protection.

"You keep that piece of shit away from me you son of a bitch," Slim yapped as he eyeballed Jackson and pointed in the direction of Jackson's pack. Now, that was a different story altogether.

FOUR
Eljuez

For most, California is pure excitement and beauty. For some, however, they don't know what the fuss is, really. Take northern California for example. Arid flat lands. A quilted patchwork of deficient greens and variable rawhide brown, as if the colors can't quite make up their minds. At a distance, rocky unfertile mounds give a meager accent to the sparse landscape on the horizon. The trees, like the coastline and backroads, are a gnarly and contorted mishmash, unregulated by time or nature. It's hard to imagine that life can be created in such an environment but, in the vines, you see it. Life that not only exists but sustains through adversity. Perhaps that is the draw. That or the fact that people experience the region while drunk on Frog's Leap. Like cattle country, most would tell you that it is best to enjoy the product without ingesting the production.

With the failure of Jackson's first marriage and the free time now available, Jackson expanded his horizons beyond the beaches of SoCal. Napa became a frequent escape. It gave him a place to reflect. Though Jackson's first marriage didn't last, the pleasant memory of romance remained. Within that relationship he felt at ease, as if someone really was sharing the load. He also enjoyed having another thing in common with his friend back in Kansas. Jackson didn't actively seek out a new wife but when the next one presented herself, he quickly jumped onboard. Jackson and his second wife, Jennifer, got married in 1988 during crush season. They took their vows in early September when the vineyard's harvest colors give rise to a golden mist in the briskness of each autumn morning. Neither Jackson nor Jennifer were familiar with Napa County but they were drawn to it. They first met during a legal conference at a nearby resort, the type of conference that is more pleasure than business. When marriage was proposed, the second time around for both, Napa suited their preference of a small destination wedding. Families were to attend and perhaps a few friends. Jackson was more enthused about these festivities than he'd been with his first marriage—which was more of an elopement anyway. In fact, Jackson's mom and dad didn't know about his first nuptials until after the fact, which was good since the marriage lasted all of three weeks.

Jackson hoped that Bo and Nancy would attend. An invitation was sent followed by a phone call to his hometown friend. Jackson laughed when he recalled the conversation.

"Come on. You have to come out!" Jackson pleaded. "This is the best time of the year to visit Napa."

"Nancy is about ready to pop. She won't want to be on a plane for three hours while eight and a half months pregnant."

"Then you come out. I don't think either of my brothers will be there."

"I'll think about it."

"Come on, Jennifer wants to meet you. You didn't even get to know my first wife."

"Excuse me … You didn't get to know your first wife."

After a while they stopped laughing and moved on to Jackson's real purpose for the call. He wanted to know how much cash Bo had if a great investment came up.

"What is it this time?" Bo said sarcastically. He was remembering a few times when they both had been burned by some of Jackson's earlier get-rich-quick schemes.

"This one is legit. In fact, I'm already in at the ground level. I own B shares of Jupiter Equity Ventures."

"What's a B share?"

"It's a non-voting share ownership with no dividends. But that doesn't matter. It's the information that is important. I have access to all the investment analyst's information, all the research data. I just can't vote on their direction. I can't vote on what they ultimately invest in. Fifty thousand dollars minimum buy-in."

"That would about clean me out of my personal savings, but I could come up with that. Nancy could never know. I mean it, you asshole. She would kill me. I loaned some of our family money to one of our friends in Topeka and he skipped town. She still brings that up."

"You can do your own research if you want before you say yes. JEV Incorporated. They're positioning themselves to go public so a lot of their information is available. It's all going to be internet technology investments. Most of the start-ups are based here in Silicon Valley."

Bo knew before he asked "what's it this time," that he would be sending Jackson a check. There was never any doubt with those two. The idea might fail, the action might be dangerous, the notion could be crazy, but if one was all in, so was the other. It all began in third grade when they both walked down to the zoo in the middle of a snowstorm because Bo wanted to throw snowballs at the monkeys and were punished accordingly by their scared parents. From that day forward, they would find trouble and triumph together.

Bo wanted to go to the wedding. He was being pulled by his own desire and by the draw of his friend's request. It was so rare that either would deny an honest request of the other that Bo couldn't remember the last time it happened. It felt good to hear Jackson ask anything of him. While they were in school, Bo wouldn't have had the courage to ask a favor of Jackson. Bo saw his role as the supporter-in-chief and was happy to have the responsibility. For Jackson to ask a favor of Bo or to make an actual request was like receiving an award. After hanging up, Bo would cherish that feeling until the day he made his decision not to go. It just wasn't feasible. Nancy would give birth to their first child about one month after the call and just before the wedding. They named her Jenna. Bo also had just started his new position as assistant district attorney of Shawnee County and wouldn't have been able to spare the time away from his new responsibilities. It would be another year before Bo would find out the exact structure of their investment. He never asked. It wouldn't have mattered.

JEV, as a venture capital corporation, evaluated scores of applications every year from tech companies throughout the region; each looking for investment capital to fund expansion or product development. JEV would try to have approximately ten start-ups in the pipeline at any given time. 50% would fail completely; 40% would fail to make the return on investment that the firm was projecting. It's the last ten percent that makes or breaks them as a venture capital organization. Ten shares. Fifty thousand dollars. Jackson's bank account was flush with his earnings over the last five years. He had yet to make any investments to date, no house, no stocks, no fancy cars or boats. He just kept putting it away for the time when an opportunity on the horizon came within reach.

JEV didn't pay dividends for B shares so appreciation came only when cashing out. This posed a problem for someone as impatient as Jackson. He didn't want to wait another five years to build up a large nest egg. He needed to find a way to make his access to the firm profitable without eliminating his position. That was the instigation of the call to Bo. Jackson had determined a way. Slightly risky. Very illegal. But it was a way to possibly make them a lot of money. Once Bo's check arrived, Jackson drafted a contractual agreement for the two to sign. They were becoming partners in their own investment company. Fifty thousand into the B shares and fifty thousand into their separate investment capital.

Over the next few months, Jackson's second marriage went along well. Though it only lasted for a few years. Both Jackson and Jennifer kept very busy, devoted to their own careers. It was not the marriage of convenience that his third attempt would be nor the one of passion his first marriage was. This union was more of a matching of similar mindsets. Neither wished to have children. Both wanted a fulfilling and impressive resume. They bought a house in Santa Monica shortly after the wedding. It would prove to be an incredible investment and allowed for a line of credit that was enjoyed by both the contented couple and their delighted banker. Time together was exciting and intellectually stimulating. They would bounce ideas off each other in ways that made them look more like partners than lovers. Neither one saw that as a problem. Jackson would share every one of his successes at work as well as each one of his investment ideas that were hatched outside of it—except for the one concocted for Bo and himself. Jackson felt that if there was going to be impropriety, he should protect his wife (and his reputation) by keeping corporate secrets secret.

Jackson, busy with work, and Bo, active as a new father, created a gap in their communication for the next year. Their new investment company was faced with a time certain deadline. Documents needed to be signed and notarized within the year of the business's formation which was instigated once Jackson deposited Bo's capital on their behalf. That meant by December 31, all signatures had to be in place. Jackson could have flown out to Kansas City for the signatures but they both had a much better idea on how to accommodate the need for business closure with the desire of personal fulfillment. Jackson and Bo had never been to a World Series game. You might recall that in 1989, the 86th World Championship of Baseball was considered the Bay Area Series. Jackson's beloved American League Champion Oakland A's were pitted against the National League Champion San Francisco Giants. In California, it was all the rage! Jackson worked diligently to procure tickets to at least one of the first two games which were being played at Oakland Alameda Coliseum. But the weekend tickets were essentially sold before they went on sale. They settled on Game Three tickets which was to be played on the following Tuesday at Candlestick Park.

Bo flew out on Monday so they could have one business day to utilize Jackson's firm's notary and complete the official formation of their investment company. After the formalities were complete, Jackson took Bo to his favorite deli located down the street from his office.

"OK." Bo began after picking a booth and scanning the activity within the busy downtown establishment. "Now that we exist, what is it that we do?"

"Remember I told you that I can't vote as a B Share holding owner in JEV. But, and this is a very big but, I get access to the most sensitive and opaque corporate information of the best start-ups in Silicon Valley. Only about one out of ten start-ups really make a significant return on the venture capital invested. The remaining losers are killed off pretty quickly, so the high flyers start to stand out on the active investment balance sheets."

Jackson paused to take his first bite of his Reuben. Bo was mostly finished eating by that time and waited for Jackson to continue, which he didn't. "I still don't get it."

"Oh, here's where you come in. I'm legally obligated to take the investment analysis of these start-up corporations to the grave. I cannot lawfully act upon them without violating almost every insider trading legislation on the book."

Bo looked slowly, methodically, and deeply into his best friend's eyes. "You are using my 50K to keep your ass out of jail and place a noose around my neck."

"Sort of. But here's the thing. It's not your neck in the noose and you would know that if your redneck legal education would have motivated you to read the documents that you just signed."

"OK. I give. What did I sign?"

"You are the sole proprietor of Eljuez investments, which is an unchartered and federally undocumented company located in the Cayman Islands. You exist but can't be found. At least not easily. My 50K will stay invested in JEV while your fifty thousand is deposited in an offshore account earning four and a half percent as we speak. Once I determine the company with the best trajectory, you will invest in that company once it goes public."

"And you're sure that I won't go to jail?"

"Hell no." And as always, their laughing brought about tears and stares.

"Oh, here's the best part!" Jackson continued. "Any income we make from the investments not only compounds but is tax-free. Eljuez is a not-for-profit entity. We may have to give some shit away from time to time."

"What the hell is Eljuez?"

"Damn, your Spanish is worse than your legal competence!"

"Listen," Bo complained. "I, unlike you, didn't grow up with a mother who was Mexican and spoke Spanglish all day long."

"OK. Here is your Spanish lesson for the day. It comes directly from your second mother, Gabriela Ayala Talamontez Stillwell.

"Are you ready?"

"Yes," Bo answered in the middle of an irritated sigh.

"You know what el means, right."

"Fuck you."

"Juez means Judge."

Bo went limp and fell back heavily into the cushions of the booth. He looked at Jackson and shook his head in disbelief. Jackson reciprocated with a smile and an affirmative nod.

"That's hilarious," Bo said. "Too funny."

The prospects of attending your first World Series Game and spending the rest of your life in Winfield minimum security are not a recipe for a great night of sleep. The night after Jackson revealed his investment *opportunity* and before they were to fly up to San Francisco, Bo tried to rest his mind in Jackson and Jennifer's guest room. He would not have let anyone know, especially Jackson, but for a brief moment Bo had thought about saying no to Jackson's investment proposal. If Jackson would have asked for the money to use himself for any personal need, Bo would have given it gladly. If Jackson would have said we should burn this cash on the steps of City Hall as a political statement, Bo would have done that too. This however, was the first time that Bo would consciously agree to do something that he knew was against the law.

Bo has always believed in rules of order and the law. The concept that American society has slowly evolved to a point in its existence and has democratically created a reasonable set of rules to live by should be good enough for anyone as a list to adhere to. As a law enforcement officer and perhaps because he actually believed it too, Bo's father never set down any regulations in his home that weren't consistent with the laws of Sumner County. If there wasn't a curfew in town, there wasn't a curfew in the house. As long as you were up bright and early to go to school or do your chores, it was acceptable. If the state said you can't drink or smoke before you were eighteen years of age, then you were required to abide by that. Not because the father of the house said so, but because the society that you live in has stated so.

Bo even prepared this long thought out speech that night to present to Jackson the next morning. He would state that he thought the concept was financially sound (or flawed) and that the risk was minimal (or excessive) but in the end, he didn't feel comfortable with doing something deliberately unethical and unlawful. Nothing new here, actually. It was the type of speech Bo had given in the past. He used to say similar things to his peers growing up back home. It never bothered him to say no to the offer of drugs or alcohol. It never seemed uncomfortable to live his Christian faith on his sleeve, to say he actually read the Bible for direction and purpose. It was easy to turn away from purposeful humiliating situations; bullying that would cause embarrassment or distress to others outside of their cliquish circle. Though he rarely said anything, he always hoped that those inflicting the pain would notice and realize what Bo thought about their actions. Why would this be different? What would be so important as to cause a departure from his long-standing moral beliefs? In the end, it would be a turning point. One of many that Bo would experience in his turbulent future.

FIVE

The Earthquake

(Fall 1989)

O n the flight to SFO, there was little discussion. Jackson was
reading the sports page and Bo was looking out the window
at the Monterey coastline as the contentious accord of earth and sea
meandered toward the back of the plane. Halfway through the flight,
Jackson was chasing his second Scotch and soda with a Sauvignon Blanc
while Bo looked on. He thought about asking if Jackson felt all right
but decided against it. Bo was never one to comment on the imbibing
habits of his friends. One of the most commonly regaled baseball stories
of their youth was a summer ballgame when Jackson and Slim arrived
extremely late, barely in time for the first pitch. Other than pitchers,
Coach Bolin always used the same starters for each game so both late-
comers were allowed to play. It didn't take long to realize that they
were both higher than a skyscraper. Between those two, they had five
errors, two strikeouts, and a black eye from a soft infield fly that never
even touched Slim's glove. And that was only the first two innings. The
Bisons lost the game yet Bo never said a thing. Even those times when
someone would be put in danger by their consumption, Bo's acceptance
with the actions of his close friends was irrefutable, if not truly wise.

They all remembered the Christmas miracle of '77. Christmas fell
on a Sunday that year and it was early on the previous Saturday morning
that Bo received a call from Jackson. "Come pick me up at Five's. You
have to help me find my car." As always, Bo didn't hesitate. *Find your
car?* He was thinking, but didn't say a word. Jackson, Slim, Five, and a
few others closed down Ted's the night before and, on their way home,
somehow lost Jackson's dad's car somewhere between the bar and Five's

house. It didn't take long to find the car. It was cold and there had been snow on the ground for a few days so there were tracks, the car had to be in the neighborhood.

Jackson remembered driving and turning left at some intersection before parking in front of what he thought was Five's house. They found it three blocks away. When Jackson turned left at the intersection, he forgot to wait until he arrived at the intersection. Jackson's dad's Mercedes was inserted perfectly (though on the wrong side of the street) in between a red VW Beetle and a yellow Pacer which were parked (correctly) on the intersecting avenue. You could follow the tracks in the snow as they conveyed across the residential corner lot, just missing a huge mulberry tree, trekking *through* a pickup parked in the driveway, and over the curb to its final resting place. They both stood there for a while, dazed by the complicated mental calculations required to visualize the event from the previous night. Obviously, the truck had arrived sometime after Jackson had passed through the yard? Obviously, the combination of red beers and acid enhances one's ability to parallel park? However, there could be no rationale established to explain the tree. There was less than one inch between the tire track and the undisturbed bark on the tree. There were exactly three and two thirds inches between the edge of the tire and the outer point of the Mercedes' undented front bumper. God does pick his moments.

"Who's pitching today?" Jackson asked of his knowledgeable friend who would always know the ins and outs of each important baseball game scheduled.

"Welch and Robinson."

"Do you want to get something to eat on the way or dogs at the park?"

"Dog and a brew sound good to me."

Noting, yet not mentioning Jackson's continued drinking, Bo drove the rental car to the stadium. Traffic was smooth, almost minimal, and they arrived about an hour before the first pitch. They found their seats; then Bo went for the food.

"I think I saw Al Michaels in the john!" Bo claimed as he was doling out the dogs, beers, and sunflower seeds.

"How do you know it was him?"

"He was short."

"Yeah, every man in California is at least six foot two."

"Give me a minute. He had on a tie and a blazer that had an ABC sports emblem."

"Impressive?"

"I didn't look."

"Cute."

They both sat comfortably for about fifteen minutes reading the programs and watching the fans pour in. Some local crazies sat in front of them and glared at Jackson's Oakland A's hat. One fully inebriated Giants fan, clearly expecting to get on TV with his home-made cardboard sign, held it up for Jackson to see. It read "A's SUCK." He laughed and shook Jackson's hand. "Pretty original, don't you think?" He turned out to be the nicest of the group and bought the second round of drinks for Bo and his friend with the "obnoxious" hat. The day had been hot but the seats were becoming shaded by the concrete overhang of the deck above as the time approached five o'clock. What was about to happen to these two Sumner Plaines expats and the other 44,000 baseball fans waiting for the game to start was unimaginable and would easily be the most memorable event of their lives.

Bo was leaning forward to talk to one of the Giants fans sitting directly in front of him when Bo lost his balance and almost fell into the guy's lap. The embarrassed Kansan quickly righted himself thinking that the second beer was starting to kick in. Jackson would have thought the same of his friend but for two facts. Bo hadn't started on his second beer which was now laying on its side and pouring onto the row beneath their seats and Jackson himself had been thrown toward the seats in front. Less than a second later, the exact thing happened again. The action should have caused a concussive impact with the heads of those sitting directly in front had they not been thrown forward also. The third jolt didn't move them as much because by that time, all were gripping their chair arms with the authority of sumo wrestlers. At that moment, a chunk of concrete the size and shape of a rosin bag fell from the deck above and landed in between Jackson's legs. That was when everyone understood this was the real thing.

The 6.9 earthquake from the depths of the San Andres Fault was centered in the Santa Cruz Mountains not thirty miles south of

Candlestick Park. Jackson, as a resident of Southern California had felt his share of small quakes. Some had rattled a few plates and swung a few fixtures but none had physically displaced his body. This was a first for Bo. You would have thought that the two friends were romantically involved for the time that they stared into each other's eyes. Both maintained a strong grip on their seats. A minute or so after the shaking had stopped, they allowed themselves to look up and try to assess the structure directly above. Portions of the fascia were missing. It was time to go. As they gingerly rose, the Giants fans in front claimed that this happened all the time and that the game would only be delayed by a few minutes. The police vehicle on the field and the fact that the grounds crew were taking up the bases led Jackson and Bo to opine otherwise.

The twenty-mile journey to the hotel took nearly six hours. They had to exit at the airport halfway there to refuel. Fortunately, for Bo, who was still driving, there were a couple of gas stations with emergency generators to provide needed resources. Fortunately, for Jackson, who was in need of a drink, the gas station chosen also had a convenience store to provide needed resources. Cell phone communication was nonexistent, and as the sun set, illumination was limited. They could see off to the west a glow on the horizon, seemingly out of place for a city without utilities. That glow came from a series of fires that sprung up in neighborhoods where gas lines had ruptured. The roads themselves were surprisingly unaffected by the jolt. The buildings atop the unbroken terrain, that however was a different story. Increasingly more damage was noted as they inched their way south. The farther they traveled away from the ballpark, the closer they came to the epicenter of the earthquake. Neither one thought to consider the status of their hotel before they arrived at 1:50 a.m. The hotel itself was uninhabitable. And even if it had been, there was no electricity or water available within the structure.

They parked their ride in the fully occupied lot and the two sojourners prepared to lodge inside their vehicle for the remainder of the night. This was not the first time this Sumner Plaine duo had spent the night in a car. Historically, when any of the gang were compelled into accepting such meager accommodations, it was by unplanned obligation as opposed to a deliberate decision. There were times, when they were young and poor, namely while in high school and college, that several of them would drive to Colorado and sleep parked in the lot of a Motel 6 the night prior to skiing. The following night they would repay the kindness of the property owners by lodging more appropriately in the establishment. Eight skiers, two beds, one room. This was the first memory of many that would be revisited that long sleepless night.

"Remember that time we took Willy skiing?" Bo asked of Jackson.

"Willy Harper? Did he go with us? Oh yeah! It was that last time we went, wasn't it?"

"He skied in jeans and a sweatshirt. The guy about froze his ass off. He loved it though and caught on really quick too."

Jackson, who was completely drunk, reverted back to his old haughty high school days. "Willy had no business tagging along. He might have gotten hurt, you know."

"Willy's a nice guy. Just needed a few breaks. If he had a normal family life, he could have been just fine. Other than Five," Bo claimed, "Willy is the most honest and selfless person I have met. It always surprised me that a conversation with Willy would eventually make its way back to me. I would ask him about something of little value and the small talk I had intended became something important regarding me or my family. The things that he hoped for or talked about were not about him but about someone else. Anyway, I always liked him. He used to walk to school with Valeria when we all talked as if she was a skank. I respected that. If not then, I do now."

"You still want some of that don't you."

Bo quickly spoke up without being defensive. He was still cautious about his past reputation, perhaps even more so than his current one. "I never had the hots for her. Besides, that was a long time ago."

"Yeah, but you got a taste of some of that didn't you?" Jackson spewed with slurred accusations. By not answering, Bo could claim deniability yet at the same time impress his friend into thinking he scored a notch but didn't want to brag. All young men find ways to improve their street cred even long after they have left the confines of the marked territory of their youth. But for some reason, Bo felt drawn to the question.

"You know, she wasn't anything at all like we portrayed. Well, maybe a little. But she was more than just the girl from the neighborhood we all talked about. She was apparently really smart. She was a year younger than us but so smart that they moved her up a grade. She helped me in freshman Spanish class. Then she would help me in English class. When she was picked on by the other girls, I would stand up for her. For some reason when the guys did the same, I looked the other way. I regret that." Bo surprised himself with his honest recollections and with his comfort in doing so. It might have been because he knew that in this state of intoxication, Jackson wouldn't remember a thing that was said. Bo, however, was saying things that needed to be said. And things not necessarily to be heard by Jackson, just things Bo needed to speak.

"You still want some of that, don't you," Jackson spluttered as he finished the last swallow of booze from the bottle labeled with his own name.

The police and ambulance sirens that were once prevalent in the city had quieted. In the concrete kiln of the San Francisco suburb, the calm ocean breeze had little impact, failing to scale back the bruising heat of the day. Their car radio was the only communication they had. By this time, the entire world was talking about the events of October 17. One section of the Bay Bridge had collapsed. The majority of the top deck of the Nimitz Freeway had completely failed and flattened its lower artery. There was no estimate yet on loss of life but most were expecting it to be very high.

"How's your dad these days?" Bo asked.

"Hell if I know. Haven't talked to him for a while."

"Good ole Charles. Wasn't it Slim that called your dad Charles?"

"He thought that he acted like Charles Nelson Riley. I never really got it. He also said that Coach Kilgore (their old basketball coach) shuffled like Bob Hope. I never got that either. Good ole Slim, he had a nickname for everyone." Jackson talked slowly as if to convince Bo that he wasn't drunk. "I wouldn't mind talking to Dad more often but the time never seems right. It's funny. When I was growing up, he was usually around but never said much. For some reason, after games, he would leave me notes on my performance instead of telling me directly. It was weird. Now that I'm on my own, there doesn't seem much point to talking. We're like two adults with all of the answers so, we don't need to ask any questions. How about your old man?"

"Dad's fine." Bo didn't like to talk about his dad either. Bo thought that everyone knew more than they actually did when it came to his complicated and heated relationship with his dad. There were times when Bo would suffer through his father's punishments and went to school seemingly wearing the results on his sleeves yet no one was the wiser, not even Bo's mom. "I talked to mom before I came. She said to tell you hi. She also said that she saw your mom at the store the other day. I didn't know that they were in the same high school class!"

"I knew that all of our parents graduated S.P. High but couldn't have told you which classes. My dad moved to town when he was a junior. He did graduate there but commented that he felt like an outsider most of the time. Mom and Dad didn't date until after she graduated. They only dated for four months before they got married. I don't think she was pregnant but that's pretty fast. I would kid Albert that he was a shotgun-wedding kid. He would shoot back by saying that no one knew who my father was." Of course, they never joked like that in front of Mom or Dad.

Bo added his family history also. "Mom makes fun of Dad saying that he dated every girl in school, including your mom. He denies it. Dad always acts as if he fell for Mom in junior high and there was no one else since then. I don't think my parents knew your dad but they both have the same memory of your mom. I guess Gabby worked at the ice cream parlor on Main Street. According to them, if you went there on your birthday, she would buy you an ice cream cone with her own money."

"That's how you tell if a girl likes you. She pays!" Jackson said, slurring his opinion.

"Dad said he bought your mom lunch once to repay for all those ice cream cones but he didn't think that constituted a date. Mom apparently thinks it counts. And by the way, the way you know if a girl likes you; when you share a motorcycle, she holds on to you instead of the seat strap."

Neither one of them slept that night. Just talking and questioning each other's recollections of life. When the sun rose, Bo wasn't sure he could drive. Somehow Jackson found the capability after a quick trip to the alley behind the hotel. He said that he needed to relieve himself but Bo knew that additional resources were needed to bring Jackson back to life.

That morning, Jackson wanted to show Bo the location of a couple of the tech start-ups that were currently part of JEV investment portfolio. It was a complete waste of time. Traffic was still snarled. Even the undamaged roads were closed except for emergency traffic. They returned their car to an unoccupied Hertz drop-off lot and walked the rest of the way to the airport. Emergency generators as well as unruptured runways allowed the airport to operate with only a few hours' delay. Vending machine cuisine sufficed for their wait in a lounge area next to their gate. Jackson, loaded up on Mountain Dew and cocaine, laid out his investment plan before his friend. Bo was only slightly interested in the details. Jackson would pick the top two or three candidates each year for the next two years. The hope and in fact the goal of all venture capital is to catch one flier out of ten. "It takes several years, but it happens. I'll let you know which ones we choose, you buy ten thousand dollars' worth of each of the first five, and if they cash flow, we'll buy a few more."

Jackson rattled off the first three he was considering and their bona fides. Bo had forgotten their names by the time they got on the plane. A year later Jackson made the call to Bo with the first investments. Jackson had chosen four companies and Bo made the share purchases for each. A year later, Jackson chose two others. In order to make the purchase, they both had to pay another five grand apiece because out of the first four, none had positive cash flow and two of them were already out of business. Bo hesitated but only for a moment. Of the final two, one would fail as quick as the first four but the last company Jackson chose in 1990, Cisco Systems, proved to be the flier they were looking for. It would become the investment trade of the decade, maybe of the century.

They both slept soundly on the short flight home to L.A. They arrived at Jackson's house at dinnertime. Jennifer had a meal ready. She had worried all day until Jackson called from the airport in San Francisco. Jennifer made the two sit immediately. She wanted to know everything. The lack of sleep didn't affect the memory of either. They both rattled off every detail, play by play. Only once did they contradict the other and that was over whether Bo actually saw Al Michaels. The two had just finished the bulk of the story when the phone rang. Jennifer answered.

"Jackson there? It's Five."

When Jennifer said who is Mr. Five, Jackson grabbed the phone while Bo explained to her that Brad Andrews's nickname came from the position he played on their hometown baseball team.

"It was originally E-5 because of the number of fielding errors Brad would have in the books after each game. We eventually shortened it to Five. The name stuck."

Five immediately gave the phone to Slim, who was there at the house. They, like Jennifer, had to hear the whole story. Jackson and Slim talked for over an hour. After all had been said about the events of yesterday, Jackson made him promise that they would all go backpacking next summer. It had been several years since their first two trips. Bo agreed. Five offered a thumbs-up to Slim. It was set.

"I'll get Bo on the plans right away," Jackson pledged before hanging up.

"When are we going?" Bo requested.

"I'll check the calendar but they want to go next June." Jackson recalled as he dove back into his cold supper.

"You going to bring the Judge again?" Bo asked while he helped Jennifer clean up in the kitchen.

"Have to. There's bears up there."

"We have never seen a bear and you know what happened the first time you brought it!"

"What about the time when the bear knocked down our tent! Huh!"

"I'm pretty sure that was the wind and faulty assemblage."

SIX

The Milo Field

(Fall 1992)

I n the East, football homecomings and Christmas are favored occasions to draw yearning souls to their places of origin. In the Midwest, it's class reunions and Thanksgiving. Western Kansas usually appears stark and ugly by the time late November arrives. 1992 was the warmest and wettest we had experienced in some time. There had been only one mild freeze so far that fall and farmers were just starting to harvest their fields of milo. Slow harvest seasons are precarious for farmers but grain in the field and temperate weather made for the best situation for time-honored Thanksgiving activities. Pheasant hunting early Thursday morning and Friday afternoon football in the park. These were enduring events not to be missed by any Sumner Plaine red-blooded, testosterone driven Homo sapiens.

Alongside those ventures, and not far removed in importance, was the annual gathering at Ted's Tavern on the Wednesday night before the holiday. Red beers and shuffleboard occupied the event while talk was ever expanding, based on the number of each that was consumed. Slim and Bugs were the first to arrive that year. Followed closely by Five, Jackson and Bo. Ben, Burn, and Marcos would surely be there. And Carlos Garcia, a lanky, long haired left-hander with a blazing fastball and uncontrollable slider-there was no doubt-would report at least two hours late. There have been stories told about Carlos where he would make it to an event so late that no one remained, yet he stayed around thinking he was the first one on the scene. This constituted the bulk of the 1976 Sumner Plaine Bison championship baseball team.

Back in the day, these Wednesday night gatherings would close the bar down. At age thirty-four, plus or minus, the need and the capability had waned. Especially if anyone was hunting in the morning. Jackson wasn't much of a hunter although he participated from time to time. Slim, Bo, and Burn (Kevin Hatcher, the team's catcher, who was called this because his pick-off throws were so hot, they would burn the hands of infielders) would be the ones hunting that next morning. About eleven o'clock most had left the bar. It became an act of attrition determining who would be able to remain long enough to meet Carlos walking through the door. By this time, only the infield remained; Five at the hot box, Slim at first, Whiskey and Wright as middle infielders. Jackson was a born shortstop and played it since he was a fetus. Bo, like all sons of Little League coaches, played second base. It would take him years to develop into the position. Talented enough to start but not enough to star.

Slim and Five hung around while Jackson and Bo saw Carlos drive up as they walked out the door. Bo needed some sleep before a six a.m. wake-up call and Jackson's mom was waiting for him since he so rarely came home. Besides, they had things to talk about before the evening concluded. It was a private conversation not particularly suitable for Ted's. After, both went to bed with unspoken thoughts and unanswered questions. A man's life, so they say, is a competition between tomorrow and today; knowing who you are and realizing who you should be. But tomorrow's prosperity requires today's sacrifice. For success to be legitimate, it must be continuous and tied to one's identity. But what creates identity? Where does it come from? What made these two who they were?

Thanksgiving dinner was always a formal activity at the Stillwell home. The meal was catered and the décor was festive. The only addition to the festivities that Jackson's mom provided were homemade tamales. In her mind, throughout all of Sumner Plaine, no one could make tamales as good as she could. It was a family tradition and recipe passed for generations. Gabby made them every year. They disappeared long before the turkey. The attire, though not formal, was not casual either. There were frequent times when Jackson and his brothers were required to reclimb the stairs to rework an unacceptable attempt. But pleasing their mom was a joy. Even Jackson, who lived and died by his father's approval, loved to be on the receiving end of mom's appreciative smile. The finished product, commencing promptly at one o'clock, was suitable for framing, a true Norman Rockwell painting.

Depending on whom was present each year, the table discussion could be lively or a complete dud. Most commonly the discussion was about the young men at the table, siblings and cousins, and what their most recent activities were. Johnathon, the table's paterfamilias, was usually tranquil and reserved. But during festive occasions, he tried to encourage the conversation's evolution; at least in a general direction that helped him understand more about each youth. He also took every opportunity to inject moral lessons to the discussion. He would never come out and say exactly what he wanted them to understand about his version of life. Choosing rather to allow his sons to discover their own paths. It was more his nature to offer his life as an example instead of his words. That was just fine for Jackson's older brothers but didn't sit well with Johnathon's West Coast son. Jackson thought it a cop-out. He thought that his dad was too afraid to be direct on the off chance he actually was wrong.

There were more similarities than differences between the brothers. All were driven. Each had a good work ethic. Albert, the oldest, who actually married Jackson's first high school girlfriend Cindy (which made for some awkward moments each time one of Jackson's wives was made aware), ended up in the military. Benjamin became an artist after graduating from medical school. An act surprisingly accepted by his dad (after he'd exhausted every attempt and utilized every tool available to talk him out of it). Yet it was obvious to everyone at the table that Jackson was unique. He stood out in every large crowd let alone this small table of kin. When asked, Jackson would always claim that Albert was the best athlete and that Benjamin was the smartest, but no one believed him. Not even Jackson himself.

On the other side of town, in the same neighborhood where Five, Slim, and Carlos lived, the Wright household gathered much later and with much less formality in comparison to the Stillwell family. Depending on the time when Bo, his dad, Slim, and Slim's dad made it home from the hunt and whether or not they were successful, the meal could be at two or six. Bo's mom had three large tables ready each year, one each in the kitchen, dining room, and living room. There was even the occasional kids' table set up downstairs. It was always a gathering of the masses. Direct family. In-laws. Close friends and unattached co-workers from the sheriff's department. Slim and his dad were regulars each year; ever since Tony Batchelder's (Slim) mom left them. Those two were so different in every way but one. It would not be a Thanksgiving without the stories provided by Slim and his dad. No one could spin a yarn like those two. Brad Andrews (Five) and his family were always invited also. Mrs. Wright made it a point each holiday season to visit and invite Brad and his mom. Five's dad died suddenly in 1974 when Five was a junior in high school. Since then, the two had self-isolated and become secluded from the rest of their friends, but Mrs. Wright meant to make sure they always felt welcome, always felt wanted.

All were welcome and Mrs. Wright was the perfect hostess. In her holiday preparation, traditional fare such as turkey and dressing, yams and green bean casserole were accompanied by unique cuisine that changed with each successive season. Sometimes there was a pork loin from a wild boar hunt or venison gifted by a friend, and of course fresh pheasant stew if the birds were available. Once, in the midst of a terrible hunting season, they had turkey and enchiladas, lots of them. It was a classic that they all remembered fondly; not for the food itself but for the blessings that she provided to the forty-three attendees that year. It was their largest gathering ever. All were welcome and all wanted to be there. It was as lively as Ted's on a Friday night, each and every year.

Mrs. Wright was the homemaker everyone wished they were or were related to. Her house was always open to friends and strangers alike. She kept her home like her Christian belief. Clean without being sterile. Nothing held back or saved for special occasions. Never any excess yet always plenty. She deeply believed that one's faith should be clear, not translucent. With Mrs. Wright, what you saw was what you got. And it was yours as much as it was hers. Everyone loved her— except Bo. He adored her. In his youth, he patterned his life as much after her as anyone. It was why everyone Bo came in contact with loved and respected him.

Bo's dad, as typical alpha males go, was unimpressed by his wife although, for the most part, he was good to her. Will, as his family always called him, or Sheriff if you were anyone else, was somewhat detached from his daughters as well. He felt his role was as a provider and protector and would have done anything to properly fulfill those responsibilities. It was assumed that the reason behind his painfully hard treatment of Bo was because there was never any emotion spent on his wife and daughters. It had to go somewhere.

Theirs was a fraught relationship but Thanksgiving was different for Bo and his dad. The season like no other brought them physically and spiritually together. If only for one day a year, they were the father and son all hoped they would be. They woke together, drank coffee together, hunted, cleaned birds, and ate together. They would regale the day's activities with a laughter and love that was never present the other three hundred sixty-four days of the year. And neither one of them knew how to change that fact. Deep inside, they both wanted Thanksgiving to last all year but something within each of them kept it from happening. It's sad when the best day of your life only lasts a day.

Friday morning came and life continued uninterrupted for those who reside in Sumner Plaine, even after a wonderful Thanksgiving. Johnathon Stillwell had a contract due in court on Monday that he still needed to draft. Sheriff Wright was back on the job at the county courthouse early that morning. Most travelers went back to their respective homes on Friday but those like Jackson and Bo who were visiting from afar and chose to stay through the weekend got to relive all the attainable joys of home seemingly unextinguished by time. The wives' plans included morning coffee at the inn, Christmas shopping downtown, lunch, and then Christmas shopping at the mall. Jackson, Bo, and pretty much all of the Ted's Tavern crew met at River Valley Park for the touch football game of the century. Word was out and the gamers kept coming. Each year found additions to the players' roster that no one knew. However, people don't remain strangers long during an aggressive two-hand touch below the waist competition.

Bystanders would sit on the park benches bordering the field of play, not for the competition, but to laugh at the ruthless banter between opponents. Comments like "you run like your sister," or "well you used to be able to throw it that far," were common. And as always, the crowd favorite post touchdown dispute "I got you," "only with one hand," "I got you in front and back," "I only felt one hand on my ass," "well, if you had a dick you would have felt the other," and similar vulgar verbiage were enjoyed annually. Once Bo had ripped both of the tennis shoes that he had borrowed from Five and Slim *accidentally* stepped on and broke the glasses of the new guy scoring all the touchdowns, it was time to go. The decision was confirmed when Carlos showed up. They all made their way over to Five's house to watch the OU vs. Nebraska football game. It was old times.

The Andrews' house was their primary meeting place all through their youth. Five had graduated from the local community college and chose to stay home to help take care of his mom. He had become the inventory manager of DK Sporting Goods downtown. He was content with his solitary life. The guy that could get any girl he wanted in high school no longer was interested in dating and became a confirmed bachelor. Everyone thought that it was at the time when his dad suddenly died that things changed for Five. His senior year in baseball, as with most every member of the team, was the best of his career. He was recruited and played at the community college for a year then dropped out. That's when he stopped talking.

Five's dad was everyone's favorite dad. Mostly because he bought them beer and provided a completely unsupervised and unregulated environment. Needless to say, the Second Street gang, as he would label them, found this home to be their safe zone ever since their ninth-grade year. No one rang the bell or even entered the front door. The side entry directly into the family room was always unlocked—day or night. As you can imagine when they walked through that family door after Friday football in the park, everyone found their former positions and resumed their past personalities as if it was 1976.

"I'm taking OU plus the points," Jackson offered for any takers.

"How many points you asking?" Slim asked, always interested because he loved to gamble. Even though Jackson was considered wild and uninhibited, Slim was the craziest and lived his life on the knife's edge. He was the first of all the friends to smoke grass. Not to be outdone, each of the others followed along. Except Bo. He was the kitty amongst the hounds. It never seemed to bother him though and eventually his sobriety became the accepted norm.

"Ten points."

"Ten Points! Bullshit! The game's in Norman!"

"Unranked team versus twelfth in the nation. Ten points."

"Still too many. What do you say, Carlos?"

"Who's playing?"

"Do you ever pay attention?"

"Sorry I just got here."

"How many points, Five?" Slim surveyed.

Five contemplated for a moment. "Eight and a half."

Bo concurred and the bets were on. Jackson was the athlete, the true athlete in the group. If he hadn't found a love of baseball, he would have been a great two guard or half-miler. But it was Bo and Five that really knew sports inside out. Especially baseball, which those two would talk about into the night, analyzing players and stats and pitching matchups. That was until Brad's dad died of a massive heart attack. It apparently killed him before he hit the floor. They were all crushed. Five's older siblings were in college or living out of town at the time. He and his mom were left alone. It took quite a while before any of the gang were comfortable enough to return to the home base of their youth. The home where all concrete maturation occurred. The home where each young man developed the personality that they would choose. Without this place, none of these connected souls would have been the same.

Bo cracked open the first beer and offered the same toast he had offered every year since Five's dad died. "To Ron Andrews, a dad to us all, number two in our minds but number one in our hearts."

"To Ron."

Ron Andrews died the Friday after Thanksgiving, 1974.

Things became more jovial after the toast; especially when Jackson pulled out a bag of Colombian hash. Everyone partook with the exception of Bo who, not quite the choirboy of old, was yet smart enough to know that the position of an assistant county prosecutor could not be retained if he would fail a state-required random drug test.

"Oh okay. I understand. But you're still a pussyboy." And with that familiar comment, Jackson kissed Bo on the cheek and went to the fridge for another beer to chase his tequila. When the game ended, Nebraska covered the points and Jackson had to pay up. Of course, everyone loved taking money from the richest member of the club.

"I'll take mine in big bills," Carlos said, not realizing that the payout was only ten bucks.

"You're looking a little low over there, Boomer Sooner," Slim remarked as time ran out.

"You do look a little down, Jackson." Bo continued with the assault. "I don't know, guys. He's lost games before. I think he's still bothered by the fact that his old girlfriend has been spending time down on the bottom with Albert." Bo could barely continue without laughing. "How is Cindy these days?"

"Kiss my ass," was all that Jackson could get out of his mouth without slurring his words.

A few others would come and go. Jackson drank harder than usual and needed a ride home. Before leaving, Bo gave Five a hug and asked, "Do you still miss your dad or does that feeling eventually go away?"

Five, who drank almost as much that day as Jackson, stammered a little before he got out what he wanted to say. "Broken hearts never heal." It was the longest sentence he had spoken in over a month.

Bo and the rest of the crew were shocked to hear Five utter more than a one-word reply. The story goes: Ever since Ron Andrews died, Five had gotten it into his head that words had something to do with it. At the funeral, his uncle Cliff, who was there that Thanksgiving when his brother died, mentioned how it seemed that Ron liked to talk so much maybe he had just used up all of his words. It was true. Five's dad was a talker. In fact, he was in the middle of one of his antidotes about life when the heart attack suddenly took his own. Ron was the type who would carry on long past the point where the point had been made. He knew stories. He told jokes. He had opinions on everything from politics to pole dancers. After a while, Jackson and Bo would get annoyed but never Brad. He and his dad were buds. Closer than brothers. Close in a way that almost seemed unnatural. Brad was totally spoiled but Ron didn't care. Ron was irresponsible as a husband and provider but Five didn't notice. When his uncle said "maybe we all have just so many words we are allowed to say before we die. Maybe, Ron talked so much that he just ran out of his allotted words." Everyone thought Five took it to heart.

After that, Five would ration his words. Whether out of fear or anguish, a word from Five was finite and purposeful. Most notably, what came out of his mouth always had significance.

Bo and Jackson spent the last full day with their respective families. Saturday was the time spent replaying yesterday's activities for those who were unable to attend. Bo brought a few case files to review and he dictated a letter while most of his family napped. Mrs. Wright was in the kitchen cleaning up lunch dishes when the doorbell rang. Everyone was surprised to see Five at the door and invited him in. Mrs. Wright always loved Brad and felt a need to mother him a bit. She offered him some pie which he declined by shaking his head. He did say "thank you" which caused many heads to turn in disbelief. What next came out of his mouth shocked everyone more profoundly than the fact he was speaking at all.

"They found a dead body in Uncle Cliff's milo field."

SEVEN

The Victim

(Winter 1992–93)

E ven after a shocking and tragic event in the life of a community, apparently all things must and will return to normal. Jackson and Bo were back in their respective cities working on their prospective projects. Bo was starting to gain his rhythm as a prosecutor. The new career was developing a change in his perspective on society at large and the immobile norms of Kansas's Midwestern population. Bo changed political parties and no longer was a Democrat as his mother. In part, it was because he was starting to believe the rhetoric, but mostly for the simple fact it was easier to be a component of the crowd than a member of a club. The change allowed him to partner up with a more politically motivated and upwardly mobile congregation whose zeal was far more than religious. When natural human hypocrisy is not only accepted but celebrated, it's easy to thrive. He could see that his potential for success would be much more advantageous looking down on society instead of directly in its eye.

Jackson, on the other hand, was refusing any change in his life. It was just as he wanted it to be. Those indiscretions and character flaws he had developed over time, in his mind were necessary evils to create the image and perpetuate the opportunity for success. He and Bo's new-found (though not yet fully realized) wealth proved just that. They were on their way to big things if Jackson could just keep up the connections needed in the world of venture capital. Neither Jackson nor Bo were able to digest the horrific event that was brought to light as they were leaving Sumner Plaine that Thanksgiving weekend. They did not appear to try either. They chose to disperse the normal perception one might have of such an incident into an amorphous fog. They allowed these newly conceived thoughts and images to fade into a blurred haze and as such were able to isolate and ignore any feelings they had toward the victim or the incident itself. Jackson was talented at this exercise and Bo was learning. It was easy to place images deemed indistinguishable in a mental alcove out of reach. And even easier to forget they were there.

Bo and Jackson did not go home for Christmas that year. Their in-laws benefited from their presence that season. St. Louis for Bo and San Diego for Jackson. Both took vacation time after Christmas but were back to their respective homes shortly after the first of the year. By the first of February all aspects of their lives were back to a routine order of daily events. Evenings for Bo and Nancy had been disrupted as of late. Nancy gave birth to their second child, a son, two weeks prior so work and sleep schedules had been altered to say the least. Bo had dozed off after watching the news one evening when he was awakened by his wife handing him the phone.

"Hello... Hi, Dad, this is a surprise. What's up?" Bo tried to hide his bewilderment but failed completely.

"Not much, how are you?"

"I'm fine. Is Mom OK?"

"Yes. She's fine. How's that new baby? How's little Jack?" Soon after Bo's wife had given birth, Mrs. Wright came to help but the sheriff was tied up at work for obvious reasons and as of that time hadn't seen his newest grandchild. Bo's dad mellowed a bit when talking of his grandkids. A characteristic that Bo didn't recall seeing when he was young. A few more niceties were extended then there was a pause in the conversation. It was a hesitation which seemed to occur more to gather one's thoughts in preparation for the next words than because there wasn't anything to say. "I wanted to let you know that they made a positive ID on the girl found in the field. It will probably be in tomorrow's newspaper."

"Oh yeah. Who was it?"

"Valeria Hernandez. Mom thought I should call you because you may have known her."

"Yes. She was in our class. We all knew her. Her family rented a house on First Street next door to Willy."

"Who's Willy?"

"Willy Harper. You remember him! He was the black kid that played ball with us a few seasons in junior high."

"Yes. Now I remember. He was fast wasn't he. Didn't Bolin use him as a pinch runner from time to time when you were in high school."

"That's the one."

"That family has had lots of run-ins with the law as I recall. Bad lot. Seems like his brother is in prison somewhere. Didn't he have something wrong with him?"

"He was born completely deaf and no one realized it until he was eight or something like that. He's a great guy. We don't usually see him but I did run across him at the gas station once last summer. I think he's working at the packing plant."

"Yeah, I remember now. He was really hard to coach. His mom wouldn't let him play sports with his hearing aids! She thought that he would lose them or something."

There was another pause before Bo continued. "So, was there ever a missing person reported? Did the family know she was missing?"

"The parents of the girl are illegal immigrants. They all lived with her uncle's family and she worked in his restaurant. Her family moved around quite a bit but she stayed put for the most part. We have a record of someone coming to the office last summer sometime; asking questions about a missing girl or whether there were any reports of an injured girl. We checked the hospital and there wasn't one. They didn't provide a name or want to file a report."

"I thought the body was all torn up. Five told me that the header on the combine did a real number on the head and torso and that the only thing they could positively determine was that it was a Hispanic female. He didn't think you would be able to identify the victim? Of course, he didn't actually say all that. It took thirty minutes of constructing questions that he could answer with a yes or no."

"It took the KBI a while to work the scene of the accident but eventually they let Cliff finish harvesting the field. After they were done, Cliff went back out to the spot and found a bracelet that was embedded into the mud. The bracelet had her name on the back."

"Wow. That's amazing! What do they think happened?"

"They don't act like they know but if they do, they're not saying much. I think that the KBI is trying to link the death with these earlier murders in the state. Something about an I-70 serial killer."

"We've been following that here in Topeka. In fact, they confiscated me and one other of the attorneys in the DA's office to help with the cases. It's pretty big news around here. No one has mentioned the Sumner Plaine incident in conjunction with the serial killings though. That's interesting."

"I'm not so sure. Let's see. I've got the coroner's report here. Yeah, Hispanic female, age 30–40, 5'6", 125–135 pounds, let's see, cause of death, presumed blunt trauma, no bullet or stab wounds detected to the head or torso. When I look at those other serial killer cases, this one doesn't seem to match the MO. The others, however, don't show a consistent pattern either. There are a few murders in Nebraska and Texas they are looking into with the same assumption."

"So is your part over or do you have to continue with the investigation?"

"Oh yeah. We're supposed to keep digging. We ask for more resources from the state but get bupkis. This new DNA technique that they are using to identify vics and perps is the wave of the future, I guess. They want us to seal evidence in a way that retains the cellular viability of the remains. We don't really know what that means or how to do it. We are running low on rape kits but I thought we could use those to retain the evidence. We had the coroner collect the samples. I don't know. It's the only thing we could think of. Do you have any suggestions?"

It was the first time in Bo's life that his father was asking him for advice. For a brief moment, it was Thanksgiving. "No not really. I'm involved in the punishment side more than the investigative side. I'm sure you're doing your job well. You've always been a good sheriff." Now, the feeling was mutual.

"By the way," Bo's dad said as he was winding up the phone call. "The girl was pregnant. We came across that in the autopsy. We took a sample from the unborn child and placed it in its own rape kit as well."

The conversation ended as unremarkably as it started. The look in Bo's eyes as he hung up the phone was ambiguous enough to create a pause in his wife's activities and concern in her thoughts. It was the longest phone call she ever remembered Bo having with his dad and the look on Bo's face seemed unsettled, as if he was unsure that the call itself actually occurred.

"What was it?" Nancy asked while moving closer to sit on the ottoman in front of her husband.

"What was what?"

"Don't do that. What did your dad want to talk about that took twenty minutes? Is everything all right?" Bo used to try harder but his deficient skills in the art of marital communications had gone wanting as he became more engrossed in his career. It usually took quite a bit of encouragement from Nancy to pry loose her husband's tightly held thoughts and words.

"Everything's fine. He was telling me about the case involving the girl in the milo field. She was a classmate of ours." Bo stopped for a moment to collect his thoughts. For some reason, he felt the need to posture his words for the remainder of this discussion with Nancy. "Funny. It's the first time we've had so much in common within one conversation-other than baseball. I guess that's why it took so long. It almost felt good, other than the subject matter, obviously."

"So, you knew the girl?"

"Well, yeah. I guess you could say I knew her. She lived in our neighborhood. She was nice. Actually, very smart for her situation."

"What situation is that?"

"Oh, you know, poor household. Her parents split time in Sumner Plaine and somewhere in Mexico. They were migrant workers, I guess. When you speak Spanish only while at home then have to turn around each day to speak English at school and work, it takes some intelligence to do that. I can remember when we were in junior high, we used to walk to school together but always across the street from each other. It's funny now but it felt normal at that age. Anyway, one day she crossed the street and we walked together. That was until the boys at school made fun of me for hanging around her. But we got to know each other then. At least as much as you can when you're twelve or thirteen years old. I don't remember her much in high school."

Nancy noticed that within that last statement Bo appeared to be attempting to convince himself that what he was saying was true. Bo was still questioning something. That was easy to tell. However, what that question was and why its presence was rolling around in the back of Bo's mind was another thing. As a former defense attorney and now prosecutor, he had developed a unique awareness and capability of looking at a situation from opposite sides. Two trains of thought. Two perspectives of consideration. It had done him well in his career; so much that he used the technique in almost everything he did. A level of foresight and wisdom emerged from his deliberate temperament. It had kept him from trouble in the past and slowly created a perceived level of invulnerability, at least in his own mind. As if he actually had the ability to manipulate a circumstance and create any desired outcome. Arrogance. It feeds upon itself. Nothing new to the world of legal due process. It's just that it had never been part of Bo's nature.

***

On the West Coast, Jackson heard the news of the identification through the *Sumner Plaine Gazette*. Jackson's parents from time to time would send him specific issues of the paper when they thought he might have an interest. The news article, which was solidly displayed on the front page, made it much more difficult to discount than the initial report that had traversed the grapevine back home. He read it twice, as if he needed to convince himself of something, then left it on the table as he made his way out the door for a Sunday morning jog. Jackson's second wife, an attorney herself, was not the athletic type and usually slept in on Sundays. Her legal expertise was elder law. She handled wills and trusts for a small firm in Santa Monica. After reaching for her first cup of coffee, she noticed the newspaper on the table.

When Jackson returned, he found her at the kitchen table, cup of coffee in hand, reading the *Gazette*. She was completely engrossed and read both pages of the article. She hadn't noticed that Jackson had entered the house and didn't immediately respond when he said "Good morning."

"How awful! Did you read this?"

"Sure."

"Did you know anything about it?"

"I'd heard something when we were home for Thanksgiving," was Jackson's short and sweet answer.

"Why didn't you say something?"

"I didn't think it was important," he stated with a nonchalant shrug lacking.

"Did you know her?"

"No."

EIGHT

The Toast

(Summer 1996)

I t was a feeling difficult to detect or clearly describe. Those around the two accomplished attorneys were surely oblivious to the situation. No one noticed the deliberate glint in both of their eyes, the kind that takes years of unconscious development to perfect. There was a casual confidence to each of their facial expressions, something clearly born out of generations of family ascendancy. Those uniquely paying attention might have been influenced more by the richness of the surroundings, tainted by the aroma of frugal cigar smoke. But the gentle concussion caused by the touching of extravagant crystal and expensive scotch muffled by corrupt air and unclean hands, should have suggested the uniqueness of the occasion. A toast. The point in time when attitudes morph into ideals, when desires become motivation, and resolve emerges from hope. Yet, at that point when energy begat sound, the phenomenon unnoticed by everyone but them, was not the agreed aspirations of two differing individuals. It was a moment of complete balance between two comparable forces; a bliss that came from true equality and the mutual acceptance of kindred souls. It was parity of accomplishment and potential. It was equity of intellectual and social status. It was a harmony of body and spirit. And it was symmetry that throughout their developing friendship neither thought would occur. "To S.P."

"To S.P."

It was early on Saturday evening during their twenty-year class reunion when Jackson and Bo made their way to the local country club just south of town. They hadn't missed a reunion since graduation but had eventually found that the Friday night activities were enough to tide them over for another five years. Besides, neither of their wives ever attended these reunions making the stuffy dinner party on Saturday night even less appealing.

Prairie Winds Country Club was the jewel of the county, in fact of the western part of the state. The clubhouse itself was built on a small and slightly elevated perch subtly accented by native cottonwoods. Its façade of brick and glass overlooked a sprawling carpet of green cut into the sand dunes left behind by the receded waters of a prehistoric riverbed, eventually to be named the Arkansas. The club is where the high society of western Kansas met to drink, socialize, and do business in between games of gin and cribbage. It was fitting that Jackson and Bo would end up at the club during this and future hometown visits for they had become much more attuned to the finer things in life. Even their much beloved Ted's Tavern had lost its appeal to these socially advancing young men with storied histories.

The typical conversations between Jackson and Bo were short and to the point. In fact, that evening, there was even less than the normal amount of banter and debate. Just, "to S.P." But those who knew them best would have realized the depth of feeling that was displayed in those two words. This home and its history that they shared were the constant and perfecting links that would keep them closer than any other relationship each would be involved with throughout their entire lives. Words were not necessary to validate the fact. Their affinity toward Sumner Plaine was undeniable but the place they called home, at least for this time in their lives, had become an image in the rearview mirror of a car whose tires had been driven to baldness, stored away in a garage whose door was rusted shut from lack of use.

"I talked to Five today," Bo claimed while scanning the golf course through the nearby window.

Jackson put his drink down on the table and swallowed his sip before answering. "No way! What did he say?"

"Ingurgitation."

"What?"

Bo regressed. "I was at Hank's for a turnover this morning. He was walking in as I was leaving. I said we missed you last night. He didn't

say a thing. I said, what have you been up to and he said, ingurgitation."
Bo couldn't finish the word before he broke out laughing.

"Is he still doing that shit?"

"Apparently so."

"What does it mean?"

"Hell if I know."

They both stopped talking for a while and watched the golfers walk off the finishing hole. Both Jackson and Bo played golf. Not because they loved it or were good at it but because it was required of them. Something in the small print that stated in order for a man to do well in life or show that he has done well, he must play golf. So, they did. In fact, they were planning to play the next day until Bo heard that the wind would be out of the southwest at 25–30 mph. Then, Bo wouldn't play. Jackson would, especially if there was money on the table, but that weekend it was just those two and Bo knew better than to bet against Jackson in any sporting event.

Jackson, now nursing his second glass of J.B., relaxed back into his chair and smiled. It was the first time this evening that he had looked his lifelong friend in the eye. "Royals suck," he stated with a chuckle.

"A's too," was Bo's response matching that same grin while shaking his head affirmatively yet still sitting forward in his chair.

"We should meet in Kansas City for a game this fall."

"You know what I'd like to do?" Bo offered in return while shifting around to find a bit more comfort and finally looking forward into Jackson's dark handsome face. "I want to go backpacking again. Try to find that lost trail up by Long Lake."

"It's too late for this season. It's going to get cold pretty soon. I'd do it next year if you want to set it up." After a short pause in their condensed chat, Jackson continued. "You could come out to San Francisco and we could catch a game at the 'Stick."

Jackson's observation was apparently forced out through an unrestrained grin. Bo's response was in disbelief. "Not on your life," he said. "I need another game at Candlestick Park like I need another hole in my head." Still shaking his head as if to say, I hadn't thought about that for a while, Bo proceeded. "That was the longest night of my life. I thought we never would make it home."

For Jackson and Bo, life was mostly about the present. Little discussion occurred regarding things farther off than a day or two. They were quite comfortable with their pasts and confident in their futures so their discussions usually centered around today. The accomplishments of their youth could fill multiple publications. The potentiality of their future claims were to be unrestrainable. Yet in each other's company, they lingered in the vicinity of what they could see and hold. Time was precious to them and not to be wasted on actions that couldn't be changed or dreams that might not be satisfied.

"How's your mom?" Jackson requested in a voice that was a combination of sympathy and interest.

"She's fine. And yours?"

"Great. She's great. She wants you to come over tomorrow for lunch after church."

"I'm in."

Bo continued with barely a pause. "What's new at work? Any Hollywood clients?"

"I wish. How's the prosecutorial business? You going to run for A.G. or do you still have your eye on that judgeship?" Jackson only received a slight shrug in return and watched as his friend's unaltered face moved his gaze again out the window onto the darkening vista of the empty eighteenth green.

In 1983, these two young men became attorneys but for two completely different reasons. Jackson's father, the founding partner of the western Kansas law firm of Stillwell, Cobb & Benson, had emblazoned on each road sign of Jackson's future path the idea that being a reputable tax attorney in a country where taxes are the only thing guaranteed to exist and constantly change, is the most lucrative job a man could obtain. It was what Jackson's dad wished he would have done. He took every opportunity to mentally inflict into his son's mind the discipline necessary to accomplish this one dominant goal. There was no choice; at least in the mind of Jackson there was no choice. He would tell his mom that the path he was placed upon led only to one opened door. The rest were locked.

So, for seven straight years Jackson had spent his days searching for ways to game the system. No matter how wealthy it made him, it was beginning take a toll. It was this concept of a perpetual unchangeable future without doing any real good, that created the positive and empathetic transformation that people were starting to notice in Jackson. A change most didn't believe could ever occur.

William Beauregard Wright, on the other hand, had always planned on being a teacher and coach as his father once was but a deterioration in that relationship lead Bo to a midstream change early in his college career. Bo decided at the end of his degree track in political science (also at KU) to apply for law school at Washburn University. However, Bo's grades didn't impress the acceptance committee as he had hoped, and he was not granted a seat in the class of 1983, leading to his decision to stay in Lawrence and study for a master's degree. Johnathon Stillwell, a generous Washburn alum, through the persuading of his wife Gabby, interceded on Bo's behalf and a special waiver was granted which allowed him to join the class at semester. It would take all the effort and resources available to Bo in order to make up for the lost time and graduate with the other members of his class. It was an experience not looked back upon with joy. Unable to participate in the normal social activities of his classmates and the fact that his admittance was granted by the graces of a third party and not his own merits, left Bo suspicious, insecure, and with a big chip on his shoulder; a change in personality that no one would have thought possible.

"Do you still think about it?" Bo said, displaying no emotion or caution yet looking deeply into Jackson's eyes.

Jackson answered, "Think about what?"

The uneventful evening came to an end for the two best friends. Plans were reconfirmed for lunch tomorrow and the trips returning home to Los Angeles and Topeka on the following day. The last act, as always was the case, a hug that was both abrupt and enduring. Their parting was always touching and tragic. Touching in a way that all could understand. Tragic in a way that no one could resolve. In a Dickens fashion, they were the best and worst of each other. They were envious and distrustful of each other. They were composed and insecure when apart. They were glorious and calamitous when together. They created each other, belonged to each other, defied each other, and reviled each other.

NINE

The Closed Door

As far as state capitals go, Topeka isn't much to speak of. Other than Brown v. Board of Education, Kansas is not known for ground-breaking political or legal decisions. The city itself seems to have been an afterthought of its founding fathers and no thought at all from its current leaders. Topeka doesn't seem to try very hard. With a population that hasn't changed since 1960, it's good at existing but not much more. Bo was to find that out and regret the reality at some point, but initially he and his family were content with their home. William B. Wright, licensed Juris Doctor, had experimented within several aspects of the legal profession after graduating, and finally reached a place of some professional stature in the county prosecutor's office. This cachet had earned him a reputation within the local bar as well as the political elite at the state house. His past history, which added a great deal of diverse professional experience to his resume, would have made most proud if not envious. And he was proud of his professional life, to a point. This emotion was fading, however, and was not enough to overshadow the fact that in reaching this position, Bo was slowly becoming disillusioned with the career path he was on. It was the inner workings of "the game," as he called it, that chapped the skin of which he was required to pro-vide. And no matter what he was able to accomplish within the legal community, it never supplemented the personal inclinations of the boy from Sumner Plaine. He never would have admitted it to anyone but Bo had become bored. Bored with his work, bored with his life. Even his recently enjoyed stock market success and subsequent wealth was not enough to loosen the firm grip that this funk had upon him.

Bo's wife, Nancy, wasn't aware of her husband's dismay so the source of his change was not initially known. When it started to become obvious to her, she encouraged him to go back to what he loved in his initial years as a lawyer. At least it was what she thought he loved. But that wasn't what he wanted either. The truth is, William B. Wright, JD, didn't know what he wanted or what was best for him. The wisdom yielded from yesterday's answers is not always adequate to the task of today's questions. No, going back was not the answer. Accepting one's lot in life, embracing the here and now, that didn't seem to help either. Too much confusion. Too much conflict. Too much uncertainty. Bo struggled with his present, didn't have a clue about his future and something about his past wouldn't let him proceed. Legal cases and judicial reviews were rarely the primary focus within his current span of attention. Yet he went about his responsibilities unhindered. Few could tell but Bo was becoming disoriented without realizing he was lost. To an outsider though, each of Bo's days were consistently stable.

The arduous drive from home to work became more monotonous each day. Five and seven-tenths miles. Six left turns and eight right in total. Half directly into the eastern sun, half angled obtusely to one side or the another. The traffic rarely changed, and if it did, it never made a difference. Seventeen minutes it took each day. Too long and not long enough. As Bo arrived every morning, the vista of his emergence was always the same, regardless of the season. Only a handful of trees blotted the concrete canvas of his nine to five. His office building looked like ... well Topeka. The exterior was square, plain, symmetrical, monotonous, and tan. Inside, it was worse. It looked like the home of frugal government, which was precisely the intent. It made one feel defeated and impotent just for breaching its portal, which was also the intent. The duly elected district attorney of Shawnee County had her own parking space but the rest of the supporting staff, including Assistant District Attorney William B. Wright, had to fend for themselves. Meaning, sometimes Bo made it to his desk in five minutes and sometimes fifteen. This constituted the beginning of each day for the last five years, one month, and twenty-two days.

The recent remodeling of the second floor allowed for Bo and two of his other colleagues to have their own offices for the first time since anyone could remember. Originally, they all worked together in open pods with portable walls and flexible privacy. There were five attorneys and seven support staff including Peggy. She was, for a short time, Bo's legal assistant and an attractive distraction. It was a one-off at a Kansas City hotel during a continuing education meeting. The affair was so quick, it hardly seemed a mistake. Those who knew them both would have assumed it morally impossible for either. Those who grew up with Bo would have been shocked. Peggy left shortly after and neither of their lives were deflected. Perhaps that was the point in time when Nancy noticed the perfected aura of her husband dimming a bit. The change was occurring so imperceptibly, no one noticed but her. Jackson might have. The two of them had been on the phone a lot since just before the last class reunion. As always, most of their conversations were compact and efficient but there were enough of them that they would have been able to feel any altered mood or progression of the other, unconsciously if not fully aware. They were like that. An enviable trait that only the closest of relationships could offer.

Once inside, the tedium continued within the inefficiently functioning area of the assistant DAs. Even for Bo, who had become the most senior in a pool of transient employees, his routine lacked interest. The same mechanics occurred each morning. Good morning. How was your evening. Get a cup of joe. Walk into the office, leave the door open. Empty your hands, set things on the desk in precisely the same order each day. Turn on the Dell. Open the briefcase. Take the first sip of coffee while waiting for the worthless computer to warm up so you can read your emails and be ready for it to hit the fan at nine a.m., plus or minus.

That day's emails included a periodic KBI report which, amongst other things, covered the state-wide registry of felony arrests from the previous week. The scanning was monotonous but Bo plodded through it as if he was searching for a specific name. The banality of that scrutiny obscured his retention of the remaining emails. That is until he came across a directive from the state bar association. It was a common request with an uncommon appeal.

The 3rd Judicial District Nominating Commission is seeking nominations to fill a district judge vacancy in Shawnee County created when Chief Judge Ansley McCue leaves his position to become a justice of the Kansas Supreme Court on November 9.

Justice Jacob J. Collinsworth, the Supreme Court departmental justice responsible for the 3rd Judicial District, composed of Shawnee County, said individuals can apply or be nominated, but nominations must come on a nomination form and include the nominee's signature.

A nominee for district judge must be:

at least 30 years old;

a lawyer admitted to practice in Kansas and engaged in the practice of law for at least five years, whether as a lawyer, judge, or full-time teacher at an accredited law school; and

a resident of the judicial district while holding office.

Nominations must be accompanied by a nomination form available from the clerk of the Shawnee County District Court, the clerk of the appellate courts at the Kansas Judicial Center, or the district court website.

One original and one copy of the completed nomination form and supporting letters must be submitted by noon Wednesday, October 28, to:

Justice Jacob J. Collinsworth
Kansas Judicial Center
301 SW 10th Ave.

Topeka KS 66612

The nominating commission will convene to interview nominees at nine a.m. Friday, November 13,
in the Shawnee County Courthouse, 200 SE 7th St.
Interviews are open to the public.

The commission will select from three to five nominees
whose names will be submitted to the governor to fill
the position according to statutory qualification and
residency requirements. If there are not three nominees who reside in the district who are deemed qualified by the commission, the commission may consider
nominees who reside outside the judicial district. The
governor has 60 days after receiving the names to
decide whom to appoint.

After serving one year in office, the new judge must
stand for a retention vote in the next general election
to remain in the position. If retained, the incumbent
will serve a four-year term.

The 3rd Judicial District Nominating Commission
consists of Collinsworth as the nonvoting chair,
Thomas Cole Spencer, Erica Jeffries, Andrew Clement,
Emily Drees, and Brian Ackerman, all of Topeka,
Mathias Hopkins of Rossville, and Anna Caroline of
Silver Lake.

It was what Bo had been anticipating and hoping for. At least, that's what
he presumed. It was a feeling not deep to the core but just under that
thin lamina that separates inward motivations from the external expectations, where all poorly thought out and impatient decisions are made.

Earlier in his marriage, Bo would have called his wife to discuss the
recent event and allow her to participate in the decision that he had
already made. Today, he called his boss's secretary and asked for a sit

down later that morning. Once the time was set, Bo sat back in his chair and stared out the windowed wall of his office onto the chaotic venue of his daily life. He wasn't sure what to think. He wasn't thinking at all. He was sedate if not solemn. It was as if he had just arrived at his seat on a train for a long trip to an unknown destination that had been planned by someone else. He was subdued perhaps because he felt little control over his direction; even with this next step which was his decision to make. His life had become limited in a way he couldn't change. Each day felt like the next intersection on a one-way street. Go or turn. But Bo didn't believe in destiny. Living, like faith, was a choice. He wasn't sure why he was going to do this. Other than it was different. At that time, anything different seemed right.

At 11:45 a.m., Bo crossed the street to the courthouse and walked into District Attorney Lindsay Paige's office. She was cordial but needed to be brief. "How can I help you, William?"

"I assume you are aware of the upcoming vacancy in the third district."

"I am. Why?" She then looked up into the serious face confronting her. District Attorney Paige's demeanor softened as she sat back into her tufted leather chair. The paneled walls supporting dark chestnut bookshelves glutted with hundreds of unread law journals surrounded her with authority. The space advertised the intended erudition of the atmosphere. It was an office that few wanted but none wished to give up. She smiled. "I always thought you would be after my job."

"I wouldn't apply without your approval."

Without hesitating or considering the difficult position in which she would be placed, attempting to find such a consistent and reliable replacement, she said, "I'll even offer the nomination and rundown the letters of recommendations. Just leave it to me. Abbey!" she yelled out the door which Bo had left open. "Get me the judicial nomination forms from the clerk at the third district, will you. And call Judge Kline, that's Woodrow Kline—307, I think. Tell him I need a favor. And tell Kristin, oh never mind, I'll tell her." After that, she smiled again. "I'm going to miss you."

"I may not be selected."

"Yeah right."

Bo went back to his office and returned to his work. The rest of the day went by uninterrupted. He drove home in a mental fog, somewhat. Unfocused on what to do next (even though there was really nothing to do) Bo drove into the garage and walked through the door and into the mudroom of his tan brick and siding faced home. The kitchen was bright, clean, and smelled of tacos. Nancy was in the living room playing with their five-year-old son Jack while Jenna, their ten-year-old daughter, was at the dining table working on a school project. Bo stood there watching the three and a rare fleeting smile came to his face. Nancy looked up just in time to catch the noteworthy phenomenon and hear the news. For a moment, Bo was content. Nancy hailed from St. Louis and grew up in a wealthy suburban family. Bo worried that he might not be seen as a good provider but she was very comfortable with her middle-class life. "I put my name in to be nominated for Third District Court Judge today."

"What?"

"Is that OK with you?"

Nancy was surprised. It didn't take long though for the stun to calm. What soon replaced it was excitement at the thought of the extraordinary life possible with having a judge for a husband. And with that image, she offered to her husband the much more frequent and less ephemeral smile she was known for. Nancy loved Bo in the way that all loved him and was willing to support him even when she was not included in Bo's thoughts of his future.

Bo didn't call anyone that night with the news of his decision. He didn't call Jackson or his mom and dad. No siblings. No one. In fact, he asked Nancy not to tell anyone. Even with the strong endorsement from the office of the DA and her confidence in his selection, he didn't want to get ahead of the process, as he said. He had always been subdued but had recently become secretive which was all part of the subtle alteration his personality was going through. At least that was about the time when some started to notice the change. Bo was always quiet without being shy. He rarely spoke of his feelings or motivations. However, the introspective appearance that attorney William B. Wright presented to the world was a perfect fit for one choosing to sit behind the judicial bench. Weeks later, after his interview went off without a hitch, Bo was selected as one of the three candidates submitted to the governor and as *luck* would have it, Bo was the only one nominated who was of the same political party as the governor. It made him a shoe-in for the position. The announcement was made public on January 4, 1999. Then Bo called his parents and talked to his sisters. He chose not to call Jackson.

The days leading up to the judgeship seem to decelerate the closer they approached. For Nancy, the family, their friends, time sailed, but for Bo, it was an unending pause. The indulgent prosecutor had become the impatient judge. Nancy tried to calm him as he mentally prepared for his new task but with little success. Most people miss their opportunity to enjoy and appreciate the positive changes in life. They overlook them as they peer into the glorious future they presume to be embarking on. Nancy grounded him in so many ways. In the few weeks leading up to his first court case, she was invaluable. She knew this was the start of something wonderful for both of them. For Bo, it was the beginning of the long sought-after dream he always had, yet was never really able to envision.

Bo attended his orientation, which was rudimentary and slow. He was given his robes, which were old and smelled of cigarettes. He was granted his judicial chambers, which were austere and unmotivating. He was presented his legal and clerical staff, who were young and inexperienced. In all this, Bo could have been disappointed but none of it mattered. This was it. It truly was like Nancy had said. It was going to be the pinnacle achieved from years of preparation, struggle, and sacrifice. It was the positive change Bo needed. The final corrected reality that all his mistakes had led up to. A reincarnated life as it always was meant to be.

Bo's first deposition on his first day in preparation for his first trial was set for ten o'clock. At nine fifteen, Judge Woodrow Kline walked in through Bo's continuously opened door and promptly yet quietly shut it. The stealth action struck Bo as strange and a little intimidating. Doors for Bo had always been ajar if not fully open. He believed in full transparency with all honest actions. He strived to present an open-door policy to all who would seek his assistance. To him, a closed door always seemed elitist. As a child, what started as a fear of the dark, morphed into a habit. As a teenager he read with the door open so as not to miss out on quiet discussions in the next room. A closed door symbolized a selfish closed-off life to Bo. It also brought back memories of arguments and violent outbursts ineffectively shielded by a closed door. When Bo's mom would discipline, there was a point to it with a proper, if not enjoyable, resolution and the door always stayed open. When Sheriff William Bedford Wright closed the door well, that was another thing. Bo never wanted any such impressions made of him, until that day. What happened in the next half hour would change all of that. From that day forward, those who wished to approach Judge William Beauregard Wright did so through a closed door.

TEN

City of Angels

(Spring 2000)

N ear downtown Los Angeles, in a conveniently located posh residential high-rise, there was a stunning apartment filled with
modern amenities, modern furnishings, and all the trappings of wealth
without the aristocracy. And it was mostly unoccupied. The apartment was one of three residential properties that Jackson owned in
California. The others weren't occupied much either. Jackson's current
wife, Gwyneth, preferred the new-built home on Laguna Beach. The
home in Napa was just for long weekends of which there were none.
Downtown L.A. is reflective and sterile. There is an echo around almost
every corner. Concrete and glass. Stone and steel. There is always a push
to add more green space to the vicinity but as of yet, not much is visible. Inside each building, however, these edifices are immaculate. No
expense has been spared for the business industry of this city. Which is
strange. The home of Hollywood celebrities and entertainment technology, where external appearances are far more important than internal
inclinations, the visage of its architecture relates the opposite.

Jackson's law firm of Williams, Brown, and Fairfield was located
within walking distance (though no one ever walked) of his apartment.
The firm represented many of the largest corporations on both coasts.
Tax law is consistent if not exciting. In the beginning, Jackson held
completely to his dad's assumption of the occupation. Jackson's intellect
allowed him to grasp the oft-hidden nuances of state and federal tax
codes while his competitiveness provoked the work ethic and desire necessary to advance within the structure of the firm's promoted agenda. In a
word, Jackson had developed a niche. The firm utilized him as their lead

attorney for large residential real estate businesses. And with few exceptions, corporate tax consulting was all he did. Traveling from real estate sites to corporate headquarters to business dinners with the high and mighty throughout the rapidly expanding Southern California region was his routine. It eventually became his Delilah. Seductively enjoyable at first but eventually it would kill him (or at least feel that way).

A corporate residential apartment conglomerate, Barton Properties, Inc., which was based in Santa Monica, was one of the firm's most lucrative clients. It owned apartment and condominium complexes all over the state. With corporate headquarters located in the affluent and sexy Los Angeles suburb, Jackson found himself there consistently. Back in 1986, as a young addition to the team, Jackson was the one who chased down the CEO on a lead distributed to him by the firm's partners. The relationship proved advantageous in many ways. It was the start of Jackson's climb up the corporate ladder and his introduction to the community he chose as his home for the next six years. New opportunity breeds excitement, and while the chance to live and work in the most exciting city on the West Coast was enough for most, it was the ocean that had caught Jackson's eye.

As such, Jackson always enjoyed his business trips to the seaside community. The fourteen years, first as a headhunter, now as a partner, never seemed mundane. Santa Monica was the only community he ever felt a part of—other than Sumner Plaine. Four weeks prior, Jackson was on-site of a potential investment off I-10, near Fourth Street. The board of directors of Barton Properties had recently moved in a different direction, intending to diversify their holdings to include commercial real estate. Most notable in the change of investment profile was a large retail mall in this area not far from the beach. California was growing at such a pace and the corporation had been so profitable, it only made sense (in their minds) to consider new types of investments within their real estate template. Jackson was puzzled. It wasn't that he was unfamiliar with the property. It wasn't far from his first home in a neighborhood he knew well. He would frequent it on weekends for the restaurants and clothing stores. But all of the other investments that he had been involved with representing Barton Properties had been residential within their business platform. The tax ramifications and contractual distinctions would be completely different and would require a great deal more time and effort to diagnose. That was, however, Jackson's job: to determine whether the contractual purchase agreement could be profitable as proposed and create the return on investment needed to meet the criteria of the corporation. Jackson had become a business as well as tax analyst. He was the best and most reliable that the firm could offer. It was to be an exhausting three days of work in Jackson's old neighborhood.

The location of the mall was in a pleasant middle-class area that would be considered unremarkable to most Californians. Jackson felt a comfort here that downtown L.A. could never offer. He stayed at a hotel not far from the mall and up the street from the RAND Corporation building. The pace of time sped and the days ran together like a child's watercolor painting. Late on Thursday afternoon after his final review of contracts and corporate tax returns, the weight of the job hit him. He was mentally exhausted and decided not to take the long traffic-ridden trek back to downtown L.A. On his way in to procure one more night's lodging, a familiar sound vibrated loose a memory of home. Romantic images of the past can be elicited by any number of senses. Certain sounds resonate to incite joyful, agonizing, or serene recollections of the place from where they hail. Specific smells, particular images, all can bring home to mind. School bells. Fresh basil. A full moon. Any number of sensations might be the trigger. For Jackson, the only res- onance capable of taking him back to that place of delight was the crack of a bat echoing unimpeded through the warm air as a fastball leaves the yard.

Jackson had noticed the baseball field behind the hotel property. He even had a vague memory of noticing the field being played upon when he used to live nearby. The image itself, though, wasn't enough to trigger some emotion or memory. It took a certain sound to make Jackson take notice. Entering the hotel, he quickly finalized his room selection, exited the hotel, and walked over to the watch some of the game. The location was the home field of the Santa Monica High School Vikings. The stands behind the plate were mostly empty, which surprised the former Jayhawk infielder. There had never been a home game played by the Sumner Plaine Bisons that wasn't fully attended by family, friends, and community. Frequently there were more fans at a home game at Lewis Field for a Sumner Plaine playoff game than some of the regular season games in Lawrence.

The field was of standard dimensions. The fences were 325 down the lines, 343 in left and right, and 365 up the gut, with a circumference of fences fully connected thirty feet behind home plate. The seating allowed for about a hundred fans with a few temporary risers erected down both lines. It was a hot California afternoon and once Jackson was seated, he started to regret his decision. Both benches, covered in plywood and corrugated tin, were the only shelter available from the intense Southern California sun. The stands and the dugouts were newly painted in the Samohi school colors. The dark blue and bright gold didn't deflect any of the heat. Jackson took off his suit jacket and loosened his tie to try to make himself comfortable. An elderly gentleman sitting just across the central isle stared conspicuously at Jackson obviously wondering why someone would dress in such a way for a baseball game.

It was already the bottom of the fifth inning when Jackson got situated. The visiting team was getting schooled. There was no announcer or program for one to utilize in following the game. The left-center scoreboard was the only informant on the field. After a moment, with the bases empty and one out, the elderly gentleman motioned across the aisle to Jackson to bring attention to the young man coming to the plate. "Number two there, he's my grandson."

The boy was small without looking frail, young without looking inexperienced. He wore his hat under the batting helmet so it would fit better and carried a bat that seemed too big for him. Jackson felt sorry for him because he was a left-handed batter facing a hard-throwing, much larger, left-handed pitcher. That was until the first pitch never made it to the catcher's glove. It was a hard shot, line drive, which caught the chalk down the right field line. Following the play in the field instead of the batter, Jackson's eyes, like the ball itself, arrived at third base long after the boy reached standing up. "Wow, that was impressive! You say he's your grandson?"

"Yes. He's my only grandchild."

"Pretty sharp hit for a small young man. What grade is he in?"

With the pride that only a grandfather could portray, he claimed, "He's the only freshman to make this team of juniors and seniors." Jackson's eyes were wide open and his face sculptured a smirk of disbelief as he returned to the game at hand. The next hit easily brought the boy in to score and the umpire called the game right then.

"What happened?" Jackson inquired, since there wasn't a PA system to advise the fans of anything.

"They run-ruled them. A fifteen-run lead after five innings and they call it."

"Shoot! I would have liked to see your grandson in the field. What position does he play?"

"Second base," was the man's reply as he was gathering his things and preparing to leave.

"A southpaw at second base? That's unique."

"He bats left and throws right. He's working on switch hitting but hasn't quite got that figured out yet." And with that, the man was quickly down the steps and over to the team meeting behind the third-base dugout. Jackson watched the man's movement till he joined the small gathering of ballplayers and supporters. He put on his jacket then headed for the hotel. Again, he was feeling tired and wanted to call it a day.

On Friday, Jackson woke later than usual to start his unremarkable day. He found that to be true. The only time he slept well was when he was away from his apartment. He was refreshed and his mind was at ease. That Friday, traffic was slow but not terrible on his way downtown, which allowed Jackson the leisure to ponder and remember his first and perhaps only love, baseball. He thought about the boy and his grandfather. He remembered his games at Lewis Field when his grandparents would drive hours just to sit behind home plate. Recalling the joy he felt when named as the starting shortstop for the Kansas Jayhawks in just his sophomore season and the phone call to his dad with the good news, the smile never left his face, that day or this.

Jackson didn't succumb to the temptation to go home or call Gwyneth to meet for lunch but went straight to the office. He grabbed a sandwich at the deli downstairs and took it to his ninth floor office overlooking the sprawling Los Angeles skyline. This was a common lunch venue for Jackson, two comfortable chairs, a small table between, and a floor to ceiling portal to thirty minutes of blissful life without thought. The Pacific. It is the end of the city and the beginning of the remaining world. Its horizon, unlike home, sharply demarcated and unquestionable, suggests that this world is finite and limited. Unlike home, where the horizon is shrouded with dusty uncertainty, giving the vague impression that there is no separation of heaven and earth.

It took him most of the afternoon to finalize his recommendations to Barton Properties and document his billable hours. There were a few other details on other projects that needed to be finalized before the weekend. Jackson didn't like to leave things undone. Procrastination and patience were not part of his mantra. "My impatience is going to kill me some day," was always offered when Jackson was asked anything about himself. "However," as he would also submit, "those things that are our downfall frequently are the things that make us rise."

The door swung open to an empty apartment. Looking to the fridge for something to eat and a chilled bottle of Peter Michael, Jackson came across a familiar note. In fact, he wasn't sure if the note was new or reused from last weekend.

GONE TO LAGUNA BEACH
BACK ON MONDAY
LOVE YA

Somehow the apartment felt emptier than it was last week or the week before that. Quiet is fine. Subdued is acceptable. Even abandoned seems temporary, but empty can be overwhelming. Jackson wasn't one to freely discuss his day with Gwyneth, even when she was around. He could call her but rarely did she pick up. He would have liked to call his dad but Johnathon Stillwell wasn't the kind of dad that you call just to chat. His mom was great to converse with but she was always able to diagnose by the sound of Jackson's voice problems that existed in his world and then would worry about them excessively for days. The solitude in those days started to take their toll on Jackson. Never to look back. Never to regret or second-guess. That was his way of forgetting those images that needed to be forgotten. Memories. Just because they have been pushed aside or even abandoned doesn't mean they don't exist. They are imbedded in time's capsule just waiting for someone or something to come along and open the lid. Possibly it was the drugs and alcohol so frequently consumed. Perhaps it was the exhausting work that week or the baseball game. Maybe it was the loneliness of an empty apartment or the lazy shadows moving across the kitchen table. The debased images that were triggered by the darkened room lit only by the peripheral illumination of the foyer started to release, or retrieve, those memories. Jackson's head was heavy and his vision unfocused as the things he thought of came gurgling back to the surface. The bottle was two-thirds empty and both of the evening's ludes had been popped before the decision was made to call Bo. There was no answer. Neither one of them ever left a message or at least rarely was one left. This time Jackson needed to say something. From the perspective of someone on the outside looking in, one might have assumed the message would have been one of hope and love brought about by a beautiful memory, or a yearning desire of reconciliation from a misstep in the past. One clearly could have predicted a passionate cry for help with an unresolved problem. The message said, "Cisco split for the ninth time. Sell it all."

ELEVEN
It All Seemed So Easy

(Fall 1977)

All through that night, Jackson's recollections of his past preyed
upon him. Yet yesterday's reintroduction to what once was such
an important part of his life, brought back his college years most vividly.

Jackson and Bo returned to the KU campus for their sophomore
years. Jackson had actually arrived early. Once his stint with the summer
league Wichita Broncos was complete, Jackson was required to be in
Lawrence for the fall baseball season preparation. He also had responsibilities of a more social nature. The athletes' fraternity, Alpha J or
Jock Alpha as it was commonly referred to, was the Greek du jour that
Jackson had chosen the previous year. It was not exclusively reserved
for athletes, but a large number of current and former players joined
each year. Frat life fit Jackson perfectly. Not so much for Bo. His perception of Greek life was ultimately the reasoning behind Bo's disgust
with the fraternity environment. It reminded him too much of his dad.
The social aspect to Greek life would have been enjoyable and perhaps
seductive in its allure, but the supportive fun-loving façade would have
quickly given way to a derogatory, self-absorbed, and abusive core.

With the exception of Bo's mother and sisters, only Jackson realized
how often Bo was beaten by his father. Jackson's compassion was initially obvious but he made that mistake only once. It happened during
the fall semester of their junior year. It was on a Monday at school
before first hour. Jackson attempted to console his dispirited compadre.
Bo had arrived on that day with a fresh shiner under his left eye. "Don't
you dare feel sorry for me," Bo yelled at Jackson after slamming him up
against their locker and walking away. There would not be a second time

when Jackson would show outward sympathy toward his friend. Not that he didn't want to. He just knew from that time forward when to let things be. Sumner Plaine knew some of the burden Bo and his family lived with. Though pretenses were made, the family could not conceal all of the flaws of Bo's dad. Sheriff Wright was a sweet-talking, hard-drinking womanizer. He always had been, though with varying degrees of discretion, even from his days in high school. He would spend his evenings drinking and chasing while claiming to be on patrol. Each election cycle, people would marvel at his ability to be re-elected while clearly displaying such character flaws. But in Sumner Plaine, an R after an incumbent's name is more important than the reputation before it.

While most boys that age would have joined the fraternity if only to seek out the approval of such a social specimen as Jackson, Bo only truly wanted acknowledgment from one individual. That never came. It didn't bother Bo when his friends made fun of him or laughed at him. Part of the reasoning behind that benumbed exterior was that with the type of friendship they all shared, unconditional love and support was always implied; kidding at the other's expense was part of the splintered wood that yoked them together. But primarily, Bo was unconcerned with things said about him because the opinion of anyone other than his father was immaterial. Bo could recount the times during each baseball season when he would listen intently for his father's voice and be disappointed. After a sharp base hit or an impressive defensive play. Silence. The high praise he would hear rising out of the dugout or reverberating throughout the field diminished quickly. Admiration from Coach Bolin or Five or even the star shortstop on the team, never quite filled that empty void of his dad's absent recognition.

Regardless of outward appearances or differing opinions, Whiskey and Wright carried on as if it were just another inning in a baseball game. No explanations. No excuses. No consideration of past choices or actions. They remained as close as ever. Their separate living situations kept them physically apart, but inside, within the soul of their companionship, nothing was severed. Bo worked hard at his studies. Any free time went to his new girlfriend, Nancy. Jackson, with the exception of the recurring Saturday night binge gatherings, worked continuously on his All-Conference abilities and his academic requirements. The demands of each obligation fell hard on the accomplished shortstop's shoulders. It took effort that Jackson was not used to in order to continue improving and prevail as one of KU's best infielders of that decade.

From time to time, Jackson would hear Bo while he sat in the stands on home game weekends. Bo would applaud every one of Jackson's defensive plays yet deride his lack of power in the box. In his last two seasons, Jackson hit second in the Jayhawk lineup, just as in high school. In both Big Eight seasons he batted north of .300 but never had a homerun. Bo only wished for such a career, but this was the only thing he could think of to tease his best friend. After each base hit, whilst standing on first or second, Jackson knew exactly what was coming. "Way to hit the ball out of the infield! Good job, spaghetti arms." Jackson would always explain that the best shortstops never hit for power. Though Bo never let up, he was prouder of Jackson and his accomplishments than Jackson's parents were. Bo used to ponder if he could have succeeded in sports the way Jackson did, would Bo's father have been more accepting? Bo was jealous of the way his dad doted on Jackson. It was most obvious during the years when the two played on the same teams. Never was there a comment or compliment that came to Bo from his dad, only criticism. But he was full of praise for Jackson's play after each game. Jackson was the son that the sheriff always wanted. Conversely, it was Jackson's mom who fawned over Bo as if he were her favorite son.

As university life came to a close, they both kept busy. They both kept close. They both found favor in each other's eyes and graduated as one would have expected. Bo's degree in political science came with a cum laude designation. Jackson graduated summa cum laude in economics.

The entire community of Sumner Plaine waited to hear where Jackson would go in the MLB draft. They just knew he would be chosen but when and by whom, that was the exciting question bantered about at the end of that final season. Most of the community had followed Jackson's senior year. Some of the townsfolk drove east to see a game or two. Five and Slim made the trip twice. Even Bo's mom and dad came out for a doubleheader that spring. It was difficult for Bo to sit next to his dad and hear him yelling encouragement and praise to his *favorite* son. Yet each one of Jackson's games that was attended by his best friend created the most joyful of memories for both. Jackson would never talk about his achievements in college but Bo certainly brought them up frequently. Each new introduction of Jackson in the presence of Bo brought about a litany of baseball stats that Bo wanted the world to know about.

Draft day finally arrived and everyone waited to receive a call. Jackson set up camp in the coach's lounge near the athletic director's offices. He could invite any family member he chose to join him in waiting for the phone to ring. Bo was the only one invited. They sat there watching ballgames on the multitude of screens in the room. They drank Gatorade and ate sunflower seeds to bide their time. It was Saturday afternoon. The start of the two-day event was the day before. Jackson's coach had heard from contacts that if Jackson was to be drafted, it would probably be after the thirtieth round. The MLB draft was forty rounds in length. Bo was shocked that Jackson would drop that far though, truth be known, Bo had recently lost a little interest in the sport he grew up loving.

Jackson's name was not mentioned that day. He had not been chosen during any of the first forty rounds. As the final name was mentioned, draft #832, the room became silent as the grave. About fifteen minutes later and the phone rang with offers to try out for the Royals and the Cubs. Jackson was also chosen as a compensation pick with the Reds but that meant there would be no contract, no signing bonus, no guarantee of any playing time except in the instructional Rookie League. Jackson shook his coach's hand, thanked him for all he had done, and the two friends quietly walked out to make a call to Jackson's parents. All felt sorry for the local standout. Yet Sumner Plaine was more disappointed than Jackson. None within the community knew how exhausting his life had been. It all seemed so easy for the phenom that showed up in their midst. He made everything look so simple. They all wanted to be him or be with him. All he really wanted was to be free of the responsibility of being Jackson Daniel Stillwell.

TWELVE
The Judge

(Spring 2001)

Of all days, Sunday has a meaning, perhaps even a purpose, so they say. Sunday is descriptive. Not in and of itself, but of the individuals who abide within it. Whether truth or deception, reality or perception, Sunday is the day that we all choose whether or not to outwardly express religious faith. Similarly, what they say about money is true. What you do with it says a great deal about who you are. Sunday. Like no other day of the week, it is an empty canvas, unmolded clay; to do with as you choose. It exists consistently without conditions. No obligations. No requirements. Only unfettered time. And, like money, what you do with your free time says a lot about you.

Bo was raised in the church, United Methodist to be specific. Nancy was Methodist too, which wouldn't have mattered to either one. It wouldn't have mattered whether either was Christian or not. Theirs was a love that both were looking for. They were both naïve enough to assume that life with love always finds a way. It was, however, convenient that they were both raised in the same church fellowship and so their Sundays existed as they always had, with little choice and even less concern. They were the same in Topeka as they were in Sumner Plaine and the suburbs of St. Louis. The Wright children went to Sunday school. Afterward, the family gathered together for worship service. Dinner out at the family's favorite restaurant came next, then home for a quiet afternoon. It was the same each week, without fail. No obligation, just a choice to express their belief in a comfortable secure manner.

The problem with the expressions of faith, as with many things, is that it's difficult to tell how authentic it is. Outward appearances do not always match up with inward motives. Like claiming to be a patriot, a term that covers a variety of sins. If saying it would only make it so. For Bo, the choice now was not so much how to spend a Sunday but whether the activity was sincere. The exercise of churchgoing slowly was losing its importance. As a young man, his actions and intent were congruent. To be a Christian and act as one seemed a most natural way of living. His faith, though limited and untested, gave him direction and a noticeable perspective. He seemed different to those around him. Which was good and bad to a teenager. Adults thought him unique and his peers perceived him as weird but harmless. Bo's mom was always proud of his habits, but his father was always wanting to change him. Into what, neither of them could tell.

Those days had slowly faded in the recollections of Judge Wright. The act of going to church—being seen with his family in church—was more calculated than intentional. Appearances were important to the judge. The power and prestige that came with a judicial appointment would be enough for most people, but for Bo, his eyes were on an ever rising and always directing focal point. He had gained some authority in his position and he realized the wealth provided by his investments in Jackson's schemes was granting him more access than a small-town lawyer could obtain. The transformation of Bo's ambition was gradual enough that most wouldn't notice. But Bo knew the exact time when the transition occurred, the tangential point where the arc bowed in the opposite direction.

He recalled it every time he looked at a picture of his family, a copy of which sat on the desk in his office. Bo remembered. The door opened as calmly as it was closed. Judge Kline was a tall, blond, goateed throwback to the sixties. From the moment he turned sixty, he returned to wearing his locks pulled back into a ponytail. When you're a judge, you can't lose your job for looking like a hippie. His arrival and departure that day was ephemeral, like a vanishing spirit whose cautionary task was completed. He was the ghost of jurisprudence present who had disappeared without a remnant of his existence. That is, except for the bloated envelope on Bo's desk.

The scheme was simple. There were two privately owned companies that operated prisons in the Midwest. Leavenworth Detention Center,

most prominently and with good reputation, had operated under a publicly owned corporation since 1992. Notably, it existed as an extension
of the first public/private venture to facilitate America's burgeoning
problem with undocumented immigrants in the Southwest. The corporation had since expanded into federal and state correctional facilities
throughout the U.S.

The second, a privately owned company, was a recent start-up but
had developed some success in incarcerating convicted criminals at a
reduced cost in comparison to other similar institutions. In order to
maintain viability as a financially insecure novel business, occupancy
was key. A hotel breaks even at around forty percent. Prisons are double
that. The goal of PriCor, the private correctional LLC based in Chicago,
had to meet in order to efficiently run was eighty percent occupancy.
When the number of inmates in their three state prisons dropped below
eighty-five percent, an inducement payment of $5,000 would be paid to
the most "productive" courts with an additional $10,000 paid once the
rate reached ninety-five percent. The Third Judicial District of Kansas
had been developed into a "productive" court system over the years and
Bo was needed to guarantee that classification continued.

The judges, in addition, created a scheme within the scheme which
required a method of covert communication. All judges were to be
made aware of the two points of inflection. All judges would therefore alter their conviction rates and incarceration referrals appropriately.
When the low occupancy mark occurred, the judges increased both in
favor of the new start-up until the high mark had been met. Once that
occurred, the judges simply stopped their referrals into PriCor until the
low mark again was achieved. Back and forth the system would flow,
thus making payments a recurring commission.

The judges' communications were simple also. Every week they
would receive an email listing the docket of hearings and trials for
each judge. All defendants were listed along with their social security
number and date of birth. If the last defendant on the list had a DOB
ending in 1995, the occupancy rate had been met and they were to shut
down referrals. One time, Bo's more astute legal secretary noticed the
six-year-old defendant and brought it to Bo's attention. It was easily
brushed under the rug as a clerical error and the cogs in the machine

kept turning. When a smaller envelope stuffed with Benjamins was found in his bottom left-hand drawer, Judge Wright knew it was time for more referrals.

That first envelope, however, was in the middle of his desktop. It was difficult to turn away from. He looked at it for a while before removing it from sight. The money wasn't the temptation, although Bo had learned the value placed upon tax-free income. The investments that Jackson had got them into were more lucrative by a factor of ten. It might have been the awkward position in which he would place himself by refusing to be a part of the criminal activity of his cohorts. Yet, if Bo wasn't bothered by what his closest friends thought of him while in high school and college, he would doubtfully start now. No, the temptation came from the access to the influencers of this third branch of government that he would gain simply by *doing his job*. Bo remembered returning to his desk that day after completing the first trial of his tenure. He had just sentenced an impoverished, welfare-reared, Black man to four years in the PriCor facility nearest his home for unpaid parking tickets. There were thirty-nine, mind you, but the William Beauregard Wright that was reared and respected in S.P. would have never considered that an option. Bo sat at his desk looking at the picture of his family. But, it wasn't his family that Bo was focused on. It was the reflection off the plane of glass imaging from behind the photo that he saw. The face he saw staring back at him, though familiar, was a likeness he no longer recognized.

The same process continued unregulated and, more importantly for Bo, undiscovered for about fifteen months. The activity itself became repetitively banal, as do all forms of servitude. In January 2000, Judge Kline died from pancreatic cancer; one month to the day after PriCor declared bankruptcy and was forced to sell its assets to another, more principled corporation. It was a relief in a way. Bo had walked the high wire and survived. His conscience could be resurrected, if he chose to. The change had brought him back to earth but the experience added another level of invulnerability to Bo's attitude toward his future. And without the excitement added by the corrupt, under-the-table enterprise, Bo was again becoming bored with his status.

Politics had become interesting to him. Politicians would seek his council and support. He was asked to serve on numerous boards and advisory committees. The Kansas Republican Party, which was on the receiving end of numerous financial contributions from the judge, had elected him as vice chair of the state organization. Judge Wright was well known, well liked, and well connected. To that end, when the opportunity came to run for the state senate seat in the District 18 in 2000, he threw in his hat. The Republican committee was salivating at the chance to run a quality candidate in this staunchly Democratic region of the state. And Bo could continue to serve as a judge while running for office. Bo chose to request an opinion for appearances' sake. It was not deemed incompatible with the appropriate conduct of a judge according to the Committee on Judicial Ethics. Also for appearance's sake, he failed to request an opinion on taking bribes from a privately run prison eighteen months earlier. Oh well.

In the Topeka area, there was no certainty that Bo would win the election. He did all the right things, spent all the right money, kissed all the right babies, yet still lost his bid for the Kansas State Senate. It didn't hurt him as much as it made him angry. He knew his opponent personally and professionally. The man was adequate but had no credentials and won strictly by the dominance of the Democratic Party in northeast Kansas. Bo had gained a bit of arrogance by this time in his career and was able to shun such defeats as flukes and mere bumps in the road on his way toward an ultimate destination. Stones to step over. Government was nothing if not a consistently altering construction project. When maneuvering around common building blocks, it would be better to trip over a few than to be crushed by one. The secret was not to be tripped up in public too often.

Afterward, Bo continued to be active in the Republican Party and made contributions to politicians that might create advantageous relationships in the future. Most important was his relationship as party leader and personal benefactor with the Republican governor of Kansas. The governor, currently in the midst of his second term, called on his friend the judge frequently. They had become more than political acquaintances. Both from western Kansas, both with middle-class upbringing, they used each other without the other feeling used. As fate would have it, the state senator in District 18 was forced to resign in scandal before his term was completed. The Democratic Party was placed in an awkward position of needing a disgraced senator to retain his seat in government until the next election while not looking like it condoned his actions. He eventually had to resign. This made for a unique opportunity for the Republican governor to replace a sitting Democratic state senator in this overwhelmingly Democratic region with a Republican alternate. The selection would occupy the seat until the next election opportunity.

The choice of Judge Wright was an obvious one. He had run a close election the year prior and was accepted by the Democratic population of the district if not by the Democratic Party. It didn't seem obvious to Bo, nor did he welcome the decision. He hated the idea of the back-door method of winning. It reminded him of the infrequent times he would defeat Jackson at anything, like a bad blister on the palm leading to a rare score of ninety in a golf match. Or making the varsity basketball team as a senior even though he consistently hyperventilated during pre-season workouts, being approved of by the coaches because of his teamwork and leadership qualities instead of his talent. And worst of all, being admitted to law school by the grace and money of a friend's father. Bo almost turned the offer down. It was Nancy that convinced him of his bona fides. She instilled within him the vision and how destiny presents itself in different ways. She was constantly reminding Bo of what each step in this career would mean for him and their family. She was right. A political career was what Bo would ultimately find most suitable for his changing personality. It was a perfect fit. He took office and began serving his term in August of 2001. After he became accustomed to the routine, he wondered why he didn't realize it from the start, from his first undergraduate class in political science.

Bo was the talk of the town that summer. Sumner Plaine pulled out all the stops in celebrating its renowned son. It seemed as if he were more popular than the local district state senator and representative. When Bo returned for the twenty-fifth high school reunion of the class of 1976, he was the bomb! Bo even went to the Saturday night dinner and dance; partly because for the first time Nancy came with him but mostly because, for the first time, Jackson was a no-show for a reunion. Nobody knew exactly why. All would ask Bo and he had to answer honestly that he didn't know. In the midst of the major changes each had experienced within these past months, they had not talked for over a year. Bo and Nancy were invited to the country club for drinks after the dance. When they arrived, they were ushered to the same table and chairs Bo shared with Jackson five years earlier. Bo talked of that experience to the level that he could remember. Nancy could see in Bo's eyes an unsatisfied pride. Whether that emotion was stored away for Jackson or himself, she wasn't sure. This would be the first of many images Nancy would notice in her husband's eyes that she would be unable to interpret.

THIRTEEN

Thanks For the Ride

(Summer 1977)

That night when Bo and Nancy were having drinks at the club, Senator Wright was drinking more than his usual allotment. The loss of inhibition triggered a release of memories about his youthful days in his home town. Some he shared with his wife. Others, he clearly kept to himself.

After Bo's first year away at college, the time spent at home during that summer started out as the worst three months of his entire life, or so he thought. He didn't have much money and no prospects for a job, so Bo signed on to a part-time gig at the sheriff's department. Initially thinking it to be a good fit, Bo learned quickly that it would be just an extension of slave work for his father. The only respite from the strain of living and working with the same hateful man was that the responsibilities finished at noon each day. Yet every morning it was the same thing. Cleaning and filing, filing and cleaning. Bo had to pick up the office, sweep the floors and sidewalks, file court documents with the clerk, deposit evidence in storage rooms and lockers, and, his very favorite, mop empty jail cells after the inhabitants had been discharged. There were only four cells on the top floor of the courthouse. They were small units stacked adjacently, so those confined to the cells next to the one being cleaned really let Bo have it during his work. Sometimes it was words, sometimes it was spit, sometimes it was something unimaginable. He told his dad about it that first time, to which the sheriff laughed and said, "You've always been soft." It would be the last time Bo ever came to his father for anything.

The job did afford Bo his first bit of spending money. That, in addition to some gift money he had been saving, was enough to buy a used Kawasaki 350cc. Lime green! During high school, Bo would just borrow his sister's car or the family Comet when needed. For college, he hitched a ride to Lawrence with Jackson and had access to his car from time to time but, for the most part, Bo was a walker. He didn't seem to mind it either. This motorcycle, however, and the access it gave him to the fruits of summer, was his first real feeling of freedom in his life. The entire community of Sumner Plaine was at his disposal. Bo explored every inch of her too.

That summer was a lonely one for the most part. KU's baseball coach placed all of his prominent players onto semi-pro teams throughout the area. Jackson had moved into the starting shortstop position near the end of his freshman season and as such was obligated to play for the Wichita Broncos. Both Bo and Jackson were hoping that he would be able to play just a few miles south of Sumner Plaine for the Liberal Bee Jays but Liberal's depth at the six-position left Jackson in Wichita and much too far away to visit. Jackson pleaded for Bo to join him on the team. "They allow walk-ons and still have one outfield position open." Jackson told Bo that he was as good as most of those players on that team. Bo, even though during his senior year he enjoyed his best season on the diamond, was too insecure of his abilities to give it a shot, especially after taking a full year off. Bo always appreciated Jackson's patronization of his baseball talents but knew that though he was good enough for a small-town team, he didn't have the qualities needed for that level of play.

Five and Slim were rarely around during those three months. Five worked sixty hours a week as inventory manager at DK Sporting Goods downtown. The job fit him perfectly. He could be part of something that matched his skills as an athlete and didn't require a great deal of conversation as a floor manager would by necessity require. Slim had a true *summer* job. He was working for Garst and Thomas Hi-Bred Corn Seed Company. He supervised the entire rogueing operations throughout southwest Kansas. Since 1935, eager young entrepreneurs have been selling their summer days for good cash by working "in the fields." The stories that have arisen from those days were epoch. Tales of four-thirty a.m. bus rides that originated from the junior high school parking lot. They included the horseplay that occurred while teenagers walked long cornfields fully camouflaged by verdant leaves and dusty tassels. And, most notably, they contained the first exposure for all participants to a different crop, one pre-harvested and conveniently rolled for easy consumption. This was the fodder for legends in the making. Because of the hours and completely uncomfortable conditions, most youth drop out without finishing one full summer season. Bo and Five made it through less than one season, Jackson and Carlos survived two, but Slim was a lifer. This was his seventh summer. He used his experience to land what actually could have been a pretty good career. Good in the traditional sense, that it provided excellent pay and good benefits. Slim saw another advantage. It introduced him to the art of cultivation of that other crop that they all enjoyed consuming each summer.

Unfortunately, Bo's social experiences that summer were as uneventful and monotonous as his employment. He had yet to meet Nancy and, unlike Five and Jackson, didn't have a list of available hometown girls to date. He was starting to dislike summer for the first time ever. On one occasion, Bo and Five caught a Sunday afternoon American Legion baseball game at Lewis Field. They had fun reminiscing about their youthful careers on that very field but quickly became bored spectators. They left in the fourth inning. On the way out, Five waved to a girl that Bo hadn't noticed as they arrived. Valeria was sitting against the concrete wall at the top of the stadium seating. She liked and understood baseball. Her cousin was playing and she, like all of that age, was looking for things to do.

"Was that Valeria? I haven't seen her for a quite a while," Bo asked and answered in the same breath. Five responded with a nod. "Did she stay in town after graduation?" Five nodded again. "I heard that you were dating her, or at least spending *quality* time with her." Five shook his head and smirked as if to say don't believe anything you hear about me or her. "You mean she's not as easy as they say?"

"Not with me. And I tried!"

Bo was shocked. Aghast, not only that this fact was apparently important enough for Five to utter two short yet full sentences, but also that he had failed in the art of female seduction. They dragged Main for an hour or so and got a bite to eat before Five dropped Bo off at his home. Bo walked toward the front door and stopped cold. Tomorrow, Bo thought, he was going to have to work with the sheriff all morning and in preparation, he needed more free time away from his dad. Bo jumped on his cycle and headed back out on the quiet warm streets of Sumner Plaine. He was driving the neighborhood and happened down a familiar street. Bo stopped in front of a dark blue paneled house with broken shutters and broken shingles. It was Willy's home and he was sitting on the porch with his mom. Willy immediately came to the street to see Bo and his new motorcycle. As always, Willy sported the biggest smile you had ever seen.

"How you doin', Bo? Long time, no see! When did you get this?"

"Hey, Willy! I got it a couple weeks ago. How 'bout you? What have you been up to?"

"Just working. I got me a job working for Five's uncle Cliff."

"So, you're a farmer now."

"No, I haven't seen him lately." Bo, recognizing that the hum of the motor was affecting Willy's hearing, shut the cycle off and repeated his claim. "Oh! Yeah, I guess you could say so. I like the job but it makes me nervous. There is so much to learn. I worry that I'm not doing a good job. I never have farmed before and I get so jittery driving those expensive tractors. What if I wreck one? Shoot, they cost more than Mom's house."

Bo waved to Willy's mom as she smiled back. "How's she doing anyway? I heard she had surgery."

"She's good now. It took the doctors a long time to figure out what the problem was. She needed gall bladder surgery. She almost died but she feels pretty good now. She loves Sundays." With that comment Willy looked lovingly and sympathetically at his mom as she swayed in comfort on her old rocking chair. "It's her favorite part of the week. After church she just sits on the porch and watches the world go by. She cleans houses every other day from sunup to sundown so this is her day of rest. I sit with her so she has someone to talk to." Bo kick-started the engine, denoting the end of the conversation. Willy said goodbye and turned toward the house. He stopped when a recognizable face peeked out of the front door of the next-door neighbor's house. Valeria skipped and bounced quickly out to the street to be part of the gathering. She had not seen the motorcycle either. It could have been Christmas Day for the excitement that she showed. And when she said, "Take me for a ride," Willy returned to the porch and Valeria climbed on the back without receiving an invitation.

Her short stature placed her eyes just above Bo's shoulders. Her long untethered black hair was going to be a problem so she gathered it and tucked into the back of her snugly fitted T-shirt. She took no heed of the strap engineered on the seat beneath her but grabbed Bo tightly, low around his waist. The fullness of her body was pressed firmly and brazenly between the blades of Bo's back. This was the first time Bo felt the opposite sex. It was the first time he felt like a man. In the past, he was just a member of youthful society, no different from one species or the other. It was the first time he felt in charge and that someone else was depending on him. It was the first time for a lot of things that summer.

They drove all over. Through the park. Around the old high school. To the Dairy Queen. All over the neighborhood. And of course, they would drag Main. Up and down, back and forth, they rode through the heart of the community in which they grew up. In one way, Bo was excited that people would see him with a girl on his bike. In another way, he was concerned with what friends might say when they saw it was Valeria. She, on the other hand, was thrilled. The ride was as free and joyful as she had felt all summer. For her, it was the same each year. The school year was fine but summers provided ceaseless indifference. They were barren times conceived by the cohabitation of boredom and poverty. Valeria didn't want the night to end. Bo knew that since he was eighteen years old and as long as he made it to work on time the next morning, he had no curfew. She suggested they drive out to a rural area they both knew well. The oil farm, as it was laughingly portrayed, was located in the middle of a farm field just south of town. No more than a couple miles down old Highway 83, a single inactive oil well pump remained standing surrounded by the crop of the season. Depending on the crop and the time of year, the rig was frequently obscured by its surroundings. The rarely used road leading to the immobile iron horse was partially covered with volunteer plants and weeds rendering it nearly invisible to those uneducated to its existence.

That path itself led to an inactive pumpjack whose melodic and rhythmic compressions had ceased their resonance many years prior. The once untarnished onyx frame of the Trojan apparatus had slowly corroded to become a rusted fusion of useless parts, a humble effigy to its formerly proud stature. The field and the well belonged to Five's uncle Cliff and had continuously been used for dry land crops, even when the oil well was active. There were large tanks on the side of the field near the county road, which used to hold the petroleum extract and the residual water released. They had been removed from the field to allow for productive farming of the field's full acreage. But the symbol of a bountiful bygone era was allowed to endure. Bo hesitated when they came to the trailhead. He had one very bad memory of this location and would not have wanted to relive it. He steeled his brow and said hold on. They slowly traveled through the milo, down the least productive side of the path to the opened area surrounding the pumpjack. Bo immediately turned off the motorcycle and exposed them to the beautiful silence that comes with most evenings in western Kansas. The waxing moon shed ample light on their hiding place. They both slid off the bike and took in the familiar grounds. After walking around the oil derrick, they sat on the cracked and broken concrete base and leaned back against the smooth flat gearbox. The night lingered as they talked as if they were old friends. It was like the evening had taken a deep breath. The quiet pauses at the end of each discussion incrementally got longer such that the final silent interlude created a tension that was unavoidable by the two. Valeria leaned over and kissed Bo. That was all the encouragement he needed.

Only the ultimate deed was held back. They worked on mysteries without the embarrassment that could occur for a first pairing of lovers. Neither were interested in intercourse. Soft hands and hard fingers would suffice. It was difficult to find a stopping point, which made Bo proud of his abilities to repress his desire while still supplying Valeria with hers. Eventually they stopped. A nervous moment occurred when the motorcycle took three pumps to start, but soon they were on their way back to town. Valeria held on with the same passion as she had on the way out. The drop off was short and sweet and without a kiss goodbye. As she walked to the door she said, "Thanks for the ride," and quickly disappeared through the front door. Bo drove home with a strange feeling. It was another first. A new sensation so comforting that he would search for its resurrection the rest of his life. Intimacy. It would be difficult to come by in the remaining years of Bo's life. Clearly more challenging than he would have imagined on that special night. It seemed so simple, so effortless, so uncomplicated. If it were only so.

FOURTEEN

A Good Day

(Spring 2001)

Empero sin fe es imposible agradar á Dios; porque es menester que el que á Dios se allega, crea que le hay, y que es galardonador de los que le buscan.

When I was very young, my mother showed me la Biblia de familia. It would ultimately be a gift for me. We were faithful Catholics but Mama didn't think her three other children would appreciate or care for the Spanish Bible so, it became my responsibility to preserve it as one of our most prized family legacies. Hebrews 11:6 has always meant something to me. *Without faith, it is impossible to please God; because anyone who comes to him must believe that he exists and that he rewards those who earnestly seek him.* I'm no scholar, but I think what this means is that for those who feel they do not have faith but are searching for God, the fact that you are seeking proves you believe that He exists or you wouldn't be searching at all. And isn't that faith.

***

Jackson had slowly come to a crossroad in his life, perhaps without knowing it. Ever since that long sleepless night about a year ago, when he telephoned his friend and received no answer, his consciousness had been altered. A lost soul searching. Not only looking for something but also the reason for why he was searching in the first place. Do you have to know what you're seeking before starting your quest? If so, we are all destined to agony. Immobile. If we are unable to take the first step toward resolution just because we don't know where the second step will go, we would all become catatonic. Jackson started his pursuit without knowing where it would eventually lead him. But he had to start.

His recollections of better days always took him to the same venue. Lewis Field. Most recently, the closest thing to those memories (he thought) was the feeling he had when catching the last inning of the baseball game in Santa Monica. In fact, it was the culmination of that particular day that made Jackson question many of his current motivations and the methods he had chosen to bring about those desired ends. To get back to a more balanced feeling of existence again, he thought maybe he should take in another game. At least perhaps it would make him feel better. It didn't take much to scan the internet for the website posting the schedule of the Santa Monica High Vikings. He second-guessed himself shortly after, noting that there were baseball games much closer to home, including the Dodgers. Yet, something about the thought of a high school game was calling him back. For the first time in years, Jackson took a day off midweek and drove to his old neighborhood. This time he would see the entire game.

Jackson needed a new source to assist in changing his current unsound temperament. What that source would be, he did not know. In order to instigate that change however, his first step was to be a small one, the search for a calm and relaxed peaceful day with time to clear his thoughts. He hoped to find that at the Santa Monica Vikings ballfield. What he actually found, as he pulled into the parking lot, was a giddiness and excitement that only a fan would experience preparing to watch his favorite team compete. Truth be said, there was one other thing that Jackson hoped for. He hoped that the old man would be there again watching his grandson play. Before he rounded the corner to walk in front of the purple painted wooden bleachers, Jackson's hope was fulfilled. The old guy was sitting in the exact same spot where Jackson had left him almost a year ago. He climbed the steps up the center of the stands; but this time he confidently crossed over to the gentleman's side of the aisle and asked if the seat next to him was taken.

"Have a seat." The man gestured by casually pointing his finger before returning his gaze to the home team warm-up occurring down on the field.

Jackson made himself comfortable before asking, "Who are the Vikings playing today?"

"The Mariners, they're the Catholic high school in Santa Monica. Great school but not very good at sports."

"Does your grandson still play second base?"

The old man turned intently and suspiciously looked directly into Jackson's eyes. For a moment, it looked as if he was going to grab Jackson by the throat.

"How do you know that my grandson plays second base?" Jackson calmed the situation easily, reminding the man of the last time they met and the game that they watched together. Jackson chuckled at his response. "You're the dude in the suit and tie! What brings you out today?"

"Just here to watch a game." Jackson shrugged, still smiling from the conversation. Jackson offered to go get popcorn and a drink for both of them before the start of the game.

"They don't have a concession stand. I brought sunflower seeds and a couple cans of Dr. Pepper if you'd like to have some." Jackson politely accepted. He had forgotten the taste of sunflower seeds and Dr. Pepper. It brought back memories of when he would share sunflower seeds with his dad each time they would attend an outdoor sporting event together. At the end of each game, there would be this large, "disgusting" (as Jackson's mom would claim) pile of spent sunflower shells at their feet. The image alone was enough to make Jackson realize that his decision to come to the ballgame was the right one.

The gentleman, Al was his name, perhaps as only an elderly grandfather would do, pointed out his grandson, Jake, to Jackson each time he was about to come to the plate. He would nudge Jackson with an elbow, state again that Jake was coming up, then briskly rub his palms together before yelling, "Come on, Jake. Knock one down their throats." It was like a ritual. Each and every time Jake stepped up, Jackson witnessed the same ceremony. The liturgy apparently worked. The first two times that Jake came to bat, two sharp singles to right field. The third time up, Jackson, now getting the feel of the game, wanted to add a bit of his own inspiration.

"Come on, Jake. Just put it in play," was Jackson's addition. He was passing on the same words of encouragement frequently offered up by his high school coach. William Bolin was a great catcher in his day. He was drafted into MLB and played AA ball for the Twins before a career-ending injury stopped his dream of making it to the show. His simple but effective philosophy to batting was not trying too hard, just put the ball in play. "That's the best you can do," he would say. "The game will take care of the rest." Jackson felt good about his input—right up to the time when Jake struck out on a called third strike. Al gave Jackson a stern look. Jackson chose not to offer additional encouragement for the remainder of the game.

In the bottom of the sixth inning, Jake fumbled the ball on a routine 6-4-3 double play. He couldn't quite grasp the pill and failed to make the turn. The game was well out of reach with the Vikings up by eight but Al still pushed his grandson from the seats. "Come on, Jake! Hand on the ball first," Al complained, "He's the best infielder they have and should be playing shortstop but Jake's a sophomore and the shortstop is a senior, which according to the coach takes precedence." Both Al and Jackson could see the potential the young second baseman had. Jackson could clearly understand the desire to push Jake to excel but too often had experienced, directly and indirectly, the effect too much pressure can place on a young man. Jackson kept quiet.

The end of the game was as enjoyable and relaxing as the start. Al thanked Jackson for coming. He said that he enjoyed having someone else to talk baseball with other than his daughter. Jake's mom was again unable to attend because she had to work. Al said that he hoped Jackson would come to another game someday. Jackson nodded his head affirmatively and smiled in a way he hadn't for some time. Not wanting to overstep any lines but still desiring one last opportunity to encourage the young second baseman, Jackson spoke. "Tell Jake to try a smaller glove when playing middle infield. With a smaller cavity, it's quicker and easier to find the handle when making the turn."

"Hmm. Never thought. Where'd you get that?"

"That's a little trick I learned from the best second baseman I ever played with."

"You played ball?"

"Yea, I was the starting shortstop for the University of Kansas my last three years of college."

"Bet they had some pretty good second basemen on those teams."

"Yes, but I got that piece of advice from the second baseman on our high school team. He was the best I ever played with." Jackson's comments, though clearly untrue, were sincerely what he believed, and he would take that belief to the grave. His respect and actual love of Bo skewed Jackson's perspective of his best friend. Never afraid of lying in order to reach a coveted conclusion, but when it came to his friend, Jackson would mean everything he would say, even when the rest of the world knew better.

Reaching the bottom of the stairs and turning toward the parking lot, Jackson would have liked a double header. This was a good day and while it couldn't be considered a breakthrough in Jackson's mental health, it was clearly a start. Gwyneth called on his way home saying that she was doing nothing and wanted to know where dinner would be tonight. They met at their favorite French restaurant near the apartment. Jackson told his third wife about his day, something he rarely did. It didn't seem to register with her. She was in the middle of complaining about hers. It was a pleasant meal nonetheless. They took their clafoutis home to enjoy with a glass of wine while looking out over the city lights. They actually had sex with each other that evening, another rarity. Both had had affairs. Both had moved on. Sex wasn't even transactional anymore but their relationship was. She needed Jackson for status and income. He needed Gwyneth for something to come home to.

Growing up, Jackson's mom, Gabby, was always home. She loved being a homemaker. It was part of her Hispanic heritage, she believed. She felt most important each afternoon when the boys started to arrive home after school or practice. Her constancy was never really noticed by the rest of the family, which did bother her from time to time, but never deflected any of her accepted responsibilities. At this point in his life, Jackson was beginning to realize that. He gave a little extra effort toward the inscription of his Mother's Day cards but was still ashamed of his attitude as a son.

Jackson's dad, Johnathon, was never home—or at least not home within the fleeting memories of his youngest son who similarly was never home. We all have expectations of our parents. Jackson's of his mother were always met. Those of his dad seemed to be, if not unfulfilled then misplaced. Jackson and his dad. Each were speaking the wrong dialog and acting the wrong part for their specific roles in this family drama. And both of them knew it. There would be times when a word here or a deed there would create the inference of regret and repentance but never enough for change. Ultimately, Jackson thought that his dad's actions were displeasing. He thought of his mother in a singular fashion. On the contrary, Jackson remembered how his father was *and* how he wasn't. Who he was *and* who he was not. What he did *and* what he did not. Jackson (and perhaps his dad too) wanted everything, both ways, at the same time. You can't win in that scenario regardless of which side of the relationship you're on.

Why is it that we define the usefulness of our parents and children based on our identity, our own individual egocentric ideals? The value of others surely should be based on their purposes, their situations, their intentions. The problem is that it's difficult to determine someone else's intentions. In families, we are supposed to assume the best of each other, trust their intentions, give them the benefit of the doubt. Yet, it is so rare that we do. It is a concrete fact that if a dad doesn't live up to his son's expectations, regardless of his intentions, as a dad, he is a failure. He is a failure in both of their eyes. It would be better to have a son with no expectations at all than to fail like that. Jackson recalled some promises that were not fulfilled to his expectations while he was growing up. In truth, there weren't many but enough to make an impact. Jackson used to tell Bo during drunken bouts of candor, "A promise, even one with great intention, is nothing but a bribe concealed in a gift."

If taking a day off midweek was rare, stretching it into two was unheard of. The next day (Friday) Jackson and Gwyneth drove down to Laguna Beach to spend the weekend together at the beach house. After a day surfing for him and shopping for her, they brought home Chinese takeout and spent the night out on the deck listening to the waves.

"Tell me what you remember about your father," Jackson requested of Gwyneth. The question set her back for a moment. She couldn't remember the last time they talked about anything other than work, money, and home improvement projects. For a moment, she didn't want to answer. She thought there was something hidden within the question. Eventually, within the ensuing silence, she spoke.

"You really want to know? Is everything all right?"

"Yes. Just curious."

"Well ... hmm ... I don't remember much. He died when I was seven. He was a strong butch of a man. He used to take me into his arms so easily, I thought he might break me. He was a welder, I think. I would only see him on the weekends because he worked offshore on oil rigs. Weekends were great, really great. Just the good stuff, playing, ice cream, you know, kid stuff. I do remember the first time I missed him though. As a freshman, I was in the chorus of the school musical and was scanning the audience to find Mom. I scanned row after row of fathers and mothers before I saw her in the back. She was sitting all alone. It was the first time I felt sad for us both. I couldn't finish the song we were singing. I lipped it just to keep from crying. It wouldn't be the last time I felt like that." Gwyneth hadn't moved her gaze from the refraction of the sunset through her wineglass since starting her memory. "How 'bout you?" she asked, blinking hard to press the excess tears down into their ducts before they would show. "Did your dad ever come to your school activities?"

"Almost every one of them."

"I would have given anything to have a normal family. Even if he was worthless. I think, enduring a bad dad would have been better than missing a good one. Watching my mom as a single parent was difficult. For a while I resented her. Hell, I resented everything, even me. I felt like a chipped porcelain doll whose defects were covered in nice clothing. There was always something wrong with me but no one could tell."

Gwyneth called it an evening after the sun had been down for an hour or so. Jackson declined the offer and stayed in his comfortable deck chair looking west. He felt calm if not peaceful, a state he had been looking for prior to going to the game and he didn't want to lose it. No more wine. No Quaalude. He just fell asleep listening to the swoosh of water mixing with untouched sand. Gwyneth found him there the next morning, waking him with a kiss on the forehead and a cup of coffee.

Saturday was nice. Feeling the athlete in him, Jackson wanted to surf again. His wife stayed home to clean up the house and read. They drove home, top down, on a perfect Sunday. The start of the week really didn't feel any different but he knew that it was. Even Gwyneth could feel the shift. Things were evolving. Life was evolving.

Jackson would return twice that season to spend time with Al and watch his grandson play. Jake ended up hitting .368 for the season with only one additional error after the incorporation of the smaller glove. Each trip was a destination and a journey. A destination of relief and a journey in the direction of home. These were his therapy. They were his connection to a life he had forsaken. Everything was changing for Jackson. The best part of change is that nothing will ever be the same. The worst part is that everything will be different. And the latter was to be difficult to live with because it affected everyone he loved.

FIFTEEN

DNA

(Fall 2002)

The creation of power, like all conception, requires seed, receptive soil, and cultivation. Those with power are not born this way. It is not an intrinsic characteristic. Power must be granted or taken. The most effective way of acquiring is a transfer of power, offering it willingly to a welcoming subject. If power is thrust upon some unwilling recipient or taken from a reluctant source, the process fails. Commonly overlooked is the significant role that a receptive element plays in the formation of true power. It is perhaps the most important aspect in the veracity of the final product. If a perfect morsel is given the greatest opportunity to thrive but no receptive venue is found, nothing happens. However, power only gains its full influence when all aspects of its conception are intact. Judge Wright, as Bo was called in familiar political circles, had become the darling of the party in less than two legislative sessions. He was a most willing participant. A new prospect with a clean history and an experienced pedigree. An individual who hailed from a powerful city with the backing of a host of influencers. And being placed in the most opportune of settings, he allowed for the creation of power at its most fundamental state. The judge was the receptive soil.

Bo accepted his position as a member of the Senate Judiciary Committee in his first session with gratitude and a sense of inevitability. As he was now a cog in the powerful Republican machinery, he was given a chance to rise at a faster pace than most. In politics, the best way to be re-elected is to be elected in the first place. Incumbency is, has, and always will be the secret to political power. But in Bo's situation, it may not have been a sure bet in a district where the population was so skewed to the left that a Republican incumbent had yet to win an election. In order to guarantee re-election in such a precarious district, the Senate majority leader placed Bo as the co-chair of the Judiciary Committee in only his second session and placed him on the Confirmation Oversight Committee and the powerful Ways and Means Committee as well. Once the electorate felt that state funding for local projects was tied to a certain politician, they wouldn't walk away even if they disagreed with that individual's positions. Few had seen any newly appointed senator rise to such influence in such a short time.

Power can only remain powerful if it can maintain its authority and credibility. Once those cloaks have been stained, the seeds of power easily migrate to other fertile ground. Judge Wright, by this time in his life and career, had certain items that he needed to keep out of view of the public. Dry skeletal remains that he would rather not expose to some priestly prophet exiled in Babylon. The kickback scheme that he participated in while on the bench was only one amongst a growing number of miscarriages, some of which would be more politically devastating than others, most of which were unknown. As with the PriCor scheme, Bo found out quickly other avenues of how public servants can serve the population and serve their own personal needs simultaneously. In time, it became all too easy for Bo to look personally magnanimous and be politically ruthless all in the same motion. He grasped the nuances of government quickly. He found new and innovative ways of deflecting opinion and creating diversion, all for political gain. He was a master of formulating and skewing timelines which allowed for the desired appearance of harmonious ends that would overshadow the unscrupulous legislative means behind the action itself.

Case in point. As part of the Judiciary Committee, Bo was ex officio of the Judicial Inquiry Commission for the state of Kansas. He was in a position as a legislator to craft and modify the regulations regarding the process of complaints and charges brought up on judicial behavior of current and past judges within the state system. He drafted the first set of regulations regarding such inquiries which included: the committee of ten would be made up of lawyers and judges with only one layperson position allowed (and that person would be selected by a nomination coming through the Senate Judiciary Committee), complaints must be in writing and notarized (making them subject to perjury charges), judges (and not complainants) must be kept notified during investigations as to the charges, process, and status of said investigation, judges can stay on the bench during the investigation, however, if they choose, a judge can remove him- or herself (yet continue to receive salary and benefits), and all resolutions are to be made confidentially.

All of this became important to Bo when a complaint offered by an attorney on behalf of Henry Wilson, the gentleman who was sentenced to four years in prison for unpaid parking tickets by the Honorable William Beauregard Wright, came before the committee. Mr. Wilson's sentence was commuted, granting him early release and the complaint was erased from the committee's records and confidentially declared resolved. There would be no investigation as to the purpose behind the sentence or the facility of incarceration chosen by the court.

As a member of the Confirmation Oversight Committee, Bo could heap favor upon favor, authorizing specific appointees of the governor or other influential parties. As well, he would reap the benefit of his political support from those newly placed individuals when he called upon them. Of course, the Eljuez not-for-profit corporation continued making generous financial contributions to the campaign accounts of candidates and incumbents alike. And under lenient campaign finance laws of the state and federal governments, when the check from the unknown, unheard of, and untraceable corporation would be given, recipients only remembered the hand of the man who held the envelope. Which, coincidentally, was also the same hand that patted them on the back when they conformed or displayed a fist when they deviated.

Political agendas of governing bodies with decisive majorities are created from the top down. Leadership directs the rank and file. The representatives cajole their constituents in order to bring about a certain legislative product. But on occasion, certain public convictions develop so much energy that they are impossible to deflect let alone stop, even if they are contrary to the will of the governors. One item of interest to the public at large had been building momentum over the past few years. The advent of DNA identification as a tool in investigative law enforcement had created a will and a way to solve crime in a more object fashion as compared to the potential inaccuracies of the subjective jury system that we all are part of. The idea that within a 99.99% probability you can establish or eliminate a suspect, the concept of *reasonable doubt*, the source of such judicial consternation, becomes almost irrelevant. Many were saying that this technology would nearly eliminate false convictions and remove from our streets many more violent repeat-offenders. The science was impressive.

Rape became the most obvious and primary criminal behavior that these scientific techniques were used for. The victims and their advocates became the compelling instigators of new methods of evidence collection and statutory changes in the law to facilitate such a breakthrough method of policing. Rape kits were established and evolved over time to be effective resources for retrieval of the evidence in these cases as well as other crimes that tissue samples were available for identification purposes.

The problem laid not with the retrieval of evidence or even the storage of the tissue and clothing samples. The problem was in the complicated forensic evaluation of the evidence. There were, early on, only a few qualified laboratories in the entire United States available to do such specific scientific testing. It was obvious as time went on that a bottleneck was being created. In addition, no governmental entity was making plans on how to remedy the problem. From the beginning, most law enforcement organizations had accepted the idea of science-based identification and as such started using rape kits to supplement their standard investigations. Police and sheriff's departments, small and large, were gathering this biological evidence without much guidance from the state and federal governments, which led to imperfect and inefficient methodology and an ever-increasing volume of unsubstantiated evidence.

Bo recalled several discussions with his father while he was sheriff and his successor once Bo's dad retired. Each wanted Bo's legal advice as to their increasing volume of "rape kit" evidence. There was plenty of space but what was their legal and ethical obligation in reference to the evidence of closed or nearly closed cases? Both were surprised at Bo's cavalier attitude toward the aging evidence. His advice to them was to treat it like financial information—it could be destroyed after ten years. On the other hand, the KBI's guidance was to hang on to the evidence indefinitely though they were unwilling to set a timeline as to when it would be tested. Only actual rape evidence was passed on to Topeka. That was all that was being tested. A change would come in 2009 when Kansas passed laws that created the avenue for all felonies to require testing. It was only then Sumner Plaine authorities would send to Topeka the evidence gathered in Valeria Hernandez's unsolved murder. Testing of old evidence was prioritized by historical age of the crime being considered. The older the case, the lower the priority.

Such was the indefinite and indeterminate state of law enforcement for Sumner Plaine in the fall of 1992 when an immigrant victim lost her life and the gruesomely mangled body was retrieved from a farmer's field. The evidence, haphazardly collected by untrained staff, was placed in an early version of a rape kit and stored in a file cabinet of a warehousing room in the basement of the county courthouse. Similar cases with stored evidence were accumulating all throughout the state of Kansas. With regards to the new technology, the jury was still out in this conservative part of the country. Some didn't believe in the science. Some didn't want to change from the old tried and true. Many saw the ultimate price tag of such a new form of criminal investigation and feared that it was more than likely going to fall on the state government for funding and administration. Needless to say, Bo was in the middle of these debates and had great influence over direction and appropriations.

The Judiciary Committee first convened hearings on the question of whom and what would be tested. Originally the populace, as did its representatives, felt that this manner of investigation was most suited for sex crimes. The collection of DNA should, according to the committee that Judge Wright played a role on, be restricted to that type of crime and those perpetrators who were convicted of rape. This would limit the law enforcement effort and the funds required from the state treasury. It wasn't long, however, before more forward-thinking politicians saw the enormous value the science could play in all types of crime, including felony murder. By that time, when the issue of expansion was brought to a Judiciary Committee meeting, Senator Wright was chair of that committee. He used the argument that if too many resources were allocated for this new, unproven science, other criminal activity like drugs and gang activity would flourish. He pushed hard to limit funds for the project and urged patience. He recommended a study be implemented to determine once and for all the validity of this new direction of investigation. His delay tactics worked and the funding was limited while a national study was set for the years 2005 and 2006. With the influence of the current governor, Topeka Kansas would be directly used in the study along with four other cities across the country.

Throughout the committee hearing process, Judge Wright frequently motioned that the state consider only testing samples taken in the last ten years. He claimed that there must be some reasonable limitations, especially at the beginning of such a major change in direction. A few conservative colleagues were completely on his side. They were those that blindly would follow the loudest and most powerful regardless. For those weak politicians and their careless constituency, as long as their leaders hate the same people and policies as they do, it wouldn't matter what type of leadership they offered. A growing number however, were surprised at Senator Wright's hesitancy. He had always been a stickler for justice and victim's rights. Even Bo's mom and dad were disturbed by his position. Jackson, who followed the issue from California thought he knew why Bo was directing the legislation as he was. Jackson never mentioned it. Though his mom and dad wanted to talk about it, Jackson wouldn't let on what he knew about his best friend's motives.

When the research study developed and implemented by the National Institute of Justice was complete, the following were its summary findings:

1) DNA evidence is 5 times more accurate than fingerprinting in identification.

2) DNA evidence identified prior felons at twice the rate of conventional techniques.

3) Blood is more accurate than other forms of biological evidence especially when tissue samples are handled improperly.

4) Material collected by forensic technicians was more likely to be usefully accurate in identifying suspects as opposed to law enforcement officers.

5) The cost of adding DNA collecting and testing to an investigation likely will add an additional $1,400.00, which increased to $4,500.00 when taking into effect the added cost of prosecuting individuals who likely would not have been caught.

It was this last resultant in the summary that Bo and other staunch conservatives would hang their hats on. It's one thing to be hard on crime but it's another thing to spend money for it. It was also that last conclusion that made many cringe, especially when using it as a political stance. Why would the state choose not to properly and more accurately investigate crime just because it is expensive? The debate went on without resolution for another two years following the study while, to Bo's liking, the system nearly ground to a halt. By 2009, after the Kansas Legislature required the collection of DNA from all individuals arrested for felonies, the backlog on testing at the KBI was thirty-one thousand collected samples and growing. They were receiving more than twelve thousand new requests each month. Most advocates of change considered this to be at best an embarrassment and at worst a travesty. For Bo, this was just part of a system of governing where needs were balanced with available resources. At least that's what he told the public.

SIXTEEN

The Judge

(Fall 1974)

B o's junior year at SPHS had a rough start. Life at home wasn't
much better. Midway through his high school career, Bo, the
ever mindful and respectful son, was starting to feel his roots. New
shoots were at least attempting to sprout. And though he would never
totally disobey his father, Bo did stretch the boundaries of his family
confinement. Sheriff Wright was also noticing the changes in his son.
But instead of finding pride in Bo's development and encouraging his
independence, Sheriff Wright's narcissism coerced him into becoming
more controlling of his son's motives and impulses. "There would come
a day when the father will have no choice in the matter," he would
think. "It's the father's responsibility to ingrain within his progeny the
discipline necessary to be successful in life." The sheriff felt vindicated
by his mere existence. Abusive men find reason behind their violent
outbursts. Which is why the abuse continues. Their rationality is based
on arrogant delusion. The core of which is insecurity. And insecurity
in the deranged is perpetual.

Things came to a head one Sunday night when Bo decided not to
attend youth group at the church, but instead go to the batting cages
to get some swings in with Slim. Bo's parents wanted him to be active
in church—which he was, far more than anyone else in the family.
They surely wouldn't be bothered by him occasionally ditching out on
a meeting to improve his talent in the area that his dad had always
thought Bo was deficient in. Slim picked up Bo in the church parking
lot and drove them to the cages. After an hour of batting practice, Slim
chauffeured them around town. Up and down Main Street, around the

park and back, by muscle and vehicular memory, they burned rubber and time. As usual, Slim fired up the freshly rolled weed he kept hidden in the compartment under the car's ash tray. He was clever about where he kept his grass. Always less than a felony's weight in each location. He was much less conscientious though about when and where he would fire one up, as evidenced by the fact that his car reeked of the drug. And too, by close proximity, did anyone who spent much time in that Chevy Impala. When Bo was offered a hit, he said, "No thanks. I'll just imbibe through the upholstery."

If there's one thing that a 1960s trained law enforcement officer could do well was recognize the smell of reefer on clothing. What started out innocently enough turned quickly into a dangerous situation for Bo, once his dad got a whiff. Bo had arrived home later than usual for a youth group night and received the question directly from his mom.

"No, I didn't feel like it today so Slim picked me up at the church and we went to the batting cages instead." It was an honest answer to a direct question. Bo's mom accepted it and decided to call it an early night.

"Don't forget to review your material for your test tomorrow." She requested while kissing him on the forehead. She soon left the kitchen and Bo took her advice. He went downstairs to his room. Sheriff Wright followed behind after stewing for about fifteen minutes. He entered into Bo's room as he was taking off his shirt and preparing for a shower. The sheriff closed the door. Before Bo could react, his dad's right hand was shoving the odorous shirt in Bo's face while his left hand was squeezing the air out of his neck. There were words said, honest explanations offered, and apologies thrown to the heavens but they were of little use. The first blow was a hard fist to Bo's left shoulder; then a second that landed just below the left eye. Bo was knocked down and he lost time. A few seconds later he was on the receiving end of the sheriff's belt buckle. Bo didn't scream as he had in the past but the pain wouldn't allow silence. After the task was accomplished to the satisfaction of the executioner, there had been enough damage inflicted that the shower water was more red than transparent. This was one of the worst beatings Bo had to endure. It may have been made more tolerable by knowing that this would be the last time he would have to suffer at the hands of his father. But there was no way Bo could have known that.

The next morning as Bo came up from his room, he tried to leave without being noticed. Bo's dad was always out the door before anyone else and sometimes Bo would sneak out without saying goodbye to his mom. On those days, he always left her a note with his plans for the day and ended it with the drawing of a heart. There was no note that morning as Karen caught him as he was walking out the back door. "Wait, give me a kiss!" Bo grimaced as she grabbed his left shoulder. As he turned, she noticed the swollen purple blob below his eye. If she could have seen the gashes and welts on Bo's back, she would have been reduced to tears. She dropped her hands to her sides and buried her head into Bo's chest. "I'm so sorry, son." Bo didn't say a word, just walked out the door and drove to school. What happened next surprised everyone.

Bo would have loved to say that it was him that finally stood up to his father. Bo would have rather found out that the sheriff died that morning at the hands of a criminal. Of what actually happened, Bo was unaware for several years. Eventually, once the sheriff retired and Randolph Ray was elected, he offered Bo the full story behind his mother's actions that morning.

Karen quickly but deliberately got dressed and drove to the courthouse. Stoically walking into the first floor county sheriff's office, Karen strode past his secretary without pausing or responding to her salutations. She barged through the closed door where Sheriff Wright was meeting with one of his senior deputies.

"I need to talk to you."

"Excuse me!"

"I need to talk to you."

"Not now, I'm in a meeting."

"Not anymore." She stood in front of his pretentiously oversized desk and refused to remove her piercing glance from the sheriff's crimson face.

"Randy, I'll talk to you later. You can close the door on your way out."

"Leave the door open," Karen said with great clarity. The sheriff remained in his seat and with words sifted through clenched teeth, demanded to know what this was about.

It was at that moment that the world stood still while the small community of Sumner Plaine gained a heroine. "You know damn well what this is about." The sheriff sunk back in his chair to evaluate the situation. Before he could decide on how to react, his wife of twenty-two years leaned hard on the front of his fake cherrywood desktop. She spoke with complete control, yet with each successive accusation, the decibel level in her voice raised until with the harshest of tones she had said what she came there to say. "If I ever see, hear, or imagine that you have laid another hand on my son, if I ever notice you raising your voice in anger or criticizing him again, if I even feel that you are looking down at him with malice or hatred, I will wait until you are asleep in your bed. I will retrieve that gun you have hidden on the top shelf of our closet. I will place the barrel in your ear and I *will* pull the trigger! And I will not regret one moment that I'll have to spend in one of your jail cells because you will be no more! Do I make myself clear!" There was a pause and a silence that made the sheriff realize that the entire office was experiencing the same version. He didn't know what to say. "DO I MAKE MYSELF CLEAR!" Still in shock from his wife's demonstration of strength, he nodded his head in the affirmative and Karen walked out the door.

When she got to her car she was smiling through her tears. Liberation comes from within but usually requires actions to validate it. This one was bittersweet. From Randy's story, Bo finally realized how the events of that morning became be a cleansing moment, not just for him and his family but for his dad as well.

At home, they all had to exist with an uncomfortable silence that stunted the evolution of their family but slowly things improved. They did at school as well. As Bo's physique magnified, so too did his confidence and his standing. The remainder of the junior year was uneventful, which was glorious for Bo. He was ready for a little less drama in his life. The shock of Ron Andrews's sudden death was the only thing that marred what would be a satisfying school year.

The summer came and passed quickly as all eyes were on the upcoming senior year. Jackson chose not to play football, but instead focused on preparing for the spring baseball season. The team's previous year had ended unsatisfactorily as the Bisons lost in the first round of the conference tournament. But all starters would be returning from last year's team and expectations were high. Jackson continued his hound dog ways but had matured away from his more spiteful activities toward friends and others. And his relationship with Bo, though still feudalistic, was much more accepting if not accommodating. The bond they were experiencing strengthened that year. All things were well in both of their lives.

Christmas passed. Second semester started. Spring arrived. Baseball began and then, it was May.

It was the third weekend of the month, and the end of an era had arrived. Graduation, which no one cared about, would be in ten days. All eyes were on the conference tournament held this year at Lewis Field. Even the state media outlets were involved because this year's tournament brought together Kansas's big three. Darren Daulton of Ark City, Mitch Webster of Larned, and of course Jackson Stillwell of Sumner Plaine. Daulton was a sophomore and had yet to reach his prime but had already made a name for himself as the best catcher in the state. Webster, a speedy outfielder who also pitched, was the first true switch hitter anyone in these parts had ever seen. Though Mitch would mostly face left-handed pitching, he would bat left because of Lewis Field's peculiarity.

Lewis Field, located on the edge of Riverside Park, had a design that was not the proudest moment in the career of some little-known city engineer. It had the most unique dimensions in the league, 360' down left-field line, 433' in deep center and 289' in right field. Everyone who thought he was a player salivated each time they looked at that short porch in right field.

Jackson's year was subpar by his standards but with a .385 average and stellar glove at short, he easily was in the discussion as the third of the big three. Bo and Five, even with their breakout seasons, were never mentioned in the same conversation. The board was set and the pieces were about to move.

Championship Saturday came and the stands were packed. This would be the matchup that everyone wanted to see. Bisons vs. Indians. Stillwell vs. Webster. It was a dream game created in heaven by the baseball gods themselves. And for the first time that anyone could remember, a scout for the Royals would be in attendance. The Sumner Plaines lineup was announced as they took the field. Batting first and playing center field, Rick (Bugs) Lawrence. At shortstop, batting second, Jackson Stillwell. At third base and batting third, Brad (Five) Andrews. Cleanup and catching, Kevin (Burn) Hatcher. At the fifth spot and playing second base, William (Bo) Wright. At first base, batting sixth, Tony (Slim) Batchelder. Batting seventh and in left field, Marcos Hernandez. In right field and batting eight, Ben Harper. And on the mound, batting ninth, Carlos Garcia.

Nerves were on edge as the first inning gave the Bison faithful something to worry about. Webster hit the very first pitch. On the ground, the ball easily found its way into right field where Ben casually made the play with an efficient toss to the cutoff. By the time Bo turned to throw the ball to Jackson, Webster was already standing beside him on second base. Bo, who had his back to the play, was certain that Webster ran directly to second. Jackson just shook his head and went back to his position. Three pitches later, Webster had stolen third base and with one out was brought home on a fielder's choice. No blood was spilled by either team until the top of the third when Carlos made a most egregious of error by walking the right fielder who was batting in the ninth spot. Webster hit the second pitch deep to right field. The pill didn't go over the fence, it went over the trees! The thirty-foot elm trees planted thirty years ago and located across the road and in the park! It might still be up there because no one saw it come down. And like that, the Bisons were behind 3–0.

The team was able to scrape out one run in the bottom of the fourth when after one out, Jackson and Five had back-to-back doubles. But after both Burn and Bo struck out, leaving Five stranded in scoring position, the rally was ended. Both pitchers showed remarkable poise and allowed no additional runs going into the last inning. Mitch Webster's last at bat in the top of the seventh was stifled by Jackson who gunned the speedster down by a step. No runs, no hits, no errors, and no one left on base. It was now or never for our boys of Sumner Plaine.

Bugs led off the inning and reached first via Larned's own version of E-5. Jackson was next to the plate and shot one into left field. It got to the fielder so fast that there was no chance for Bugs to advance past second base. Things were looking better for the team. Five summarily smacked a bolt on the ground directly at the third baseman who, after picking himself up off the ground, was able to step on third for the first out of the inning. Everyone was looking for a deep one from Kevin but his second swing only launched the ball straight up for an infield fly rule.

Two on, two outs, and up to the plate walked the most nervous ball-player in the history of the game. Coach Bolin could sense the jitters of his second baseman and called Bo down the line for a conference. "It's not a championship tournament," Coach said. "It's not even a game. It's a little white ball. See it and cut that fucker in half." Bo shoved his glasses firm to his brow and stepped to the plate for the biggest at bat of his life. Bo was always a cautious batter and rarely swung at bad pitches. Webster however, didn't know that and threw him two straight, low and inside. Bo might not have been the best player on the field, and his odds facing the future MLB star were probably not good, but Bo knew the game like no other. There was no way Mitch Webster was going to walk him and put the tying run in scoring position. This next pitch was going to be meat down the middle. Every Indian fan in the stadium listened for the pop of the catcher's glove but the pitch never made it. Bo had hit home runs before yet none of those matched the velocity and angle of this 2-0 stroke. Yet there was a problem, and the problem was Lewis Field. Bo's shot heard round the world would not be a Bobby Thompson shot. It was hit to no-man's-land in deep center field. The ball easily cleared the head of the unsuspecting center fielder and hit at the base of the 433' sign. Moving on the contact, Jackson and Five scored easily with the fans cheering on Bo as he stood on third base once the ball finally made it back to the infield. The Sumner Plaine fans were ecstatic, which aided the second most nervous player in the history of the game. Slim would step into the right-hander's box with the winning run just ninety feet away.

Mitch Webster put a little red-ass in his next two pitches. Both were swung on and missed. With an 0-2 count, Coach could sense what the next pitch would be and whispered for Bo to be ready. Bo knew that this would be a throwaway pitch, He also knew that the odds of a passed ball had just gone up exponentially. Webster made his first mistake. Working from the windup, he allowed Bo's lead to stretch closer to home plate than he should have. When that pitch skipped slightly and the short-hop gently got away, Bo was off. The confluence of four players in an area of 288 square inches, formed in the shape of an isosceles right pentagon suggests a reaction of seismic proportions. When the ground stopped quaking, the dust had cleared, and the call was made, Bo's left hand got there first.

It was the culmination of youthful comradery, fateful opportunity, and luck. The boys won. The parents won. The community won. To this day, every baseball fan in Sumner Plaine can recite you each pitch of that last half inning. In western Kansas, the name Jackson Stillwell is renowned for his career and shall live on as the area's best ballplayer ever. But, in Sumner Plaine, it is the image of Bo Wright's bolt to home plate that will forever be remembered.

There were ceremonies and festivities associated with the championship and upcoming graduation, but the most fitting celebration for our victors came in early June. The infield of the legendary team chose to go on a road trip to Colorado. This backpacking jaunt had been in the works for months. The Stillwell family had habitually traveled to the mountains for winter skiing and summer camping for years. Jackson and his brothers had become quite adept in the skills of mountain camping. Enough so, that Johnathon Stillwell was comfortable with Jackson leading a backpacking expedition of four close friends to a familiar campsite near the Rocky Mountain National Forest. The family had made that trek several times. They had the proper equipment, the necessary tools, and the knowledge to offer these four young lads so as to guarantee a safe and enjoyable trip. At least, that's what each set of parents thought. Jackson, Bo, Slim, and Five were each given permission and some funding as a graduation gift. The fact that the team just pulled off the greatest victory in the school's baseball history added to the sense of entitlement these four graduates felt. After all, what kind of trouble could four sober, law-abiding, polite, churchgoing young men get into in the mountains of Colorado.

Each pack was prepared by Jackson, since he had the equipment and was using his money to buy food, which would be necessary if they didn't catch any fish. He evenly distributed all the gear by weight and balance so that each hiker would carry a similar burden on his back.

The other three were responsible for "ancillary" items, ones that might be referred to as comfort essentials necessary for the three cold nights next to Long Lake in the height of the Rockies. Actually, it was only Slim and Five who were given the charge to procure the whiskey, beer, weed, and *Playboys* to add to the packs once they were out of eye shot of the parents. Jackson knew he couldn't rely on Bo to come up with such indispensable provisions. Bo's money would be held in reserve for emergency purposes; meaning, if they drank all the booze before they got to the mountain.

Bo drove his family's secondary vehicle, a puke yellow, four-door Ford Comet with nearly eighty thousand miles logged. The time in the car consisted of one long collaborative recollection of the past year. The time on the trail was made up of multiple debates over just how much of that recollection was bullshit. The first night on the mountain provided exhausted and blissful silence. It wasn't just Five who claimed the vow of limited verbiage. Jackson, Five, and Slim were stoned, drunk, and drained. They were so tired that the *Playboys* didn't make it out of the pack until the next morning.

The rules of the camp, and there were many, included that the first one awake and up in the morning had to reestablish the fire. Even in June, the nights were cold and it took some fortitude to get out of the tent when it was thirty-five degrees outside. Of course, it was Bo. Everyone knew it would be Bo who would start the fire. Slim and Jackson both would awaken first but would pretend to be asleep until Bo got out of his bag. Five slept through it all. He could sleep through anything, except what occurred on that first morning. Upon arrival, the four had adequately gathered wood for the next day's fire but the kindling available was limited and damp. Bo had matches but needed something flammable to start the blaze. He decided to use pages from Five's *Playboy*. Each ripping vibration caused by the destruction of such sacred art was like shoving a hot needle under the nails of Five's extremities. He knew exactly what was happening as if he were metaphysically united with June's Playmate of the Month. It only took a couple of stings and he bolted out the tent as if it were on fire. He ran *through* Bo and laid him out like he used to in junior high football. "Not ... one ... more!"

"Damn it, Five!" Bo said while rising from the pine needles and brushing himself off. "I left the best articles."

Five threw a full can of beer at Bo which bounced off his shoulder and rattled around the campsite. Bo picked it up, shook it some more, and proceeded to shower Five with the suds. The rest of the day went about the same way. All fun and games. Any worries that each might maintain were nonexistent. That night while they were all resting against their respective trees, noises in the woods behind the campsite were heard. Jackson immediately ran to his pack and pulled out a handgun his father had loaned him. "What the fuck is that?" Slim inquired with eyes and mouth wide open.

"That was a bear!" Jackson replied.

"Not that, asshole. What is in your hand?"

"I heard a bear!" Jackson reaffirmed.

"Bullshit." It was the only word Five had spoken since he bulldozed Bo that morning.

"I promise you, there are bears up here or, maybe a cougar," Jackson responded, obviously displaying his fear of mountain wild animals.

"Bullshit!" was Five's final word of the evening, as he watched Jackson slowly and calmly lower his guard.

"Each time we come up here, Dad brings the Judge," Jackson explained. "He always said you need something to bring down whatever comes charging. This will do the trick." Jackson returned the gun to his pack after he was assured that no wild animals were present. He slipped it in the bottom sleeve of his backpack without zipping it closed and returned to the fire. Later on, he went to that pack to retrieve the bottle of whiskey to pass around. The pack shifted with the removal of the heavy bottle and the gun fell out of its compartment and onto the large stone at the base of the tree. The gun discharged and blew the bark off the tree that Slim was sitting against—just two inches above his head. Everyone froze. The echo of the shot loudly encompassed the entire range. The silence that followed was deeper than a graveyard at midnight. There was no sound for an eternity, followed by an outburst of laughter that went on forever. It would have also been the loudest laughter ever except only three of the four were laughing. Jackson remembered his dad mentioning something about a sensitive trigger on the Judge but this was the first time he had ever seen the gun fire. Slim never completely forgave Jackson for that nearly fatal accident and none of them would ever forget it. The incident itself was rarely mentioned after that night, and then, in code, only as "the thing with the Judge.

SEVENTEEN

Hello, Crystal

(New Year's 2003)

With the end of the spring high school baseball season, Jackson lost some of his therapy and for a time drifted back toward his old ways. He noticed the regression, but Gwyneth and Jackson's co-workers still recognized the improvement relative to his previous behavior. Though Jackson still drank more than he wanted to, it had been six months since his last illicit drug and over a year since his last extramarital affair. During the following summer, the thought that religion might help, or at least be a step in the right direction, propelled his actions. He tried to go back to church. A couple of times he attended a Scientology gathering, which was little more than a recruiting and group counseling session utilizing Dianetics as its base tenets. They met on a campus in East Hollywood. The architecture of the centralized buildings was a cross between army barracks and Lower East Side. In contrast, when he saw the facility the church maintained for celebrity members only, Jackson knew this sect was not for him. Plus, if Bo and Five ever found out, Jackson would never live it down. With other attempts, Jackson bounced back and forth between the Catholic church nearest his apartment and the Lutheran church his legal assistant belonged to. It all just confused him. To the point that, on his own, he started to study the primary scriptures of all orthodox religions. None of this changed him at his core. There was no spiritual transformation. There would be no emotional conversion but with this desire and the ascendancy of the sacred writings, he felt as if his life was now evolving around something other than himself. Even if he never found any answers, the search itself felt right.

Jackson was clearly the most intellectual of his brothers and his friends. His parents and teachers had realized this from Jackson's early childhood. He absorbed everything he read and retained anything he deemed necessary. The Holy Scriptures of each religion were a challenge, not in the reading but in their interpretation. Yet, if nothing else, Jackson found relaxation in the study. It became part of his evening leisure. Jackson was fascinated with the words of each. He respected the beauty and drew wisdom from the traditions of the midrash and Talmud. He was surprised and enthralled by the connected disciplines of the Torah and Quran. And in revisiting the New Testament that he failed to read as a youth, Jackson was touched by the compassion and simplicity of the Gospels. No one expected Jackson ever to be religious, least of all Jackson himself. In this labor, however, he was finding balance, a re-centering of himself with a mindset that was more intuitive than intellectual, more wise than well-informed.

Baseball became his only vice that summer. Whenever possible, Jackson would catch a USC doubleheader or take clients to watch the Dodgers. It wasn't the same though. He never quite found the peace of mind and spirit at each as he did while watching the Vikings play in Santa Monica. Jackson found himself counting the days until the opening game next spring. He was planning on going to as many games as possible. He even toyed with the idea of contacting the coach to see if there was room on the team for a volunteer fielding coach. Between reading the sacred texts of monotheistic religions and the box scores of area teams, Jackson's summer was the most pacified since KU. Not requiring an artificial catalyst to reach a psychological high is what success feels like when you are a functioning addict like Jackson. He felt wonderful.

As the summer ended and the fall ambled toward the holidays, travel plans needed to be made. The family had hoped Jackson could make it home for Thanksgiving and Christmas. These newfound interests in things other than work created a backlog of business which kept Jackson in L.A. over the Thanksgiving weekend. Additionally, Gwyneth had obligated them to a family gathering in Hawaii over Christmas. This wouldn't have bothered him in the past, but this year Jackson wanted to see his family and friends. The best he could do was to get home over the New Year's holiday.

Perhaps out of the long-standing guilt of not taking Christmas seriously in the past, perhaps from the evolving attitude that Jackson was experiencing in the present, he decided to go all out on Christmas gifts. Each of his brothers received a case of Chateau Montelena and the kids got so much L.A. Dodgers gear that it filled up the dining room table. But the kicker was an Aspen ski trip for all members to enjoy over the spring break, paid in full by the prodigal who finally realized how important family was. Perhaps this encompassed a few back payments, but mostly he just felt like it. He wished he could have been there at the time. He missed his hometown.

Little did anyone know just how flush Jackson and Bo had become. Their original fifty thousand dollar investment had swelled to something north of ten million each thanks to the most lucrative stock pick since the Great Depression, Cisco Systems. In a little less than ten years, it had exploded as a multinational computer technology firm by creating products that all other telecommunication firms needed. Once Bo sold all of their shares in the spring of 2000, the money sat in a money market through the dot com bubble. In 2002, Bo offered his only input to the investment fund by recommending they not risk as much on start-up ventures and place the residual funds in more conservative dividend producing stocks like J.P. Morgan, Exxon, and Philip Morris. The move, Jackson had to admit, was smart and with such, Eljuez added nearly a million dollars annually in additional equity and revenue—tax free!

This was all Jackson's idea but it was Bo who was the primary beneficiary. He had consistently been using his half of the fund for some time now. Jackson had yet to utilize any of his share. Bo started to pay much more attention to the portfolio. He needed a steady stream of income to finance his glad-handing and pocket padding crusade. Jackson was just the opposite. What once was a vital motivating factor now seemed unnecessary. He even asked Bo once if they should fold up the operation and go legit. Bo remembered that day. He remembered shaking his head and snickering. He remembered looking down at Jackson in a way that he had never done before. Not to the friend who he always looked up to and had never contradicted. It was another pivotal moment.

When Jackson arrived in Sumner Plaine just before the new year, only Five remained but he was working at the sporting goods store and wasn't available that weekend. Jackson's brothers and their families had returned to their homes. Bo was in St. Louis with Nancy, Jenna, and Jack visiting the in-laws and trying to reconnect. Slim had recently eloped (or so they thought) and was living in Las Vegas. Gwyneth didn't want to make the trip after just returning from Honolulu. Their separation was becoming more permanent. It was quiet and peaceful at the Stillwell house, not quite what Jackson had been searching for. Sleeping in his old bedroom and looking up at familiar cracks in the ceiling, he felt out of place—just as he had recently been feeling in his own bed. It was a strange feeling for a man so sure of himself and his place in the world to search for something that he knows exists yet incapable of finding. It must exist because he can see it in the lives of so many around him. It's a strange inadequacy to see something so near yet not be able to grasp. Some of the old sensitivities were welling up inside his vacated heart. He wasn't angry or sad. He felt depleted. Lacking in emotion. Lacking in direction. Lacking in purpose. Who would know that hollowness could produce such pain?

Jackson joined his parents for a pre–New Years drink before they went out to the club to bring in 2003 with dinner and dancing. Jackson had never felt so out of place. He didn't know many and didn't feel like dancing. His partial sobriety made getting drunk a little easier. Watching his parents, Jackson noticed something he hadn't before. They really enjoyed each other's company. He didn't recall them showing much affection when growing up. Sure, they showed it to him and his brothers but not one kiss or pat on the backside did Jackson recall. There weren't many arguments between the parents as Jackson thought back but not many smiles either. He tried to recall specific times when memorable events would bring back some emotions of youth but Jackson was having a hard time doing so. As he watched Johnathon and Gabby, as he now referred to them, smiling, dancing, kissing, caressing, Jackson looked upon them as if they were a different set of people in comparison to the ones he remembered raising him.

It may have been the alcohol that he was continuing to consume but, in his mind, Jackson was beginning to think that he had somehow missed out on the important aspects of adolescence. It was something for which he blamed his dad yet he couldn't quite put a finger on one incident that triggered his animosity. So, if there wasn't something specific to trigger this emotion, maybe it was because there wasn't anything specific to his rearing. Maybe they selfishly chose not to try at all. It was a lack of parental direction that perhaps he had missed or misplaced. Such an omission could be why his life was so empty.

They arrived home shortly after midnight. Johnathon and Gabby didn't stay out as late as they used to. Oldness comes upon us all, from the inside first. Neither Jackson nor his brothers noticed that their parents were aging because they tended to themselves so well. Physically and emotionally they both felt their maturity creeping closer to its end. Or was it racing away from its beginning? Gabby went immediately to the bathroom to prepare for bed. Jackson and his dad sat at the kitchen table looking at the same clock on the wall. There was a fog in Jackson's eyes and a murk to his mental state as he slowly looked at his father, waiting for something to be said. Words were not easy to come by in this household. How Jackson became such an extrovert, no one really knew. Johnathon enjoyed conversation but rarely in one-on-one settings. His father had been a quiet man also. Johnathon remembered few punishments coming from his dad. At worst, he could tell the anger of his dad when Johnathon was admonished by a "way to go, bud" or "I expected a little better out of you."

When Jackson was younger, he used to listen to his dad speak in church or hear him at gatherings but rarely heard a word from him at home.

"Why was that?" Jackson barked out as if Johnathon had been privy to his son's internal conversation all along.

"Why was what?"

"Why didn't you ever tell me anything?"

"I'm not sure I'm following you."

"When I was growing up, you didn't ever talk to me!"

Johnathon was startled at the comment but it didn't take long for him to see the reasoning behind it. In that very instant, he saw an entire lifetime of wanting to do the right thing for his sons reduced to utter failure. To Johnathon the time spent contemplating the accusation while sitting at the kitchen table was enormous but his response actually came quickly. "I thought I had told you what you needed to know. At least when you were young. As you got older, you didn't take well to direction from anyone other than your coaches and friends. Perhaps I stopped trying when I felt it was doing more harm than good."

Jackson, in his drunken stupor, snapped back, "Well it didn't work, obviously."

"What didn't work?"

"Look at me. Whatever you did trying to raise me, well … it didn't work."

"I think you are the very best of our family, we all do. We love you. Even when you are at your—"

Jackson didn't let his dad finish before he yelled back. "Why didn't you tell me how to be a man. How to be a better person?"

"I guess I did what came most natural to me. I remember the freedom my dad gave me. I knew his expectations or at least I thought I did. And when I didn't live up to them, I always felt it inside. It was as if he was teaching me without being there, without saying a word. I must have been lucky, I guess." Johnathon wasn't an athlete growing up so he didn't have any coach's advice on which to focus. He relied on his parents for wisdom, or so he thought. If he was honest with himself, Johnathon too pulled away from the teachings of his parents at a young age. "I never thought I was doing anything harmful by letting you have the same freedom I enjoyed."

"I don't think I learned anything from you."

It was that statement that cut the deepest. Johnathon was somewhere between outrage and shameful regret. He heard in that statement from his youngest and most successful son something not spoken but existing in the spaces in between the words. Their rapport was apparently missing something that he had found noticeable in the father and son relationship of others. Johnathon took a deep breath before responding. "Some fathers teach their sons how to drive drunk without getting pulled over. Some fathers teach their sons how to cheat on their taxes without getting audited. Some fathers teach their sons how to be with women and keep them from getting pregnant." The entire time Jackson's dad was making his speech, he wondered if he should have just walked away and let the controversy resolve on its own. Almost immediately he wanted to take it back but he was too far in. "I'm not that kind of a father." And with that Johnathon got up and went to bed. Jackson returned to the clock on the wall and his barren outlook.

Little was said the next day between the two. Jackson's flight was to leave early so there wasn't much time to rehash or repair the obvious chasm that was exposed the previous night. Johnathon drove Jackson to the airport. Other than flight information, nothing was shared on the way. Before Jackson crossed the security threshold his dad grabbed him, held him, and thanked him for last night. "There is nothing more liberating than honesty, no matter where it comes from," Johnathon told his son. "I love you more than you will ever know." Jackson reciprocated. Realizing that he had been dodging his own responsibilities all along, he started to apologize but his dad stopped him short. "No need for apologies; not between you and me, ever." With that, he turned and walked to the parking lot. An attempt was made, but with both the tears were unstoppable.

***

Later that spring as Jackson's work and life became more uncomfortable to him, he was still able to find a type of inner peace at the baseball games of the Santa Monica Vikings. Jackson had missed the first three home games before he was able to attend. He very much looked forward to reconnecting with Al and evaluating the developing talent of his grandson who, as a junior, had grown quite a bit since Jackson last saw him. Jackson watched him warm up and come to the plate batting third in the Viking lineup. Since Al hadn't arrived yet, Jackson chuckled as he tried to remember exactly how the superstitiously dedicated grandfather would cheer for his grandson each time he came to bat. Every time Jake came to bat, Jackson would try a different theme but to no avail. Jake reached base only once that game, on a walk. The team won but the young shortstop was 0-3 at the plate. A woman sitting in front of Jackson turned around after Jake's last at bat and noted that he was a little out of sorts and probably not playing to his potential.

"His grandfather had a stroke last week and is in the hospital ICU. They are very close."

Jackson watched Jake as he gathered his gear and walked toward the school locker room. He watched hoping to see a parent or another adult meet him but Jake disappeared into the building without any attention. When the woman in front of Jackson stepped out of her seat and down the bleacher aisle, she left behind a team program and roster of players. It was the first time Jackson had known Jake's full name. #3– Jake Evans – shortstop – junior. He paused, looked up, and took the program with him.

Jackson planned on making at least one more game this season but work and a pending divorce with Gwyneth had completely occupied him. The divorce was not unexpected. The two had separated just after their holiday trip to Hawaii. It was an amicable split both emotionally and financially. Of course Gwyneth, and subsequently her attorney, had no information regarding a specific Cayman Island account of which Jackson's share was now over twelve million dollars. Other than not revealing his total financial status, Jackson was very accommodating of Gwyneth's needs in the breakup. Jackson actually took the blame for the failed marriage when he would speak of it to friends and associates. He hoped that they could remain friends though he suspected that she would move on to greener pastures quickly. Most of those around Jackson thought that he would again find love, but in Jackson's own mind he wasn't meant for marriage. At least not now. Perhaps not ever. How can you be comfortable in someone's arms if you're not comfortable in your own skin?

As he hoped, Jackson was able to attend the semifinals of the conference tournament. Santa Monica was playing El Segundo for the right to face Charter Oaks the following day in the southern section championship of Division IV. Jackson made his way to his familiar seat hoping to find his acquaintance, Jake's grandfather. When he wasn't there, the worst was assumed, but by the play of the sharp shortstop, you would have thought that Al was sitting next to Jackson. The game was close with the Vikings trailing 2–1 in the top of the sixth. El Segundo had runners on second and third with two outs. Though Jake was two for two in the first five innings, the rest of the team was struggling against a stocky, hard-throwing right-hander. Jackson knew that if two more runs were to come across the plate, it would be difficult for Santa Monica to overcome such a deficit in the final two at bats. The infield was shifted toward right field for the left-swinging cleanup batter. Second and shortstop were playing deep, near the outfield grass. The first pitch was hit hard down the right field line but foul. The entire crowd gasped a sigh of relief. The second pitch, hit equally as hard, was a ground ball up the gut, just to the first-base side of second base. With the shift on, the only person who would have had a play was Jake. Off the bat, it seemed unlikely anyone would get a glove on the ball and two more runs would score easily. Out of nowhere (it seemed) Jake, sprinting and with precise timing, laid flat out and swallowed up the pill. He was just as quick to his feet, spun 360 degrees and fired a strike to first—one step ahead of the batter and his shocked teammates. Jackson couldn't believe what he just saw. He had never seen such a defensive play from a high school player. Not even Five, who made some impressive stops in his day (only to fire the ball over Slim's head as well as the first-base line fence, E-5). Jackson himself had made similar stops in his career but never at this age. In fact, when Jackson first saw it, he thought without saying so that it could have been himself he was watching, Jake looked so similar.

Santa Monica tied the game in the sixth and won with a walk-off single in the bottom of the seventh. Jake scored the winning run. Jackson, as well as the rest of the crowd, went ape-shit as the team rushed the field. It would be the first time that Santa Monica ever played in the finals of the Southern Section. Someone tapped Jackson on the back and he turned to see a familiar face, the woman who first told him about Jake's grandfather. She said that Al was recuperating nicely but was still required to stay home. His daughter, Jake's mom, was taking care of him. "I'll bet they both hated to miss this game," Jackson stated after shaking her hand and thanking her for the information. "If you ever talk to Al, tell him the dude in the suit got to see his grandson play today." With the finals to be played on Saturday, Jackson was sure he would be there for the championship game. He smiled as he left, watching the Vikings celebrating in the dugout. It reminded him of the celebration he, Bo, and the rest of the Bisons had during their own championship run in the spring of 1976. The next morning Jackson awakened with the same knots in his stomach he'd had when the hometown crew of Five, Slim, Whiskey, and Wright took the field for their final game together as a team.

When he arrived, Jackson first went to the tournament concessions for snacks. He talked with some of the opposing fans from Santa Anita before moving toward the seats. The line into the central stands was slowed to a crawl. Jackson questioned the pace but got his answer on his own when he saw Al, walker in tow, being assisted to his traditional seat by a woman. "It might be Jake's mom at long last making it to a game," he thought. As the crowd dispersed, Jackson slowly moved toward what he hoped would be a seat next to Al. Jackson was halfway up the stands when Al finally was seated and his helper turned toward the field before sitting next to him.

When faced with a sudden shock, people's reactions can be quite different depending on the individual and the situation. Some, after the initial jolt, simply carry on with the task at hand. Some stop cold and are incapable of moving forward. Others may try to cover their reaction with a thespian-like inventiveness, pretending no such shock occurred at all. Jackson, after acknowledging the surprise of whom he just laid eyes on, slowly walked up to the woman assisting Al and said, "Hello, Crystal."

EIGHTEEN

Ebenezer

(Spring 2003)

Jackson remembered little of the championship game. In fact, it was days later that he realized the Vikings of Santa Monica had lost so handily, 7—1 and that Jake, his son, was 1-4 at the plate. He only remembers the sound of the squeaking bench as he sat behind Crystal and Al. The bench would moan each time Jackson shifted his weight, something that occurred frequently, with every uncomfortable inning. So many things were unsettled and unsettling. Jackson's brow burned and throbbed with each beat of his quivering pulse. His mind was knotted, recoiling back and forth trying to validate memory with history. There were occasions before that day when Jackson recognized Crystal after climbing those steps, when hints of correlation and reflected imagery had occurred. The possibility that Jake wasn't just another ballplayer. That with so many similarities, there could have been a connection of some sort. From the time Jackson left the semi-final game to the moment he returned, he felt more like a family member than a spectator. He couldn't have known just how true those feelings were.

Jackson's diluted Dr. Pepper and unopened sunflower seeds sat at his feet for nine innings. He didn't remove himself from the seat he had chosen; just behind Al, who did not seem to recognize Jackson at all. Twice Crystal left her seat only to return without looking directly at her ex-husband. Yes, they had been married. Yes, they were perhaps in love, but the conclusion of that relationship was so resolute that Jackson had lost all desire and concern for her. He hadn't thought of his first wife for seventeen years. For two hours, Jackson was miserable. So many instances during the game, Jackson wanted to leave. Truth be known, he would have gladly disappeared if given the opportunity. He would have paid any amount to have never set eyes on this ballfield, never to have met Crystal on that beach, never to have been born. The game concluded with none of those yearnings being met.

Jackson sat motionless after the game concluded, not knowing his next move or what was about to transpire. Crystal rose to help Al to his feet. The two slowly inched their way to the bottom of the stairs and over to the dugout. Jackson watched as the two hugged Jake and then returned to their vehicle. It was only after he watched them drive away that Jackson realized that the feeling he was experiencing was the same as on that beach the evening after their divorce was finalized. As before, the tears did come; but this time, the only animosity he felt was toward himself. He sat on that bench rehashing the story in his head and asked himself what just happened. After finishing the scrutiny, he rose from his seat wondering to himself what *might* have been. Jackson was the last to leave the stadium. He drove home in silence. No one realized just how important Jackson's sobriety was. It had taken a solid, if not firm, hold on his character these last months. If not, he might have done himself harm just to remove himself from this anguish.

Jackson slept hard that night and dreamed of far-off lands with images untethered to reality. As if those depictions were trying to mother him. He woke to the same pain. He couldn't move so he laid there and left his mind open to what might come. He wasn't angry, as others might have assumed, nor was he hurt so much. What came to him was embarrassment and the shame of who he was. It was a similar sense that occupied him that night in the empty apartment after the first time he saw Jake play. That feeling again returned on the evening he remained outside and stared out at the ocean for hours, allowing it to mesmerize him to sleep whilst on the veranda of their home in Laguna Beach. And once again, during a drunken stupor sitting at a kitchen table with his father. Conversion, as Jackson had learned from the Koran, occurs when one faces oneself, speaks the truth of oneself, and turns around. True and complete conversion, however, is not like lightning. It does not transpire during one dance with the devil. It is a series of steps, sidesteps and missteps, that bring about our evolution as human beings. With that thought, he showered and headed out the door on a brilliantly clear Sunday morning.

Jackson retrieved the home phone number for Al from an old phone book at the office. The phone rang as Jackson's heart raced. He hoped that Crystal would answer. He assumed that she would be there caring for her dad. If not, Jackson planned on speaking to Al in a fashion that might convince him to trust the caller enough to offer up her number. Her voice was a revival and a relief to Jackson's spirit. The beginning of a new beginning. Crystal agreed to meet with him. She didn't want Al or Jake to know the reality of the situation. Not at all. Theirs was an alternate reality that she had carefully constructed using lumber without nails. Each lie supported by another. If even one shadowed myth was brought into the light, the structure would collapse upon anyone who was sheltered by its walls.

They met at one of the three Starbucks within a one-mile radius. Jackson arrived first. His breathing was shallow and terse as he waited. When the door opened and he looked upon her face, he didn't breathe at all. She sat down, taking a deep breath for both of them. Jackson had pounded his memory since sitting down, trying to recall how Crystal liked her coffee. It would be at least an opening shot of contrition if he could have ordered her favorite, based on a long-held memory of beautiful mornings they had shared together. "I'm sorry, I forgot how you like your coffee." Jackson sheepishly gave up.

"I always hated coffee," Crystal noted. Jackson swallowed and blushed. "I'll take chai please."

They drank quietly for a while. Neither knowing what to say or how to start. "How is your father?"

"The stroke and his COPD are slowly taking his life. He was so worried that he wouldn't see Jake play that last game. Now that he has been given that gift, I think he is ready to die."

Jackson's heart sank to new depths. As they talked, he learned a new respect for family that he had been missing all these years. It was a new overlaying of shame that unfortunately wasn't thick enough to cover the existing layers.

When Crystal couldn't go through with the abortion, she returned home to her father thinking how angry he would be. They talked things out without retribution and hurt. Al couldn't believe how lucky he was to get this second chance at raising a family. Like all fathers, he too had regrets and wanted to offer himself up more fully and selflessly to his daughter and grandson. Crystal, thankful for the support and love, offered to provide much needed income to the household. The cost of living in Santa Monica had outpaced Al's abilities to cope. It was difficult, but they managed to create a protective, caring environment for Jake, who being a great student and even better son, was equally protective of his mom.

"I'm sorry," Crystal continued, "but back then, I didn't know what to do. Jake thinks you're dead."

From the beginning, Al knew that not to be true but aided in the charade by not questioning anything that Crystal would say. He would just accept the fact that life is messy and he was the janitor. Crystal hadn't been with a man since she left Jackson. Not one date. She put it all into the family. One hundred percent. Her biggest concern now was not disrupting the last months of her father's life and Jake's upcoming senior year. "How about you? How has your life been?"

Jackson smiled. Not because he was proud of what his life had been. Not because of his career or the money. Jackson smiled because for the first time in his memory, if only for a moment, he had been completely immersed in someone else's life and needs. His concerns had been turned on their heads and he was no longer fixated on his own selfish desires. He wanted to find a way to repay for his absence. Over the next half hour, he did lay out his past with complete honest detail. Jackson thought that regardless of how his life looked to Crystal, she deserved the unvarnished version. He laid himself bare in a way that he'd never done before. Crystal now knew more about him than his father, his mother, his brothers; even more than Bo. Some people say that there is one soul on this earth that knows you better than you know yourself. That's such bullshit. We know ourselves, even better than God does. We just won't admit to it. Well now, Jackson was admitting to it, all of it. The weight was lifted and his countenance was released. This had been the worst and the best day of his life.

When the coffee and tea were cold, they shook hands and left the restaurant. Jackson had agreed to continuing the ruse and Crystal would make no claims. The attorney in Jackson recognized that last part was perhaps important but legally enigmatic. It didn't matter. When they reached her car, Jackson asked if he could keep in touch from afar. Meaning, he wanted to be a support to Jake at least and to Crystal and Al as well, if she would allow it. Stating that it wasn't necessary, she did allow Jackson to attend Jake's ballgames in the future but "Jake must never know who or what you are." Jackson renewed his concession from their earlier conversation. He understood that this was the best course. He wanted to hug her but was unwilling to make the first move. Crystal turned and got in her car. While she drove away, Jackson stood there silently while noticing her hand wiping at both cheeks. He felt terrible but in the best way possible. Like the last round of successful chemotherapy, he assumed. The remnant of an earlier diseased existence had found remission. Though sad, Jackson felt reborn.

Almost immediately, Jackson made significant changes in his life. He felt like Ebenezer Scrooge the day after Christmas. In fact, he embraced not only that feeling, but that name as well. He recalled clearly its significance from the teachings of the Talmud. Ebenezer means *stone of help*. Jackson continued to work hard at his profession, perhaps becoming more proficient with his earning potential. He chose to remove from his personal portfolio all non-essential assets. He sold all of his properties; including the loft apartment where he lived at the time, downsizing to a smaller rental unit in the same building. It was a practical solution to his present unmarried status. He liquidated two business partnerships regarding commercial property ownership as well as his position in some undeveloped land in Napa. None of it meant anything to him. He was surprised that the sale of the homes in Laguna Beach and Napa created no emotion, only relief. It was another releasing of built-up pressure that he hadn't realized he was experiencing.

Jackson noticed that with each action he was taking, the thought of Jake was integral in the deed: *How would this be viewed by my son? What could Jake do if this resource was available to him? If he knew who I was, would he be proud of me?* The thoughts vexed Jackson yet they were an inward sign of his commitment to his son. It was also an internal conflict because of a promise Jackson made to Crystal. That conflict played out daily during the summer and subsequent fall. Jackson worked as hard as ever, coming home to an empty apartment and reading himself to sleep. The holidays were especially hard on Jackson that year. He was alone each night. The walls would talk to him. His physical appearance started to change. The once formidable athlete was becoming flabby and careless with his health, though with others, he was more courteous and protective than ever. His concern was no longer for himself to the point that he didn't care what happened to him. He knew he was sinking but refused to ask for help—until one night shortly before Christmas. Jackson made a call.

Bo had just gotten home from a workout. His ritual each evening was to stop by the gym for cross-training with free weights or a three-mile run, alternating each day. That would get him home late at times, which meant his dinner after the shower might be eaten alone. Bo, after missing dinner with the family, didn't like shunning them for evening activities. And so, when Jackson called, Bo put him off and said he would call him later. He never did. It wasn't until Bo received another call, one that came after the first of the year, that he started to realize the depths of Jackson's problem. The call was from Gabby, Jackson's mother. Jackson was in the hospital for some tests and she was worried about him.

"Santa Maria! Bo," she went on. "I don't know what to believe or what to do. He says he's fine but he doesn't sound fine. 'No preocupe, Mama,' he says. But he might be dying and just doesn't want me to know." Gabby gave Bo all the details of his hospital location and asked him to call. "Mijo. You're his best friend. He will confide in you." Bo promised he would and, after he hung up, immediately called the hospital only to find that Jackson had been dismissed. The next day they did connect.

"Oh, I'm fine. I wasn't sleeping well and then I started to get headaches, but I'm fine," Jackson interjected, trying to convince his friend.

"What did the doctors say? Do you have any follow-up scheduled?"

"Nope. They gave me a clean bill of health. Heart, blood pressure, brain MRI, everything. They couldn't find anything wrong. They thought I might be depressed so they prescribed me some pills but I don't want to get back into that habit. I just need to get through the holidays and into some warm weather. I'll be fine."

"Do you want me to come out?"

Jackson hesitated. It was the first time that either of them recalled Jackson requiring and Bo offering help. They both were surprised by the tender. Jackson seriously thought about it. Ultimately, he said no but thought it would be great if they got together in the spring for a game somewhere.

Nothing was accomplished but Jackson did feel better after the conversation. It might have been just what he needed. Momentum can't be produced while stationary. Velocity only comes after some external energy has created the initial movement. Bo's call was the physics necessary to instigate the motion. Of course, all Jackson really needed was to survive until opening day for the Santa Monica Vikings. He called Crystal once again to make sure he was wanted. They had a short but nice conversation. They agreed that if she was there, they would sit in different stands and no conversation was to occur at all. "Agreed?" "Agreed." It was difficult for Jackson to watch his son play and not let on. Jake was, as always, exciting to watch. How do you have pride without showing it in some form or fashion? Jackson knew he was going to fail when during the first game, Jake went four for four, six RBIs, including a three-run dinger in the sixth. Jackson was glad Crystal was not at that game.

Halfway through the season, Jake was hitting .467 and leading the division in all statistical categories other than homeruns. Jackson had yet to see Crystal at a game and wondered why. She agreed to meet him for coffee on a Sunday. Jackson convinced her that it was important. This time the chai tea was waiting. "It's none of my business, but this is Jake's senior year and you haven't made any games yet. Why?"

"Dad is in hospice care at a nursing facility. I'm working two jobs to make the payments and when I am free, I need to spend time with him. The doctor says maybe two or three months. Jake understands. Besides, I know that you're there. Even though Jake will never know, somehow I feel better that you are watching him."

Jackson had never experienced the pride of a father in his entire life. It was completely new to him and it came out of left field. He didn't know what to say. "Thank you for that. How's he doing in school?"

"Top three percent! He tells me he wants to be an engineer. I know for a fact he wants to play in the majors."

"You know, with those grades and his talent, he might be able to play ball in a quality university. Maybe even Pepperdine or Cal Poly."

"He would love that, but unless scholarships start arriving, there's no way. He wants to play so he thought City College or Glendale Community College might be his best option for the first two years. Then we would see how much money we could save by then. Dad has a life insurance policy …" She stopped short of taking that statement to its end.

Jackson was sorry to hear about Al. He was equally sorry that he couldn't share a seat next to Jake's grandfather. Watching Jake together would have been a special treat this year. They finished their drinks and walked to the cars. Jackson made Crystal promise that she would see Jake play during the last part of the season. "You'll regret it and I'll feel even more guilty than I do now." She promised and they parted ways. Jackson marveled at the fact that Crystal was becoming more of a friend now than she ever was when they were in love. Jackson didn't say much but he was hatching a plan to help out with Jake's baseball potential at the next level.

An assistant athletic director at USC and friend got Jackson in touch with the head scout for the baseball team. He agreed to look at some film and watch Jake play at least one game. They both met at Santa Monica's final home game of the season. Jackson spent the time building Jake up in the eyes of the scout. Quality kid, 4.05 GPA, good student-citizen, etc. The scout told him that if he could play, they didn't care about the other stuff. After the game, he told Jackson that he was impressed but that they have too many infielders now. What they needed was pitching and big bats. Jake was neither of those. He hadn't pitched since his freshman year and only had two home runs during his high school career. The scout said that he would put in a word to a friend of his who is an assistant coach for Stanford. "Jake is just their type of ballplayer. It's just a matter of if they have an opening coming up on their roster." Jackson was encouraged and thanked him for his time and effort.

The season ended quickly for the team. Last year's graduation had done a number on the squad and they lost in the first round of the division playoffs. Jake, however, had a great year and was named to the all-district all-star team. By the time graduation rolled around, no college offers had arrived other than Glendale, but there were more chances for Jake to be noticed in the coming months. During the summer, Jake played on a semi-pro team out of Huntington Beach. College scouts were known to frequent certain venues and Huntington Beach was one of those. In addition, in June, some universities had camps that invited certain recruits to attend. But by the end of the month, Jake was losing hope and about to give in to the fact that he would be attending a two-year school to further his baseball passion.

Two major events occurred in July that would change Jake's fortunes. One for the better and one for the worse. Jake received an offer from Stanford. It was the opportunity to be a walk-on with the baseball team and acceptance in the university to attend classes. No money or guarantee but the chance to earn a spot on the roster and possible scholarship after one year. And Jake's grandfather died one week after Jake received the offer from Stanford.

The emotions of a teenager run maniacally enough without the advent of two such antithetical events thrown into the mix. Before Al's death, Jackson was shocked when he received a phone call from Crystal. She wanted him to know of the offer from Stanford. All of them were so excited just to have the letter to place in Jake's baseball scrapbook. Crystal and Al knew there wouldn't be a chance they could afford even one year at Stanford; and to go into significant debt, even for such worthwhile opportunity, would not be prudent for Jake in the long run. They were just so thrilled. Crystal knew Jackson would want to hear the news. Almost immediately, Jackson stated with authority and pride, "Send him. I'll pay for it." There was no hesitation. No regret after the words were out. It was as if finally, Jackson's life had a function. There was a purpose to all he had gone through in the last forty-seven years. It all made sense now. That feeling was short-lived though as Crystal outright denied the offer. She would not consider it in any fashion.

"I did not call to ask for help. It was as a courtesy because I knew how much you have been following his progress this year. I felt that, as his father, you were at least entitled to the news." Jackson had to stop her from hanging up, she was so curt.

"Hear me out, please," Jackson pleaded, noting over the phone that it was going to be difficult. "I realize that your concern is that Jake would find out about me and I am completely in agreement with you that this is not for the best. My intent, though I wish things were different and that I could actually get to know Jake somehow, is to be helpful only. You and he have had few dreams come true in your lives and maybe this is a chance to realize one for a change. Tell him that he received a scholarship after all. It would have to be from another source, like a government grant of some type. But tell him that it can happen. I want you and me to make this happen." Crystal did not hang up. In fact, she discussed it further if only hypothetically. She said she would think about it and thanked Jackson for the offer. Jackson smiled and hung up the phone.

The next time they talked was two weeks after Al had died. Crystal again called out of civility to apprise Jackson of her father's passing. She also wanted him to know that she did create another fabricated aspect to Jake's indeterminate and opaque relationship with his unknown father. She had told Al and Jake that he had received a Pell Grant that would allow him to attend Stanford this fall. Crystal wondered aloud whether this drama might have been the event leading to the incident which finally killed her father. Yet she told Jackson that she wouldn't dare take away the feeling they all shared in that one moment—not even for another year with her dying father. "Dad was more excited than Jake," she said through her tearful smile. And as Jackson would come to realize and accept, Jake chose not to accept the contrived grant and would embrace playing baseball at Glendale Community College because it was so close to home. Through trepidation and pain, Crystal and Jake had debated and argued the merits of a Stanford education but Jake would never leave his mother alone after her father's death. Not for the world.

Jackson told Crystal how much he disagreed with the decision, how much he wished he could talk to Jake and convince him of the error within his choice, but also how impressed he was with the selfless gesture of a young man giving up on a dream out of love for his mother.

Jackson even told Crystal that if they would have raised Jake together, he probably wouldn't have turned out as well as he did, being raised by a single and very impressive mother. She should be proud of herself also. It was another of those moments recently in Jackson's life where he felt terrible and great at the same time. Later that same night, Jackson received another phone call. Hoping it was Crystal stating that Jake had changed his mind, Jackson suffered through an even more shocking discussion. It was his mom. Jackson's dad had been killed in a private plane crash piloted by one of his close friends.

NINETEEN

Would You Say Something

(Summer 2004)

B o spent the afternoon at the Stillwells' home. It was the day before Johnathon Stillwell's funeral. Even with a houseful of the closest of family and friends, there exists an eerie discomfort in a space left partially vacant by a dying member. One never knows how to be present in the perpetual absence of another. Bo sat calmly on the couch in the beautiful living room. It was a large, open, L-shaped area with beautifully treated expansive windows overlooking the front portico and unveiled French doors inviting all to the furnished veranda and pool in back. Gabby was sitting in her favorite provincial chair. She always had marveled at the architecture of the cabriole legs and the worksmanship of the ornate scalloped back and arms. Each piece of furniture, every stitch of cushioning was to her liking. Jackson slipped over to the baby grand piano and tried to remember some old tunes he played when he was young.

The passive setting of the gathering was short-lived when Gabby got up for the third time in as many minutes to clean or rearrange something that had caught her attention. "Relajarse, Mama." Jackson pleaded after pausing his music.

"Estoy tranquila, mijo. Estoy," she claimed as she repositioned herself in the chair only to rise again and walk outside to rearrange the chairs on the back patio. Gabby was always the strong parent. She was responsible for the encouragement and the discipline. Both Jackson and Bo knew she would be fine after a limited period of mourning.

"She'll be fine," Jackson reassured before commencing to his musical pursuit. "How's politics?" he queried. It was Jackson's intent to lead the conversation away from death and his own recent history.

"The best part about it is being fully in the loop of every activity you used to take for granted. It's a feeling of power actually, having all that information." Bo leaned forward and took hold of the book displayed upon the Parisian coffee table while continuing to explain his attraction and interest in his newest trade. "As a citizen, you hear of the final products coming out of government. As a lawmaker, you see it from start to finish. It can be ugly and sometimes we know more than we should but that's the way it always has been. It's addictive, really." Jackson scooted the piano bench back by necessity before spinning his girth around to face his friend. "And you, what's happened to those six-pack abs I remember?" Bo was in the best physical shape of his life and was shocked at Jackson's *soft* physique.

"Lord, my body has been a good friend. But I won't need it, when I reach the end."

Bo smiled and asked where he had heard that before. "Is that in the Bible? No wait, the Torah?" Bo waited for a minute, half expecting Jackson to quote some Zen Buddhist or Confucius testimony.

"Cat Stevens." Jackson looked at Bo with tenderness, bordering on sympathy. "'Miles from Nowhere' ... Let's get something to eat." As is the tradition in the Midwest, families and friends had brought enormous amounts of food following the death of a loved one. "You might as well eat. We'll have to throw out most of this tomorrow." Bo wasn't hungry and allowed Jackson the chance to feed for the third time that day. Bo continued to thumb through the pristine book he had seized. He recognized it was a Bible but the binding was stiff, as if it hadn't been opened. And the language was familiar but unique enough for Bo to ask. Jackson peeked around the corner to ascertain to what Bo was referring. "Oh, it's Mama's Bible. It's written in Castilian Spanish. She has always preferred the stately sound over colloquial Mexican Spanish. I'm not sure where the book came from."

"It's beautiful. Your mom. You know, she's quite remarkable. Let's see ..." Bo thought as Jackson returned to the room with a full plate of grub. "She's an American citizen whose family derives from Guadalajara,

Mexico, yet speaks a dialect originating in central Spain and loves all things French."

"She is a worldly woman," Jackson said with a smile as he carefully replaced the sacred item. Jackson confirmed Bo's thoughts and added one more. "She loves you more than you'll ever know. I can remember in third or fourth grade. There were times when she wanted me to be your friend before I wanted to. She always asks about you in the same conversations that she would ask about her own children and grand-children. I think she's more protective of you than she is of me." There was a long pause while Jackson remained in thought and stared out the back window at his mother cleaning the patio table. "It would be a lot easier to give the eulogy at Mama's funeral than Dad's." Jackson turned back toward the piano keys and started to play again.

"That's nice. What is that," Bo questioned.

"'Homeward Bound.' The choir will be singing it tomorrow. It's one of Mama's favorites. She made me learn it when I was in high school." And with that he continued playing and started to sing.

If you find it's me you're missing. If you're hoping I'll return.
To your thoughts I'll soon be list'ning. In the road I'll stop and turn.
Bind me not to the pasture. Chain me not to the plow.
Set me free to find my calling. And I'll return to you somehow.

"It makes me think of S.P." Jackson stopped after he couldn't remember any more verses. He stared out the window in unknown thought.

"Are you giving the eulogy tomorrow?"

"No. We decided that responsibility belonged to the oldest son, so Albert gets the honor." There was another pause while Jackson looked down at the keyboard. "Would you do me a favor?" Bo listened intently but didn't move. "When I die, I won't have an oldest son to talk about me." Jackson's eyes were filling. "Would you say something at my funeral? ... Please." Without a word, Bo nodded his head and accepted the honor. It was an honor, at least in his eyes. He heard crying but noticed the sound was not coming from Jackson but from behind the couch. They both turned to see Jackson's mother sobbing in a way that neither had seen before. When Jackson made it over to his mama, she smiled and said that when the two were little boys, she would pray that they would become best friends, like they were that day. She had overheard the request from her youngest and joyed at the connection they shared. She just knew that they would be good for each other, unconditionally love each other, and protect each other. She prayed that each would be the other's shield when the world around them was throwing stones. It was a comfort to all of them that she could find such a joy at a time of such loss.

Bo and Nancy sat with the family at the funeral, but Bo spent the rest of the time with Five. The Celebration of Life ceremony was brief and simple. No singing. Some preaching. Lots of food. During the reception after the funeral, Bo and Five sat off in the back corner while Nancy made herself useful in the church kitchen. Slim hadn't been seen by either for several years and didn't make the funeral. They thought he was still in Vegas but even Slim's dad, who was present, didn't know for sure. Five had heard that he had experienced some type of religious conversion. Bo doubted such an outcome. He was just hoping there hadn't been some form of *Crying Game* episode that was keeping him away. A few others were at the funeral. Carlos was there. So were Ben and Bugs. They chose not to attend the feast after. Of course, there wasn't much to say since Five was still silent for the most part. It has always been interesting with this group of friends. Words were rarely necessary to communicate what was truly needed. They knew each other's sentiments without having them rehashed. They would finish each other's sentences without opening their mouths. Of course, the old stories had to be retold, but the base emotional connection they all shared never changed. Those sentiments didn't need to be verbalized in order to be validated.

Both Five and Bo accepted the invitation to Jackson's house to be with the family one last time before everyone left. Nancy was tired and went home with Bo's mom and dad. While Bo and Five were standing near the foyer of the home, a loud bang occurred at the door. Being the closest, Five opened the door to find that the sound came from the newspaper slamming solidly against the door. Seeing the boy ride off on his bike, Five thought, "Nice arm!" but didn't say it. He removed the rubber band, opened the paper, and laid it on the coffee table in front of the couch but immediately picked it back up to read the front-page headlines. ARREST MADE IN COLD CASE. He stood off to the side away from the crowd and read the first few paragraphs before handing it to Bo. Bo read it beginning to end, sat the paper down and said his goodbyes to the family.

Jackson asked what had happened. Five didn't say anything at first; he just showed Jackson the article. While Jackson was reading, Five said, "They arrested Willy for Valeria's murder." And with that deluge of words, Five left as well. They were all aware that Willy had been under suspicion for the murder, just because he lived next door to her and worked on the farm where her body was found. But after more than ten years, most had forgotten about it. That evening, Jackson shared the article with his mother. She remembered Willy and didn't think it was possible, though she had heard rumblings of the girl dying at the hands of someone familiar to her. Gabby remembered her own younger days, when the spite of racism and the motivations of tribalism, those that come from the pride and entitlement of a superior culture, would overtake and hold hostage reason and righteousness. She would wait to make judgment and hope that our system of justice would hold true to its reputation and right what she felt was dreadfully wrong. Listening to his mother, Jackson became more sympathetic not only to Willy's but also Valeria's lives in S.P. His regret was compounding. Jackson was ashamed to consider what his mother might have thought of the way he treated them both.

***

In Topeka, the remainder of the summer went quickly for Bo. There were several items required of him as a consultant for two businesses that held him under contract. Most of his work though was in preparation for the upcoming Kansas State legislative session. The ranking Republican leadership had much responsibility for this preparedness and as chairman of two Senate committees, a member of two others and one task force, Senator Wright kept himself busy. This kept him mentally occupied as well, which was perhaps most important since he had learned of Willy's incarceration and upcoming trial. Bo was hard to read, but this reality bothered him. He might have been sad or possibly worried, but he never stopped thinking about it when most had moved on. He hoped that the case would close unresolved. To Bo, that would have solved everything. Now that it was on the front burner again, the senator meant to quell the evidence.

The 2004–05 session started. Left over from last year's term were the residual effects of the National Institute of Justice DNA study. Committees were to interpret the findings and implement the recommendations accordingly. As lead voice on Judiciary, Senator Wright slowly fostered the debate regarding those implementations. Enthusiastically, he would publicly endorse the findings yet slow-walk the hearings and votes, and therefore the actions of the Senate branch of government. Most notably in that initial Senate bill was the wording regarding funding of such required DNA testing and to whose responsibility it would fall. Bo knew that his conservative Republican colleagues would be opposed to General Obligation funding from the State. His liberal Democratic opponents, or friends from the other side of the aisle as he would refer to, would not sign on to a fee-for-service structure where the costs were laid onto the local law enforcement and judiciary. Playing the two against each other, brilliant, in his mind.

It is difficult to completely stop a groundswell like this but, as Senator Wright found out, it was easy to slow the process down immensely. Initial directives from the state regarding the requirement of DNA testing for all felonies and those arrested for such infractions eventually became law. Yet the funding for those tests was not provided and the backlog of untested evidence continued to mount. The KBI received and catalogued so many test kits, it had to store them off-site. It became a herculean effort to find them efficiently. Some were not found at all.

The media, in particular, paid no attention to the backlog and the failure of the state to financially address the problem. For one thing, they had their hands full with the debate between evolutionists and those wishing to add "Intelligent Design" into the curriculum of Kansas schools. Anything that was of great importance but not a part of that game was easily able to remain hidden from the oversight of the media.

Also, numerous legal challenges to the Kansas School District Financing Act of 1992 had been placed before the Kansas Supreme Court and were again coming to a head during this session. Throw in a blackmail scandal, the antiabortion movement, and an upcoming bank fraud and tax evasion lawsuit involving a large energy producer located in Topeka, and you have a convoluted legislative session where a great deal could be hidden or at least placed on a shelf out of the way. Senator Wright took advantage of all these irregularities to make the funding of DNA testing obligations a low priority. Stonewalling that funding became an art and passion of Bo's. No one knew why but everyone was caught up in something other than the testing of rape kits at the time.

The arrest of Willy for second-degree murder vexed Bo deeply and perhaps his political stonewalling played a role in Willy's plight. A felony, consequentially, which required his DNA to be taken and compared with a state and national database. The problem was that there were thousands of similar obligations lined up ahead of this new case. The kit from the victim found in a milo field belonging to Five's uncle was tucked away somewhere in a KBI storage facility waiting for its testing debut. The DNA kit from the victim's fetus, however, remained in a basement storage room at the Sumner Plaine Courthouse. And so the townsfolk asked: Why wouldn't this be a priority for Bo? If he thought the findings would exonerate Willy, couldn't he pull some strings to move this murder investigation and trial out of the starting blocks? There must be some other reason, people would speculate, but few except Jackson could figure out the motivation of Senator Wright.

TWENTY
Willy's Plight

(Spring 2006)

The public defender in Willy's case presented a half-hearted submission to the court in furtherance of delaying the trial and requesting a change of venue. Both were denied. The trial date was set for May 15. Willy was initially charged with second degree murder but after additional evidence was presented to the county attorney, charges were elevated to first degree capital murder. A capital murder in Kansas can be punishable by the death penalty and has been the case since it was reinstituted in 1994. The governor, though being openly opposed to the death penalty, allowed it to become law in her term of office. The last executions permitted in the state were in 1965, which included the hangings of Richard Hickock and Perry Smith. They had been found guilty of the 1959 Clutter family murders not far from Sumner Plaine.

Any attorney willing to take the risk and found to be successful of the first capital punishment execution would instantly become infamous. Such name recognition in a state that bleeds the darkest color of red would become quite formidable on an election ballot. It was easy to see the motivation behind the alteration in charges. The county attorney, who was known locally as brash and arrogant, would be the type to take advantage of all methods to further his career. Yet, as worthy politicians do, he pawned his actions off as for the good of the community. Fredrick North was a transplant from eastern Kansas. He was average height with unremarkable features and light skin, a bourgeois appearance clearly overcome by his professionally cut suits, meticulously coiffed wavy brown hair, and cool designer glasses. Some found him handsome, others claimed there was a level of distrust in the glint of his eyes. No one could identify reasons to be skeptical of his actions, just the same political hypocrisy that one finds in most white men with ambition.

When the trial began, it was as if people had to be prompted to its presence. Even the most ardent of local news consumers had to be reminded of the who and what about the case. Perhaps trials involving unknown immigrant victims and little-thought-of Black defendants created an accepted level of indifference, especially after more than ten years. Most of Willy's acquaintances felt at one time that they wanted to offer their support for him but most felt uncomfortable being in the courtroom during the trial. Would they be seen as supporters of the defendant, the victim, or just sightseeing? Five was the only one who witnessed the trial. DK Sporting Goods was within walking distance of the courthouse; therefore, it was relatively convenient for him to attend. Even so, all of the friends thought that if anyone was going to attend, for Willy's *and* for Valeria's sakes, it would have been Five.

Five. He's hard to figure out. His style is unorthodox, his family is nontraditional, his outlook on life makes sense only if you throw out all the social and financial norms we have adhered to over the two centuries of this country's existence. Five has a faith that is as pure and simple as a child's and above all, far above all, he is the most honest of all with whom he associates. If he told a lie he would burst into flames and become consumed by an evil force that he would never have known. Dishonesty was as foreign to him as breathing is to a rock. Jackson was the most coveted of the group. Bo was the most admired. Slim was most enjoyable to be around. Bugs was intuitive. Ben was selfless. Carlos was late. Brad Andrews, the one they called every nickname in the book before Five stuck, was fundamentally all of these characteristics. But he would never have been described with any. He existed in a different realm. He was better than any of them, but no one was exactly sure of why and how.

Five sat through every hour of every day of that painful trial. Six days. Three recesses. Two weeks. The jury of seven women and five men, all white but three (two Hispanic and one Southeast Asian) was out only ninety minutes. The sentencing hearing was set for June 22. Regional papers covered the story well but the state outlets would not be interested unless the death penalty was the final settled verdict. Each day of the hearing, Five seemed perplexed and was angered though unsurprised by the guilty verdict. The defense was hapless and the jury uninterested. All of the evidence presented was circumstantial with the exception of one jailhouse snitch who shared a cell with Willy's brother for two months. The trial had all the makings of a cold case that, in some politician's mind, had to be resolved no matter how accurate the resultant justice was. Only after the trial was Willy allowed to have visitors. Five put his name on the list along with Willy's mom and brothers. All were denied. Willy, whether out of shame or anger, didn't want to see anyone. Not that Five would have known what to say in such an encounter. But he didn't believe that Willy was guilty, and according to Five, innocent people imprisoned by fate needed to know that there was someone who still believed in them. Five's uncle Cliff always thought that Willy was a good boy, as he put it. Worked hard. Always respectful. Always on time. Though Willy wasn't a core member of the group, he was known by all and as such, at least in Five's eyes, was less likely than any of them to have committed this crime.

Five communicated with Jackson through email. It was a medium that Five felt less restricted by. His personal oath limiting his verbal communication apparently didn't affect online written conversations. They both tried to communicate with Bo but he seemed too busy to respond. Five was somewhat disappointed that Jackson and Bo were less than supportive of their neighbor and classmate. Neither had shown much affinity toward Valeria and couldn't use her victimhood as much of an excuse. Willy on the other hand, as a classmate with whom they all spent time, should have elicited more sympathy. To Five, they seemed detached from the fact that a horrible crime had been committed and that perhaps another unthinkable injustice was about to occur. Of course, the posture of the entire community was similar. No one paid much attention to the presence of such a horrible event. All just wished it was over.

Unbeknownst to Five, Jackson and Bo had their own personal issues which perhaps provided acceptable excuses for their withdrawal from the trial and sentencing. Those issues became more evident when they all gathered in Sumner Plaine on Fourth of July weekend, also utilized for their thirtieth class reunion. It was less than two weeks after Willy was sentenced to life without parole. The judge's decision was a disappointment to the prosecution. Bo never heard a capital case while sitting on the bench. That would have been interesting to watch since he, in his earlier days, had been staunchly opposed to capital punishment. How does someone in authority and with the responsibility of carrying out such a legally and potentially mandated edict step over such a personal solid line? Unless they, like the law, change. And Bo's transformation over the last thirty years was undeniable. He not only took no interest in the trial of an individual he grew up with, he also took no interest in it from a judicial standpoint. Asking only one question of the county prosecutor, that of what physical evidence was presented at trial. Bo's concern of the proceedings was notably absent. Needless to say, those who knew Willy joined in with his family in their relief with the judge's decision. All thought that current status would at least allow for appeals to move forward in Willy's attempt to search for justice.

The thirtieth reunion was the most unremarkable to date. There was a gloom cast over the entire weekend. Most didn't care to spend more than the minimum required period of time in order not to seem impolite. Bo had an additional emotional effect that he was experiencing since arriving in Sumner Plaine. Walking into his old house that Friday afternoon, a couple hours before the traditional Friday night social gathering of the class, Bo noticed that his father was walking around rummaging through the drawers in the kitchen and screaming at their contents. He was looking for something, but the item of pursuit kept changing. After a while, he sat down in his favorite chair and watched television for about an hour. The TV wasn't on.

"What's going on?" Bo begged of his heartbroken mother.

"It's not always this bad," Karen assured as she sat down at the kitchen table. "We missed you last Christmas. I was going to let you in on your dad's diagnosis but I forgot it was Nancy's family's year." Bo was listening to his mom but couldn't take his eyes off his dad while he fidgeted in his chair. "Dr. Henry made the diagnosis about two years ago. Prior to that, we just considered it normal aging but the last test confirmed Alzheimer's. I would have called but I know how busy you are and I didn't think it would progress this fast."

Bo couldn't look his mother in the eyes. He just looked down at the familiar pink and green placemat, adjusting it so the corners of the mat were equal distance from the edges of the table. "What are you going to do?" he asked.

"Do the best we can for as long as we can."

"Does he get violent with you?"

"He just gets frustrated. If I can ignore him long enough, he forgets what he's mad about. I don't know if this is true for all in this disease, but he's like he was when he got drunk but fortunately, it doesn't last as long."

"Does he still have a gun in the house?"

"No. I had Randy come get that. Almost to the day of the diagnosis, I hid it from him. My concern now is that he'll find the hidden keys to the car. If he drives off, I'll never be able to find him. I'm afraid, Bo. What do you think I should do?"

"Put him in a home. I'll help pay for it."

"It's not that simple," Karen claimed with her eyes fixed on her coupled hands before her. She didn't expound further. The clock on the wall got louder. The shadows in the room stopped moving as time slowed. He knew there was another shoe but couldn't subpoena the courage to ask the direct question. Bo went to the bathroom to relieve and gather himself. When he returned, his mom and dad were in their bedroom. Bo went to the reunion.

When he came home, Bo called Nancy to let her in on the events of the party and the news about his dad. The next morning, he found himself again at the kitchen table waiting for his mom to sit down.

"Bo." Karen started but after her first word, she just came over to cup Bo's cheek and gleamed a proud smile. "You've become so important. Are you happy with your life?"

"It's fine." There was another timeless pause before the conversation continued.

"Bo. You have to promise me that if anything happens, you'll take care of your father."

"That's not going to happen," Bo snarked as he got up to get another cup of coffee.

"Your sisters are so far away with families that can't be moved. They won't be able to do much. I don't expect you to move home but I need you to be here when he needs your help."

Bo stood there and looked out the window above the sink. "Where is he?"

"He's in bed. He sleeps a lot these days."

"I'll put him in a home. I'm not going to be much help. I don't want to be much help. I hate him!" It was the first time either one of them had heard that statement and it surprised them both. Bo kept shaking his head in surprise. "I'm sorry. I didn't mean to say that."

Karen was less shocked than sad. She stared into the living room at the empty chair in front of the TV. She placed her finger hard on her lip trying not to cry. Her mind wandered back to the first time she brought Bo home from the hospital and his dad rocked him to sleep in that chair. This was the only home that any of them had known. Life seemed full of delight and potential. "Before your children are born from your body," she thought, "they are born in your dreams. I know of no parent that dreams of their children in a realistic manner. Those dreams are perfect and virtuous in ways that couldn't possibly come true. But you can't visualize anything except the most splendidly contented images. Even if God himself showed you exactly how difficult and heartbreaking it was going to be, his words would be cast aside by the bliss that you have imagined. But the first time something happens to prove God right, it's as if you're living in someone else's body and you find it impossible to free yourself from that inconceivable shell. When that time arrives as it always would, those joyful images don't just gradually fade away so that you can enjoy one last euphoric smile, they shatter and disappear so suddenly, you're convinced they must have belonged to someone else."

She turned toward her son and acknowledged his predicament. "I know exactly how you were treated and I'm sorry I wasn't strong enough to intervene sooner."

"You have nothing to be sorry for. You are a great mom. He's the asshole."

"You shouldn't say such things! You have to hold on to the love and respect that you once had for your father, no matter how difficult. It's still there. You can't give that up."

"Love. Respect. Honor. Discipline. He actually used those words. What a crock!"

Karen sighed deeply. "I guess fathers and sons are destined to disappoint each other."

"How did I disappoint him? How did I disappoint him!" He seethed. Bo allowed his words to burst with inquisition as a well-practiced prosecutor would. He stood behind the chair and slammed it into the table. "I took his abuse. I covered for his character flaws. I grew up listening to every word he said even when I knew he just wanted to hear himself talk." Bo took a deep breath and sat down quietly. "I would have been more impressed by his silence."

"When you were born," Karen interjected, "I could tell he was going to treat you differently than your sisters. And when I asked, he said that a father has to choose whether to be a father or a friend; you can't be both, he would say."

"Well, he was neither. I'm done with him and have been for a while. I can't believe you stayed with him. After all the drinking and gambling and lying and ch—" Bo stopped short and wished he wouldn't have gone that far. After a minute though, he gained some ill-advised courage. "You know how unfaithful he has been. Why didn't you leave him?"

She looked Bo directly in the eye and without blinking said, "When I take a vow, I live by it." Karen had more to say but not then and there. She left to check in on her husband.

The rest of the weekend was a wreck. Jackson and Bo didn't retreat, as recent tradition would have it, on Saturday night to the country club for a social drink during the boring reunion dinner. They both stayed home. The Sunday after, the two met Five at Ted's to drink a beer and watch the Royals play. They all were like zombies. No one could maintain focus. It was as if they hit the wall in a marathon at just the exact same time, even though they were at different stages of the race. Five was still aghast at what had happened to Willy and was still troubled with the almost flippant way Bo was discussing the trial. Jackson, though showing mild concern, seemed to have written off Willy long before the trial started. This also bothered Five. Jackson and Bo's discussion moved away from the trial and more pointedly to their fathers. Five gave them the benefit of the doubt; that they were distressed, especially when Bo mentioned his father's diagnosis. But even within that and the remembrances of Jackson's dad, the two spoke as if they despised their fathers. No memories of any good times at all.

"At least they expected something of you." Five sighed as he released his first words of the afternoon. Bo and Jackson looked at each other with question marks on their foreheads. Jackson asked what Five meant by that to which he replied, "My dad was more groupie than father. I wonder what I would be now if someone would have disciplined me toward being something instead of conceding their role as a parent. I never got punished or even chastised, not once." The audience was speechless. This was the first time anyone, let alone Five, had spoken bad about Ron Andrews. Of course, this was also the first time in years they had heard such a speech come from Five's mouth. They thought that he must have blown nine months of his life with that outburst. Bo sat there quietly, ambivalent about what he just heard and worried about the health status of his parents. Jackson was absolutely morose. Five's pontification was perhaps the final straw. For the first time in his life, Jackson was physically and emotionally deflated. It wasn't only the contrasting image of Ron. It wasn't just his father's death or his own paternal quandary he found himself in. He was bothered by Willy's predicament more than he let on. There was even some level of emotion relating to the death of his murdered classmate that seemed to persist. Something or everything had created a mystifying lathe that was hollowing his core. It was possible that this tool has been doing its bidding for some time now. Regardless, Jackson was feeling its effects. A base level of depression became part of Jackson's life from that day forward.

TWENTY-ONE

The Locker

(Fall 1973)

In a child's life, metamorphosis comes slowly, at least for most. Change is persistent. It is constant. It comes involuntarily over time. It has reason without always being rational. It has purpose without ever being deliberate. But for Jackson and Bo, Five and Slim, change came suddenly and began the moment they arrived at Sumner Plaine Senior High. It was their sophomore year. Three years of transition that occurred seemingly in an instant. Not so much as a larvae—when life requires more—but like a spark when stasis has had enough. It was the change from ninth grade to tenth. As if moving from one digit to two was the chrysalis of life itself. For them, it was walking to driving. It was single to dating and soda to alcohol. Change was all encompassing, for it was more than life, it was living. Smooth to rough. Arms to wings. Buds to leaves. Birdshot to bullets. Carefree to careless. Touch to fondle. Susceptible to suspicious. Disciplined to disciple. Existing to thriving. Reliant to reliable. Flesh to spirit. Belief to faith. It was more than transition, more than transformation. It was Renaissance.

Memories. They all remembered that sophomore year in its entirety. When asked about it though, like witnesses to a crime, each remembered individual aspects differently. Take for example driver's education classes. During the summer before the tenth grade, this program was a requirement in order to receive your learner's permit and a restricted level of freedom behind the wheel prior to turning sixteen. In the driver's instruction portion of the class, all vehicles used in the training, the type that had foot brakes on both floorboards of the front seat, came complete with radio receivers on the dash. They allowed drivers the ability to hear from instructors standing at a safe distance just off the high school parking lot. Which, as all remembered, was freshly lined in June to mimic a Le Mans racing track. Stiffly erect orange pilons were creatively placed throughout the course to imitate obstacles in the road. Which, as we all remember, had to be thrown out each August because they no longer were vertical in stature.

Most often it was Slim that was the cause of those pilons to become flattened. It wasn't that he was a terrible driver, but he was the indirect instigator of many of these collisions. No one could ever keep their car straight on the road because they were laughing so hard. You see, each week, Slim would steal an instructor's walkie-talkie and place it under the seat of his car. When he was the passenger of his pairing (Jackson was always his partner) he would make bodily functioning noises over the radio. Or he would recite his favorite Cheech and Chong one-liner. Or, in his best imitation of instructor Burlington raspy voice, he would tell the car in front of Five's vehicle to STOP!—causing Five to run into its back bumper. Once he told Bo to drive out of the lot and parallel park between two of the instructor's cars which were parked by the side of the road. Bo was so naive that he took the bait and drove out onto the street. Even with the windows rolled up, you could hear Slim and Jackson laughing as all four instructors, arms flailing in the air, ran their hardest toward Bo's car. They were shouting for Bo to stop while Slim was quietly encouraging him on the radio. "You're doing just fine, son."

Slim. He was perhaps the one most loved of his peers. The story behind his mother's disappearance never was offered by Slim. Not even in moments of drunken candor, which were common. It was also strange because Slim couldn't stop talking about anything. He was blessed with the gift of dialog. It served him well in many aspects of his high school career. He could get out of trouble, get into a date, change an F to an A, change traffic tickets to warnings, forge notes for excused absences, and forge his way into the heart of an assistant principal with ease, just by his charming ability to enlist and persuade. He always landed on his feet, regardless.

One morning Slim and his dad woke to find a note on the kitchen table. She was gone and never came back. For a while, the rumor was that she ran off with Bo's dad. Then it was her gynecologist or her shrink, but when they all remained present in S.P., the ideas went stale and the story just died. For a day or two, Slim and his dad were silent. Then, as if they turned the switch, things were back to normal—all things. All were concerned but it was hard to feel sorry for him when he was making you laugh. Some thought that was the point. Slim was tougher than his skinny appearance let on yet, it was as if he wanted to make sure all knew of this fact and that sympathy was unnecessary and not to be part of his legacy.

As you would expect, Jackson hit the ground of the Sumner Plaine Senior High campus running. Athletically, academically, socially, Jackson existed in a league primarily reserved for seniors. No one begrudged his early successes. Least of all Bo, who was honored that Jackson chose to remain his locker mate for another three years. That locker, fortuitously located two lockers down from Five and Slim's and just outside the open door to the cafeteria kitchen, was the foundational venue for every subsequent social adventure over the next three years. It was their linchpin to all things pleasurable and problematic. Each fragment of fun, every bit of trouble was incubated and hatched at this very site.

The locker, if you ask Jackson or Bo, was just a green metal box built into a wall. Whether you believe such things or not, for three years, it was a location that had its own energy. Perfectly located in sight of but far enough from "jock wall," *the locker* could draw from jock wall's essence yet not have to compete with its testosterone-glazed substance. More importantly in most minds, was *the locker's* proximity to the other more notable location in the school building. It was located across the hall from the locker of James Timothy Keillor. J.T. was the best athlete and smartest student with the nicest hair and brightest smile. He was certainly the best-looking boy in school—prior to the arrival of Jackson Daniel on the scene. J.T. was a senior. It took an entire semester for them to realize that it was J.T. who was envious of Jackson and felt lucky to be in proximity of his green metal abode.

On the second Friday of the first semester Jackson showed up with one of his mom's old stone dinner plates, to the bewilderment of Bo. "You'll see," said Jackson. After third hour, Bo returned to their locker to find two freshly baked and covertly pilfered cinnamon rolls set cleanly on a plate positioned on the top shelf in their locker. Every Friday, the cooks made cinnamon rolls and placed the stacked trays next to the door adjacent to the locker. Over the next three years, the two would steal an entire truckload of pastries. Some thought it was the aroma that nurtured *the locker* and gave it its soul. The location, if you must, was like a watering hole in an arid environment. All types of fauna would gather or pass by. Even predators would find their carnivorous appetites lessened by the calming resource of the place. And that resource? Girls. Between J.T. and Jackson, the flow of women was endless.

Routine became their commonality. School, practice, shower, home. Except on Fridays when there was a home game, which added to the routine. Game, drag Main Street, and then a party at Five's house. Saturdays and Sundays were sleep, eat, and back to Five's for the afternoon, where the discussions were always centered on girls and sports. In that order! Each weekend, they would relieve Five's dad of his beer, his mom of her food, and commandeer the television. Halftimes would bring about street football in front of the house or basketball at the nearby elementary school they all had attended. The love of activity, especially sport, would frequently overrule the return to the house. Dinner was time to check in on the homestead but it was back on the road for Saturday nights. Where? Who knew? It could be anywhere with anyone. You only hoped that you were in on the communication or you would clearly miss out.

In the early years of high school, Bo was frequently on the outside looking in. Never with malice, but Bo was just a little slow for some settings and would be left off the invitation list. It took persistence to play a role in the decision-making of Saturday night activities. When Bo didn't make the cut for the previous weekend's action, Mondays at the locker were the worst. Too many conversations about activities he was unaware of became a heavy one-sided weight on the scale of Bo's insecure ego. At times, it was heavy enough that no counterbalance could be found. But he learned not to take it personal and studied the tricks needed to become aware of the goings-on of each weekend's social scene.

It was during that sophomore year that Bo first heard the phrase "Saturday night girl." He always assumed that if you had a steady girlfriend, as Jackson and Five always had, she would occupy both Friday and Saturday night. To Bo, it was a duplicitous and hypocritical concept.

How could you date two girls at the same time? And how was it that you could be with a girl on Saturday night and mock her all the rest of the week? The guys kidded Bo enough when he used to walk Valeria to junior high that he stopped that activity cold. Bo liked Valeria and, without saying as much, thought she was pretty. Jackson, in particular, called her loose and easy. When she would walk by the locker, he would make snide comments and snap her bra strap. Sometimes he would slap her on the ass or pinch her boob. She would laugh and keep walking. Bo assumed she was humiliated and hated Jackson. Apparently not. Valeria was Jackson's Saturday night gal!

There existed an unnamed ritual utilized by the gang to determine which girls in school were worthy of public adoration. It was a ritual unnoticed even by its participants. It had no charter, no agenda or rules of order. It was never claimed as such but undoubtedly, there had to be a consensus of the organization before a member could feel comfortable in asking any specific girl out to public gatherings such as dances and parties, Friday night stuff. During the meeting of the minds, a girl's name would be casually offered for evaluation. The unwritten rule was that it couldn't be anything but a bland unemotional submission. Bo found out quickly how traumatic it would become to state affirmatively his approval of a girl only to find himself the butt of all jokes for weeks; mocking his taste in girls. Maturation, as they all would find out, was a series of trial and error. Failures were painful but the fastest way to learn how to get it right. They were necessary. The secret was that those deficiencies needed to be as inconspicuous as possible. Full-throated miscalculations could easily become permanent scars.

One Saturday afternoon, in the confines of Ron Andrews's pacifying family room, the subject of conversation moved in the direction of Valeria. Slim said, "Man, did you see Valeria at the game Friday night?" The point was offered as an ambiguous question so that no meaning could be inferred by the committee. Bo took great interest in this for he remembered well the grief he took not more than a year ago.

"She's all right, I guess," Jackson offered with controlled enthusiasm.

"She looked fine in that tight sweater," Slim returned.

"What do you think, Five?" was Bo's dispassionate motion on the floor. He was learning the trick of extemporaneous input without appearing to be concerned about the subject.

"Valeria? Are you kidding? She's awesome! Those tits have their own area code. I'm going to get me some of that someday."

"How many times you been laid?" Slim questioned. Five smiled but didn't answer; this made him look impressive to his friends even though the truth would have disappointed them all. "Where do you take that nookie?"

"The best place is my uncle Cliff's oil farm."

"Where?"

The directions were granted as each ear in the room perked to a sharp and maximumly protruding extent. "Depending on the time of the year and what crops he planted, there is a sweet hidden area located around the abandoned oil pumpjack. No one can see you. And the best part is that there is an old mattress wedged in between the engine box and the crank that my cousins use to take afternoon naps when they're supposed to be working on the farm."

That was all it took. The unofficial motion and debate constituted the minimum required three affirmative votes in the direction of a single girl which would allow for a member to make a move without being negatively branded an idiot. Little did anyone know that Valeria and Jackson had already started their Saturday night relationship. This would be Bo's first realization of just how Jackson worked. He would do as he pleased but not fully in the open. Whether it was girls or drugs or any form of misconduct, Bo would hear about it after the fact. Those activities of which Bo derived ridicule, Jackson had been doing many times over. And it wasn't just Jackson. They all did it that way—eventually, even Bo. It became a mode of survival in the early days. No one took it personal. The method was accepted and admired by each.

Without realizing it, Bo benefitted from all of Jackson's girlfriends, no matter what night of the week they claimed. Bo became the conduit to the inner workings of Jackson Daniel Stillwell, or so the girls thought. Bo would be stopped in the halls or called on the phone or even asked out on the occasional pity date just so the girls could get the lowdown on Jackson. At times, it would bother Bo to be seen as the nice guy that girls wanted to talk (and only talk) to. Early on, he resented the role and wanted his own action but after a while, he grew into character and enjoyed it for what it provided. Within a few short semesters, Bo was the most popular guy in the class, at least as far as the girls were concerned. And as far as being Jackson's social representative, this became just another position of inferiority for Bo. But it was one that he took on gladly and, quite frankly, it was a diminished status that any other boy in school would have given their left one just to have.

Jackson took advantage of Bo as much as possible that sophomore year. Bo was able to drive six months before Jackson. He knew that Bo had access to his older sister's car and so if Jackson needed a ride or wanted to go somewhere, Bo was called. Bo didn't realize his friend was taking advantage of him. He thought they were honest feelings of friendship. In some ways they were, but Jackson was all about himself in every aspect of his plans and schemes. The company that Bo offered Jackson was comfortable and enjoyable, as long as it was just the two of them. Once they were in a crowd, Jackson was overcome by arrogance and a haughty smugness that would utilize his body to do horrible things to his friends. Jackson would just laugh when a wad of gum straight out of his mouth would land in Bo's thick hair. Everyone thought it was a riot when an extra small jock strap with WRIGHT written across the front was found taped to the clock in their second hour Spanish class. That spring, when Bo received his first letter jacket for varsity baseball, Jackson made fun of how clean and unused it was. Jackson decided that Bo's jacket was too new and needed breaking in. He did so by spitting a stream of brown tobacco drool onto one of the pristine off-white leather sleeves. Bo couldn't believe it yet said nothing. Slim and Five got their share also but they fought back. Bo just took it and accepted it as the natural effects stemming from the cause of being in Jackson's entourage. The worst was yet to come.

One warm August Saturday night, just days before the start of their junior year, Jackson convinced Bo to take Valeria and him out to the oil farm. It was a Saturday night and the two had just left Ted's Tavern where Jackson illegally drank using his brother's ID. He was drunk even before he and Valeria took their drags on a doobie in between make-out sessions in the back seat of Bo's sister's car. Bo was clearly uncomfortable with the situation. That did not keep him from checking out the action in his rearview mirror. When they arrived at the farm, the milo was too tall to drive through so Bo parked on the side of the field while Jackson and Valeria walked into the hidden core. About twenty minutes into their foray, Jackson, still high as a kite, asked Valeria for a favor. He wanted his virginal friend to at least get a glimpse into the promised land, if not taste some of its honey. She was sympathetically stoned and said she'd allow some but not as much as she just gave out.

Jackson ran back to the car and convinced Bo of the benefits. Bo, who initially said no, got hard just thinking about it. His conscience said no. His mind said that this was a mistake but his crowded khaki shorts overruled them both. When he arrived, she was sitting on the mattress with bent knees crossed and pulled up to her waist. As Bo approached, she lowered her legs, exposing her unbuttoned blouse and unadorned cleavage. Bo sat beside her while she made the first move. They kissed for only a few seconds when she guided Bo's right hand to her left breast. Even before the round softness was felt on his fingertips, the tightness of Bo's shorts and the fullness of his desire created an environment where nature couldn't be held back. Bo's supporting left arm buckled and the dizzying release laid him down for the count. Valeria giggled even though she felt bad for Bo's obvious embarrassment. The light color of his shorts was unable to hide the evidence. He apologized to her and walked Valeria back to the car, blocking her exposed legs from each sharp milo leaf.

Jackson was standing outside the car when they showed up. The sight of Bo's appearance must have been similar to a Richard Prior stand-up routine, Jackson laughed so hard. Bo was glad Jackson didn't have a camera, yet that didn't matter because by the time school started that following week, everyone that they knew was calling Bo by his new name. It wasn't until the following baseball season that the callsign of Whiskey and Wright would replace the new nicknames *Gunslinger* and *Quick Draw*. Jackson and the others were unrelenting in their wisecracks. Bo's shame would last longer than the name but again, he didn't blame Jackson. He blamed himself. He was mortified for months but actually worried more about Valeria, anguishing about how her reputation was affected by the events of that summer night.

TWENTY-TWO

You Have to Be There

(Fall 2006)

Jackson's depression mollified somewhat after returning to sunny California. He no longer was in shape enough to surf but he spent as much free time at the shoreline as possible. The call of the coast never lost its appeal. It was an outdoorsman's paradise, unrelenting in its enticement. Jackson's seemingly unquenchable thirst for the beauty of the beach and its inhabitants was always satisfied with each outing. A close second to his desire for the excitement of seaside life was the relaxation of an afternoon at a baseball game. Last spring, during Glendale's baseball season, he was able to inconspicuously watch Jake play three games at the close-by community college. It was Jake's second season with the team. Jackson was astounded at the physical transformation Jake had gone through since graduating high school. Jackson himself didn't grow much after his first year at KU but his son now was 6'2" and 225 lbs. He was going through the Barry Bonds phenomenon. When you have an eye for the ball and a sweet swing, you only need size. Adding the power would complete the trifecta. Jackson hoped that Jake hadn't developed a taste for anabolic steroids but thought that if it would have been offered to him when he was in his prime, no doubt, he would have partaken in the synthetic enhancement to his body.

Jake led the league in all the power stats. His size slowed him down a little so the coach moved him to third base. Glendale's left side of the infield was the envy of the league. They beat Antelope Valley for the divisional title and won the conference tournament that year without a loss. Their team received quite a bit of interest from the MLB West Coast teams. In fact, there were four scouts at the championship game where Jake was chosen tourney MVP. For the week, he hit .405 with two home runs and nine RBIs. He had one error on a bad hop that should have been considered a base hit, at least according to his dad. Jackson smiled when he thought about the scorekeeping of the game and the memory of how they used to laugh at Bo's expense while in high school. It was back during Bo's one and only breakout season in baseball. It was their senior year. Prior to that season, Bo, at best, hit .275 from the plate and was leadoff batter only because he walked a lot. In their final season together, Bo saw a little Bonds growth himself. He was moved to fifth in the lineup because of his new swing and some semblance of power at the plate. That season ended with Bo sustaining a .404 batting average for the season and tied with Five for home runs and RBIs. Jackson (who was close behind in each stat) and the rest of the squad used to kid Bo about those stats; which stemmed from the fact that Bo's dad was the team's official scorekeeper. If Bo was found standing on the bases after an error or a fielder's choice, Jackson would jokingly yell out, "Don't worry, it was a hit. Your dad brought his eraser."

There were two competing emotions each time Jackson watched his son play. Every joyful game that Jackson was able to watch also was a dagger in his side. He so much wanted to meet Jake's coaches, to talk to Jake's friends, to cheer Jake on and offer advice. He dared not. Jackson lived up to his agreement with Crystal and then some. Glendale was close enough to Santa Monica that she should have been able to attend but there was never a meeting of the two parents. That concern never materialized. Jackson quietly enjoyed the spectacle of his son's play without being able to show it. He did, however, talk to the scout for the Dodgers just to find out who they were looking at. Jake was on the top of their list. The upcoming MLB draft for outstanding high school and college players would be an anxious day for players all over the country. The scout thought there was a very good chance three players on that year's Vaqueros team would be drafted. That year's draft was scheduled for July 9 and would last three days. With all that was going on back home, Jackson had almost forgotten about the draft and how it might affect Jake's future. He could have kicked himself for not watching while each selection unfolded on ESPN. His initial anger occurred after he picked up Tuesday's L.A. *Times* and read the sports headlines. That anger quickly turned to elation when he saw Jake's name on the list of local products drafted into the league. Jake went in the twenty-third round to the Oakland A's. Jackson was in his office when he read the news. He crunched the paper like a paper bag and screamed with excitement. The enthusiasm was quickly subdued when he came face-to-face with the reality of the situation. What a glorious day it would have been to share this with the world. "My son is going to play Major League Baseball. He's going to play for my favorite team since childhood. You can't imagine how thrilled and proud I am." Jackson would have loved to say all those things. How he would have loved to call Bo to give him the news. They both would have reveled in the glory of that day. Jackson made up a story about a stock pick and walked out the door. In the elevator, the depression hit again. He didn't know if he would ever be able to truly enjoy Jake's success. Jackson took the rest of the day off and went home.

The only benefit Jackson would enjoy from Jake playing in the majors as opposed to a small community college was that those who wished could follow him more closely. Even the single-A Kane County Cougars had a live audio feed that Jackson could hear online. Jake's stats would be available the next day. Jackson was never able to ascertain that kind of information before. A call to Crystal had to be made when he first was made aware. She was happy but had hoped the location of Jake's team would have been closer than Geneva, Illinois. When she was offered the chance to meet at a computer bar to listen to Jake's first game, Crystal turned it down. Jackson could tell she wanted the experience of at least hearing her son's first game in the majors, perhaps hearing the crack of the bat with his first hit as a professional. But she was unwilling to risk slipping down that emotional hill once she had survived the climb and made it to the top. Any relationship would be too hazardous. And since she didn't have the technology to connect herself, it appeared she would just have to miss out on the big game. A recent call from Jake made her happy though. He was going to start at third base on Saturday. The thrill in his voice brought tears to her eyes when she finally let go of the phone.

The following day after lunch, when Crystal returned to her work, she found an envelope on her desk. It was sealed. It had her name written on one side and a message on the other. It read, YOU HAVE TO BE THERE. Inside there was a first-class ticket to Chicago which would leave early Saturday morning. There were directions to the field, a hotel reservation nearby, and a number for a car service that Jackson had used before in his travels. That plus five crisp one hundred dollar bills filled the thoughtful package. The round-trip flight was scheduled to return Sunday night, late enough she could catch both of the Sunday afternoon double header and make it home for work the next day. She couldn't believe it. About the same time the contents of the parcel were spilling out onto her cluttered desk, Crystal's boss walked in and offered his congratulations. "Your brother came in while you were gone and asked me to place the envelope on your desk. He also asked if I would be willing to let you miss out on half a day's work next Monday morning, since you would be getting in late on Sunday night." Crystal's boss did one better. He gave Crystal an additional paid day off in case she wanted to stay an extra night in Chicago. Crystal thanked him. "No thanks necessary," he stated as he walked toward the door. Her smiling face was nearly stretched to the limit when her boss yelled from the hallway, "I didn't know you had a brother."

The gift was one of the most enjoyable things Jackson had ever done. It was made even more so by the thank-you card he received from Crystal after she returned home from her trip to see Jake play. The card was beautiful in its sentiment but the words paled in comparison to the gift that was inserted within. It was a picture of Crystal and Jake. They were standing near third base. Jake had his arm around his mom's neck and she had the biggest smile Jackson had ever seen on her face. The depression was real. The sadness was enduring but from time to time, there was joy in Jackson's life. Yet with each satisfactory step forward, there were always two regretful steps back. The idea that he had given up so much when he was young and immature saturated each pore to the point it could never be eliminated. He kept the picture on the stand near his bed. It was part of the ritual to end a day, to say good night to his absent family.

As Jake's life found a routine, so too did Jackson's. He remained busy with business during the day and following Jake at night. Regimen is the answer to most levels of despondency. A mind can only accommodate multiple thoughts if they are substantially similar. When the mind is exposed to dissimilar attitudes, the most physically active of the two usually wins out. That's why when a person is feeling depressed, positive actions can overcome. But Jackson had been in the habit of staying busy, though his busyness was always selfish in nature. There was never a desire to help others. You could say he was just out of practice but unfortunately, Jackson had developed a selfish lifestyle early on and that youthful habitual status is always difficult to overcome. What all learn as children becomes so imbedded in the immature core of a human that it is nearly impossible to extricate as the personality develops around it. For Jackson, those occasional moments, once exposed to the unrestricted vacuum of idleness, drew on that core. One can't remain constantly busy. It was inevitable. Those hidden demons would eventually surface. He would sit in his apartment and sulk. He felt sorry for his plight and saw no way out. And for those who knew him or lived with him, they recognized that the regret in Jackson's life went back much further than the missed opportunity of having his own family. There was something or some things that haunt him even more.

For those unfamiliar with his history, on the outside looking in, Jackson was rolling! His life, with the exception of appearing lonely, was what most would wish for. He was wildly successful in his business, he had slowly but proficiently deleveraged his real estate positions in all his investments. That, on its own, would become huge in financial terms as everyone approached the housing crisis of 2008. Additionally, he started to sell off his holdings in Eljuez. Intellectually, Jackson knew the statistics of being completely out of the market but he found himself less stressed by isolating all of his resources in one location, even if it was a bank account of twenty million dollars only returning 2.1% on his investment. And with the crash of 2009, he would again look like a genius.

***

Bo, on the other hand, had rapidly depleted his share of Eljuez to keep his political influence at the highest level. Which was something he felt necessary in order to divert and direct legislative momentum at the state house in Topeka. His power was becoming unfettered, yet his paranoia was palpable even in the presence of a climbing status. Similarly, as most saw in Jackson's life, each noticed with Bo that there was something other than the desire of political power that claimed his attention. More than the allure of control over the direction of an entire state, there was something else deep within Bo's core that was creating a conflict in his thoughts and actions. It was easily seen that Jackson was trying hard to extricate himself from his past or at least make positive changes for his future. Bo, on the other hand, had lost much of his benevolent and generous character from his past and was giving in to the villainy of his future inclinations and destiny.

***

Crystal and Jake were living the dream. Contrary to the plights of our Sumner Plaine core group. Jackson, who was searching for his future, and Bo, who was suspicious about his. Five, who was disappointed in his existence, and Slim, whose existence was recently in question. Willy, whose freedom was ending, and a murder victim, whose life had ended. Crystal and Jake were happier than they had been throughout both of their lives. The stats of the Kane County Cougars' most recent infielder were impressive enough to move him to Advanced-A ball for the start of the 2007 season. This became the sprinkles and the cherry on Crystal's ice cream sundae. Advanced Class A ball for the Oakland A's was played in Stockton, only a five-hour drive from her home. Crystal's assumptions of life had been pragmatic at best since she made the decision to fight for the child within her, now more than twenty years ago. She never had those pristine images of a Norman Rockwell home or the perfect child being enriched by a wonderful mother. There were no moments when she would look at her beautiful son and wonder more than what it was going to take to keep him fed and safe during the upcoming week. There were no prophetic dreams of the two of them smiling in the face of a poetic sunrise. Only fearful contemplation of what was on the other side of each exhausted sunset. Yet endurance is more than a verb. It is a gift that yields; not just perseverance, as the apostle Paul had told us, but like character that leads to hope. Endurance, it would seem, creates tomorrows.

TWENTY-THREE
Alexa's Law

(Winter 2007)

" I thought we got rid of that notion in 2005!" Senator Wright expressed, feeling the frustration of the moment.

"We did," the Senate majority leader reiterated. "Back in 2002 also." They were referring to the House's third attempt to pass legislation designated as the Unborn Victims of Violence Act. In 2002 and 2005, the Kansas House of Representatives easily passed the bill that would instigate the legislation but both times, it failed to get out of committee in the Senate and therefore, never reached the governor's desk. Senator Wright was instrumental in its defeat. That year, during the 2006–07 session, what was essentially the same bill as before had been dubbed Alexa's Law. So called sympathy names, those of victims of crime attached to legislation to give greater notoriety, were becoming commonplace. By making personal the impersonal words of a House or Senate bill, laws that failed in the past are being rendered more effective throughout the country. Some states are actually bidding to rid themselves of such practices, stating that they create an emotional imbalance to what should be a level dispassionate exercise.

"We should be able to use the same argument to stop it again, right?"

"I don't know. My last polling of the caucus this session shows more support in the Senate. Even a few Democrats in swing districts are on board. I think it could be a political win if we back it this time. We could say we were waiting for a stronger bill to come from the House, as our excuse for not passing it before."

Bo stood up from his chair and moved around to where the majority leader was sitting. "I still don't like it," he claimed as he sat on the edge of his desk. "Why don't we pacify them by making the current law more punitive. You know, increase the penalties for crimes against women who are pregnant."

"We served that up last time. They surely won't swallow it again."

"What if we take the other side completely! We could say we're suspicious of the precedent because it would make it easier to prosecute the mothers of unborn fetuses for negligence or some such nonsense."

"You'll completely lose your base and probably get voted out of the party," the leader said jokingly. "This is, if not the primary core of the Republican Party platform, the most motivational component. This legislation would effectively define all unborn as victims regardless of gestational age. It would by law change a fetus into a person. You have to vote for it if you want to continue to lead your party."

"Who is this Alexa anyway?" Bo questioned.

"She was the unborn daughter of a fourteen-year-old who was killed in a murder-for-hire plot involving her boyfriend last year in Wichita."

"So, we're going to prosecute the boyfriend for double homicide yet we weren't willing to accuse him of statutory rape. That makes a lot of sense."

"You know this has nothing to do with the crime and everything to do with the politics."

"I know. I know."

The leader finished his discussion and left just as Bo's administrative assistant came in to tell him that his mother was on the phone. "Tell her I'm busy in a meeting with the Senate majority leader and can't be interrupted." The assistant didn't raise a brow. She had become numb to telling casual lies to the ever-increasing list of people that Senator Wright did not wish talk to. Bo wouldn't even take calls from Nancy or the kids.

Discussions among the politically savvy grew more perplexing as members of both branches became mystified at Senator Wright's reservations on this particular issue. A staunch conservative on everything cultural and fiscal, Bo had dug in his heels on this issue. And for what? No one really could tell. It didn't make much sense to those who evaluated each motion and vote at the capitol building. It was very similar to his stance on testing of rape kits and the financial and moral obligation of the state. Both issues fit well within the Republican platform, which touted the tough on crime and anti-abortion sentiment demonstrated by the majority of the electorate throughout the state. Yet, all political figures have their pet issues, especially those that find some personal level of importance in them. Most however, don't have Senator Wright's power or the position to directly act on them.

As the session moved into the spring, Bo could see that the train was leaving the station without him on board. His credibility was at stake. And since his stance on this issue was personal and not based on principle, he could resist the momentum no more. As such, Senator Wright jumped in with both feet, ankles and legs up to the knees, loudly proclaiming he had always been a proponent but was waiting until the law was *strong* enough to live up to his high standards. The legislation passed both chambers with easy majorities and was signed into law by the governor. But not before Senator Wright made one last bid—a clandestine meeting with the highest power of the state to pitch an idea that might stop the statute from being placed in the books.

The governor and Bo had a chummy relationship ever since they met. At that time, Bo was a district judge and the governor was the state attorney general. Bo had always been an important constituent of the governor and one of his biggest benefactors. Over the years, Bo had donated above and below the table funds in excess of one million dollars. He clearly expected considerations in return. To no avail. The governor was a sensible man and could see the future for him if he didn't sign the bill into law. Bo's noticeable anger aided in the remarkable climax of the meeting. It would be the end of a fruitful relationship for both and an enduring memory to Bo as he eyed his future political career.

It wasn't until later that year, several months in fact after the governor's signature authorized Alexa's Law and placed it on the books, that the reason behind Bo's aversion to the law became apparent. At least it became more obvious to those familiar with his past. Kansas's Unborn Victims of Violence Act made the death of an unborn child occurring during the commission of a capital crime—such as first-degree murder—a capital offense, in and of itself. Therefore, someone found guilty of murdering a pregnant woman, no matter how far along the pregnancy was, would be guilty of two murders and presumably punished for both. The situation that made Bo's reluctance more understandable came in the form of a memo left on Senator Wright's desk. It was a request to return a phone call and mentioned the refiling of murder charges in a familiar Sumner Plaine case. County Prosecutor North had petitioned the court to refile capital murder charges against Willy. This time, the victim being represented by the prosecution was the precious unborn child within the womb of the murdered girl. In Fredrick North's view, Alexa's Law created an avenue for him to bring Willy to trial again. North would again attempt to get a death penalty conviction since two murders had now been committed. Double jeopardy would not come into play since, in the eyes of the prosecution, this was a different victim and therefore a separate crime.

As Bo read the notice, he turned a noticeably altered shade. His already light complexion became truly pale and the moisture on his brow provided evidence of his blood pressure change. Bo sat back in his plush swiveled office chair, behind the desk where he so frequently and so easily greased the gears of government, and stewed. He thought that the issue of Valeria's death was faded history. This is what he feared might happen with the passing of the newest addition to the state's criminal code. After being relegated to the dusty shelves utilized for unneeded and invalidated evidence, the test kit of Valeria's unborn child's DNA would now be placed back in the queue to be evaluated at the KBI lab at some future date. Senator Wright could again slow down the process by restricting necessary funds, but with the new legislation that rape kit would continue to inch forward toward its eventual reso-lution. Bo was concerned.

With the unfunded mandate requiring the testing of all rape kits or ancillary DNA evidence of all capital crimes, this new statute would be an added burden on the system. It would create the type of resource depletion that could put off trials for years. When dealing with such limited resources and increased demand, a new prioritization system was needed. Something must be put in place in order to insure an equitable and appropriate hierarchy of evidence development. Bo was immediately on the phone with the head of the KBI to discuss the issue. Bo assured the director that necessary funding could be made available but that those resources must be placed toward crimes most recently committed. The director disagreed stating that there may be a point when the evidence of older crimes might become tainted or lost through time. Those crimes needed to be cleared from the books before moving on to more recent evidence testing. Senator Wright countered with the hypothesis that older crimes assumes older criminals, individuals that probably are no longer a threat to society. Where contemporary crimes are sired by younger perpetrators and thus placing the citizens of Kansas at greater risk prior to an arrest being made. To which, the director offered that these criminals have already been arrested and are ready to go to trial even if the evidence cannot be fully processed.

In the end, money ruled the day. Senator Wright guaranteed that if old or unsolved crimes were placed on the top of the priority list, funding would not be assured. Bo used the same argument when discussing the specific case with the Sumner County attorney. Mr. North was livid. He too had personal reasons for wanting those kits to be tested further. He was convinced that the unborn child belonged to Willy and that evidence would easily sway a pro-life judge toward a second guilty verdict and subsequent death penalty. The two went back and forth over the phone with no resolution to the conflict, leading to Bo's refusal to accept Fredrick North's calls in the future. When a call came from the sheriff of Sumner County, a good friend of Bo's dad and the entire family, Bo knew what was coming. Randy, the one who had been so helpful to Bo's mother, the one who conveyed to Bo the story Karen's fearless confrontation with her husband, the one who removed the gun from their home; he wanted to put in his two cents. It wasn't that he had a dog in the fight. All of this happened long before he became sheriff. His point was that the community couldn't move on unless this issue was completely put to rest. "We need a resolution," he said. "Whether you realize it or not, Sumner Plaine has a millstone hung around its neck and it's standing near the stern of the boat waiting for someone to push it into the ocean. This girl needs justice and if it's your friend Willy, then so be it. We need your help. No one would blame you for pulling a few strings."

Bo thanked Randy for the call and promised he would look into it. Months went by and Randy received no communication from Senator Wright. The trial date was set even though there was no certainty of evidence being presented at trial. At Willy's first trial, no DNA evidence had been presented at all. That of the unborn child, at the time, was inadmissible. That of the victim was inconclusive. Bo had hoped that the judge chosen for the new case would see the futility of the charges as well as the likelihood that no significant change in the status of the defendant would occur. Bo hoped the charges would be dropped or that the case would be thrown for lack of evidence or on constitutional grounds. It was, after all, trying a man twice for the same act. If an arsonist burns down a house, you don't charge him again just because you find out later that there was a Rembrandt hidden in the basement.

None of these arguments changed the course of events in Sumner Plaine. Answering a motion from the defense before the judge, the prosecutor falsely guaranteed that fully qualified DNA evidence would be available by early 2008. Regardless of the motion and the legal ramifications therein, the judge apparently felt as Randy did. A court date was set for trial, May 6, 2008. If you surveyed the community, they would all say the same thing. "We need to get this behind us," or "why has this dragged on for so long?" No one could have told you the primary reason behind the delay. No one knew just how culpable Senator Wright was. He was able to drag his heels in order to slow down this process while blaming his worn soles on poor cobbling. As all good politicians do, he was able to deflect criticism and defend his position with cunning and skill.

***

As luck would have it, an open United States Senate seat became available after a veteran of Kansas public service chose to retire. When they caught wind of the pending abdication back in early 2007, the state Republican leadership contacted Senator Wright and encouraged him to run. Very little encouragement would be needed. Bo again was noticing an obvious lull in his level of excitement and motivational feelings toward state politics. Boredom had once again showed its face. Bo needed a change.

Part of his campaign would be his position on DNA as an investigative tool. He would contend that the backlog of rape kit testing could be blamed on the federal government and that only he, with his knowledge of the obstacles and direct experience with the issue, could satisfactorily solve the dilemma at hand. It seemed brilliant to his campaign advisors. Senator Wright, the source of the actual problem, could now be seen, by his candidacy for the open U.S. senatorial seat, as the solution. In the back of his mind, he knew if the right strings were pulled and he could be placed on the appropriate committee, he might again have direct influence over the expenditures and dissemination of funds for all Department of Justice programs; programs which may or may not include money for backlogged DNA test kits.

As the hearing date approached for Willy's second trial, it became obvious that no specific DNA evidence would be available. The charges were dismissed with prejudice such that if the evidence presented itself in the future, the charges could be reinstituted. Senator Wright, by skill or by luck, had prevailed. Willy, by culture or by color, had lost and sat miserably behind bars in the El Dorado maximum security correctional facility.

TWENTY-FOUR
Tragedy

(Fall 2009)

Jackson, Crystal, and Jake were forced back into the routine with the start of the 2008 baseball season. The bubble surrounding Jake's current dream location burst as his accomplishments on the diamond continued to impress, which meant that his time in Stockton was short-lived. It was on to Midland, Texas, for Double-A ball. The problem with baseball in the Great Plains is twofold. It's in the middle of nowhere or at least on the way, and there are no direct flights from L.A. to West Texas. In fact, it frequently took two flights and a rental car or three fights and a huge bank account to arrive. Also, most of the locations for AA competition within the Texas League are miles from Midland in towns that you can't reach by plane either. Needless to say, neither Crystal or Jackson had any opportunity to watch Jake play that season. They both buried themselves in their work and slowly drifted toward the reality of their lives. Jackson tried to connect with Crystal a time or two but was turned down.

Jackson wasn't so much lonely as needy. He could exist by himself but there were few people in his life that he could claim as his own. Family. Close friends. Peers. No one met the qualifications essential to mean something to him. Deep down, Jake and Crystal were becoming important to him. It was a fact unrealizable in the past. Of course, how could you understand the importance of something without knowing of its existence. And there was the rub. The only people who could validate his pitiful existence, the only individuals that created some semblance of an identity were off-limits. What he needed was just out of reach. It was a miserable feeling and Jackson didn't know how to deal with it.

He retreated back to readings and his search for meaning. Something he could identify with. Something that might give him purpose again. An athlete's resolve is built in until the competition disappears. An entrepreneur's desire is inbred until money no longer satisfies. But, as Jackson found out, a father's hope is innate whether the son knows of it or not. Hopelessness was becoming the core to Jackson's reality. You could see it in his eyes. He wasn't sure he could live a life without hope. He wasn't sure of anything.

Jake succeeded in his trade while those that brought him into the world merely existed. Lots of people do that. Day in and day out, the mundane becomes the catalyst for the next day. No poetry. No song. No desire for the fragments of life that give it color and diversity. These diversions have somehow been removed from the lexicon of thoughts and dreams. After a time, the absence of vitality ceases to be abnormal. Especially when you see similar deficiencies in so many individuals around you. Maybe the dreamers are the strange ones. Maybe they haven't yet learned the value of converged and restricted order in one's life. The value of realizing that the only things of true importance are visible and only moments away.

Jackson and Crystal became comfortable in their indifference. Indifferent to what? Who knows? But you could see it in their eyes. They went through the motions without design or expectation. The only joy they harvested from their worlds was centered around the exploits of a twenty-three-year-old baseball player. It was the only joy that each would allow. It became the manner by which each would punish themselves for their past sins; an emotional flagellation that hopefully would lead to absolution; a spiritual exercise with the intention of rebalancing lives selfishly tilted by youthful indiscretion. It's easily done actually. It's seen it in first generation immigrant populations, their children are not allowed to see past their noses. The future is off-limits. Hardships are compounded when you reach for something beyond your fingertips, even if your fingernails can briefly touch what you are desiring. Those are the dreams that are most dangerous of all. The ones that seem plausible. When you start thinking, "why not me?" you have drifted in over your head. And it's all your fault. You've been told not to imagine. You've been warned not to yearn. And aspirations—those will kill you!

For Jackson, it didn't used to be that way. He was allowed to have dreams. His parents made sure that resources were available to assist in the realization of those ambitions. Now that kind of dreaming was all right. The type where there was never a doubt as to their eventuality, where the advent of desire and hope always came to fruition. Those dreams are acceptable. Those dreams may even be rational. Yet, what the fortunate of the world eventually find out is that faith in something that already exists is not faith but fact. And what good is that. What's the use in hoping for something that has already been set in motion, something that is guaranteed to happen. That may be why Jackson had lost his sense of wonder in his world. Living a dreamed life had come too easily. He had lost the ability to imagine something that may never come true. All his imaginations in the past were just about to touch his nose. Where's the faith in that?

Jake continued to surprise his coaches and within two and a half seasons he was playing Triple-A ball in Sacramento. For one more season, Jake and his mom lived an existence where prayers were actually answered. A short flight or a six-hour drive and they were together. Crystal's acceptance of her unsatisfactory life gave way to contentment and Jake's contentment became happiness. It was more than either had expected when they were living a simple life in Al's home.

Jake had truly become a physical specimen. Everyone could see that he was *subsidizing* his growth but testing for performance-enhancing drugs in the minor leagues was not a priority since, for the most part, the players were out of the media spotlight. Crystal noticed how her unassuming son had become a beast but never imagined that it was due to anabolic steroid derivatives. She always expected the best from her son because he always granted it. He was a wonderful child who became a respectable teenager and a responsible young man. These growth changes were just part of his blessed existence.

The drugs aided in Jake's physical stature but were beginning to leave their mark on his psychological state of mind. He angered more easily, he was careless about anything other than baseball, and he became reckless with his actions off the field of play. There were numerous auto accidents. He lost a tooth in a fight that he didn't remember. He treated his girlfriends horribly. Most of these incidents were out of view of his mother but clearly obvious to his coaches and teammates. Jackson would not have recognized Jake if the opportunity to see him would have come about. He hadn't seen Jake for nearly two years. It wasn't until Jackson received a message from Crystal stating that she wasn't able to attend Jake's Pacific Coast League's championship game due to an obligation at work. She thought it might be enjoyable for Jackson to watch his son play while she wasn't in attendance. He accepted the invitation gladly and promised only to observe from a distance, and without connection. Jackson knew immediately what had caused Jake's transformation. Jackson was trapped between two emotions, those of a former athlete and a biological father. He realized the potential these supplements were providing for his son's career. He also was aware of the harmful effects that they were doing to his son's body and mind. Would Jackson have done the same thing? He couldn't resist the thought that his career would have been extended if only he could have enhanced his strength and power. There was no doubt. If he could have bulked up to the level of Jake's body, Jackson would have been drafted and given the same opportunity to make a career in the MLB as his son now had.

This conflict added to Jackson's misery. As a father, he would have been involved with these decisions (he would have hoped). As a husband, he would have conferred with Crystal about the best way to parent and advise (he would have hoped). But as a complete outsider, even more of an outsider than a casual fan, Jackson was placed in a one-way bubble that he could not escape. One where he could only see out and no one else could peer in. His fraught existence within this partially translucent shell would eventually leave him unable to cope. He left the game at the seventh inning stretch. Jackson didn't even wait for his flight, choosing to rent a car and drive home. He needed time to think. But what was there to think about? Is there any value in pondering a dilemma where there is no possibility of aid? He was miserable. He was floating in a lifeboat and watching while the *Titanic* teetered on the brink.

As is commonly the case, the solution to a problem becomes less necessary as the proximity to that problem grows more distant. All problems fade in time without continual exposure and as the problem fades, so does the need for a solution. Jackson chose not to confront Crystal with the perceived plight of her son. Jackson retreated to the shadows as he was accustomed. Jake's fate pained his father greatly but even that waned with time. In Sacramento, Jake's formidable skills became matched by the breadth of talent that he suddenly had to compete with. He started to doubt his abilities and wondered about his chances for playing at the next level. Jake was batting in the seventh position and found that he was left out of the lineup against certain pitchers. This only fueled his resolve to succeed at any cost. He would take on more risk by consuming more experimental supplements and dedicating more time to aggressive workout sessions with his strength coach. Crystal was beginning to notice the change. Not necessarily from Jake's physicality but more an alteration in their relationship. The postgame phone calls ended precipitously. Jake's demeanor on the field and after each game was in opposition to what his mother had been accustomed to. But a .255 average from the plate and only one error all season kept the fledgling Athletic in contract for another two-year extension.

After the 2009 season ended with the A's failing to make the playoffs, Jake was offered lodging in Oakland with his strength coach during the off-season. Jake could be close to the team's training facility and be available for continued assistance from the teams training experts. Jake was becoming obsessed with his ambition to play in the big league. Nothing else mattered. It was a job however. Which meant that every night the training and coaching would end. Jake didn't have a Bo to entertain and motivate. There was no Wright to his Whiskey. His mother had always been in that role. The long empty nights needed to be filled. Jake had lost his license to drive the summer before with his fourth DUI and his third accident. He used his signing bonus from his two-year extension to buy a motorcycle. Apparently, Jake felt riding a two-wheeler did not constitute the type of driving that required a license to operate. As fate would have it, Jake was stone sober as he drove home from a Saturday night movie and was clipped by a drunk driver. It was just enough to send him into a spin that pinned his left leg under the chassis of his Harley and dragged it for about thirty yards. The result was tragic. So much damage occurred that there was a question of whether the surgeons could save the leg. Weeks led to months and it was determined that the leg would need to be amputated below the knee.

The ultimate decision was anticlimactic. Even with a leg fully conserved, the complete functioning of the limb could never be regenerated. The amputation was fate's final confirmation of the obvious. Jake's career was over and so were the final solitary hopes and dreams of his parents. The three individuals that made up this disjointed clan sunk into deep depression. Jackson perhaps more than the others. He had to suffer through the tragedy alone. He couldn't help. He couldn't be helped. He offered the only thing he had but Jackson's money was unnecessary. Jake's benefits from the team's health and disability insurance made the financial burden of no consequence. The emotional hardship was something else. Jackson was left to observe his son's torture with no manner in which to help and no possibility of looking away. For Jake, it was the beginning of the end. For Jackson, it was the final straw.

Crystal tried to be the invisible adhesive force for this unconventional family but she had her pain as well. The misery took its toll as she saw her son attempt suicide twice. There would be no consoling the young man. His attempts failed but they were utterly successful in inflicting anguish upon his devoted mother. Jackson would not hear of this until weeks later as he met Crystal for coffee in a hospital cafeteria during one of Jake's numerous surgeries. As they allowed the sadness to wring fully the contents of their hearts, individual tears were replaced by family blood. It was a metaphor that brought to mind one of Jackson's readings which recently took him through the Gospel of Luke. It was the first time Jackson empathized with the Savior his mother attempted to introduce when Jackson was just a boy.

Jackson offered everything he could think of. Crystal, now more than ever, declined all support, which broke Jackson's heart as he walked out of their lives for the final time. He would not get a chance to see his son or encourage his son or hold his son. Love offered from a distance without touch or warmth is of no value unless Divinely conceived. And even that falls miserably short for such sorrow. Jackson resigned his business partnership the next day. His co-workers were shocked; and the fact that Jackson couldn't give them the real reason for his departure made it all the more inconceivable. He cried in the presence of the entire office but without explanation. He went home and broke down. He became sick. He vomited and nearly passed out. He woke in the middle of the night still curled around the toilet. When he finished a shower, the pain took hold again. He became aware that what he was now feeling would be his consistent wake-up call each and every morning for the rest of his life. His despair was complete. Even good memories that he tried to kindle by revisiting the picture album of his youth retrieved only the worst recollections of a wasted life. The last photo in the album was one of his entourage during their last backpacking trip. They were all there. Bo, Carlos, Slim, Bugs, and Willy, who was the only one smiling in the photo. The rest of them were either too cool or too spoiled, unaffected by the joy of the moment. Jackson closed the photo album. He slowly walked into the kitchen and, after pausing for almost a minute, threw the memories into the trash.

TWENTY-FIVE

I Can't Live With This

(Spring 2010)

Home. A specific point on a star named Kansas. It is a place, more than any other location on that star, that provides comfort. A comfort that is resilient in its existence for all who claim its source. A comfort that offers contentment which emanates from each neighborhood and every inhabitant. Most commonly, it is found in the eyes of its residents. You easily notice that characteristic the closer you are to home. Eye contact is a hallmark of the home experience. Topeka, especially within the capitol building itself, is far removed from home—everyone's home. Even those who live in Topeka lose that sense inside the capitol. No one looks anywhere but straight ahead, as if all heads are fixed in position the moment you accept your assignment. Like, here's your ID, these are your computer passcodes, and now let me remove your sternomastoid muscles. The residual abscission does allow your head to move up and down. After all, you are required to evaluate committee and legislative material placed in front of you. But even with direct communication between individuals, there is little eye contact. This facial attitude has totally laid its claim to Senator Wright. He was as removed from his home, physically and spiritually, as you can get. His landslide victory last fall took him to the chambers of the United States Senate, but his behavior was derived from and developed within the halls of the State capitol in Topeka.

Senator Wright had to retool for his new and improved location. What had become effortless at the state level now had to be reworked and refined in Washington, D.C. New relationships were needed. Pertinent connections had to be made. The resources necessary were the same, money and political favors, but the subtleties used within required a different methodology. Because of poor oversight in campaign funds, Senator Wright was able to pad his Eljuez account through the years. But the 2008–09 housing crisis and stock market crash had decimated his Nixonian slush fund. Unlike Jackson, Bo had let his stock picks ride, seeing no need to follow his friend's move to divest himself from his equity market assets. It would be years before that funding source would be sizeable enough to be of significant political help. Other methods would be necessary to maintain his position of power and influence.

Senator Wright's appointment to the Judiciary Committee was as expected. He had direct oversight of all social and legislative momentum regarding the issues that have interested him the most over the years. Bo's experience in the legislative process involving DNA testing and its application to the law gave him unique status within committees. He found himself having influence in the area he most wanted. He gathered power the old-fashioned way. He bartered his vote. Republicans were in the minority of both houses and so the only power that could be gained was from the middle. Bo offered his vote when needed to either side.

All eyes were on the financial crisis, except of course, President Obama's, who changed focus midstream to his healthcare horse. The conflict between the two political issues created an environment that placed all other legislative agendas behind the scenes where savvy politicians could run wild. Each time a bill was created to address the housing or healthcare crisis, Bo was able to slip riders onto bills that had nothing to do with the actual legislations being proposed. And these add-ons could be purchased. Any PAC or corporation that needed a change in regulation or alteration in tax law could find their needs met with "campaign donations" directed to Senator Wright's appropriate accounts. The heightened desire of the majority party to provide universal healthcare coverage and the minority party's wish to stop it at all costs created cover where legislative riders went, if not unnoticed, clearly unchallenged for months. Senator Wright used his willingness to hold hands on both sides of the aisle to put himself back in power.

Bo became so engrossed with the power grab available to him he ceased concern of almost everything else. His wife and children stayed home in Topeka where Bo maintained his address for appearances yet came home only at Christmas and for fundraising. Bo developed new political and social circles in the D.C. area. He was successful in developing inconspicuous relations with Democrats, with influential CEOs and lobbyists, and with legal representatives of criminal enterprises. He enjoyed extravagant dinners, expensive liquor, and "off the books" female companions. He took to lining pockets and cocaine with equal proficiency in order to balance all plates he had spinning above his head. His talent at such became legendary. His impression in the public eye was impeccable, his perception with his constituents was impressive, his image amongst his peers was dubious yet acceptable since they were just less proficient at the same game. Within a very short time, Senator Wright was able to create for himself a lock on power that he couldn't have imagined a few years back.

Able to consistently bring home the bacon to his adoring state of Kansas, Bo was a shoo-in for re-election every six years. Only one thing could ever stop an incumbent of the majority party within a strong majority state—scandal. And Bo knew it. There could only be one aspect of his life that could rise to a level of defamation that would bring the plates crashing down on his balding head. It consumed him. Even more than his desire for wealth and power. Most people didn't know of his secrets; he was successful in that concealment. If they would consider it possible that Senator Wright could even have skeletons, those mysteries surely would not rise to the level of political concern. A few did know but, as of yet, no one would think about coming forward with information or evidence.

Bo found it interesting that many of the same issues that vexed Kansas were also creating problems in Massachusetts and California. All states were grappling with the technology of DNA testing and the explosions of unfunded mandates by states wishing to harness its potential. But none were willing to sacrifice the funds necessary to make it all work. Pressure was being administered on representatives in most states to come up with financial solutions to the problem. As the minority chair of Judiciary, Senator Wright was instrumental in crafting the language of such legislative assistance. Of course, these bills must take appropriate time and measures to create adequate steps in vanquishing the problem. In being granted a position of such influence, Senator

Wright guaranteed to the party leaders that he would not use his power to fund his own state until all other states represented by committee members were cared for. A promise that he gladly lived up to. Funds for the testing of backlogged rape kits and overdue felony evidence started funneling out of Appropriations during Bo's first tenure on Judiciary. Kansas would not receive specific funding until Senator Wright's second term in office. The language of these appropriations was boilerplate and the funds themselves had few restrictions, providing minimal limitations to receiving states. This meant that the state of Kansas had full authority to create its own criteria determining which evidence was placed at the front of the testing protocol. And as Bo knew all to well, state legislators and bureaucrats were easily manipulated.

Bo's connection with the people of Kansas grew weaker. The longer he lived and worked in Washington, D.C., the shorter his recollections were of his family and home. Bo missed anniversaries, birthdays, proms, and reunions. He failed to show for his daughter's graduation from college and his son's graduation from high school. He wasn't fazed or shamed by these absences. His life was locked into a pattern that was completely indulgent and self-centered. His change was complete and he knew it. This was what he desired out of life. It kept his interest. All past images and memories were of no value to him. Bo planned on living out the rest of his days as Senator Wright. He had fooled his faithful and enriched himself.

Even when he could be tracked down and forced into taking calls from his family, he spent as little energy on the communication as possible. When his sister told him of his mom's condition, there was only a slight pause in Bo's reaction. He did recall his mother's conversation around the sheriff's diagnosis. When she'd claimed that the decision to place him in a home was not that simple, Bo hadn't inquired just why that was. Now, according to Bo's sister, their mom had been diagnosed with ALS. A diagnosis that came more than four years ago. There were few things that she could do for herself. Even with advanced dementia, the Sheriff was able to help her with the tasks she couldn't do. She was able to work around his fits of anger then convince him that his job had always been to take care of her. She could keep him safe. He could keep her alive. They were two halves existing as one life.

Bo took no interest in their plight. Whether his apathetic emotions further tarnished his feelings toward his father or his narcissistic sentiment newly separated his concern for his mother, his parents' problems had to be resolved by someone else. The saddest episode came when Senator Wright found out that his daughter was married and he had not been invited to the impromptu ceremony. He was furious. Not because he missed out on an important family event but that it might someday generate negative publicity. Those images could be devastating to an upcoming campaign. After a while, that didn't even matter. His transformation was complete. Even phone calls from Jackson were avoided. History had been severed. Only his future political career mattered.

Senator Wright's aides and staff members were the machine that made this all work. Bo was able to neglect routine items of senatorial business because his staff was authorized to make all motions on his behalf. They did the work. He voted as directed by them. Unless however, the issues before him were specific to his direct enhancement or survival. Any actions from staff regarding these items, without his approval, would mean instant dismissal. He expected them to know the difference between trivial and imperative. Turnover amongst the senator's staff was high because it was not easy to recognize that difference. For example, Senator Wright always made time each afternoon, at the end of committee hearings, for VIP conferences. Which meant those who had donated six figures or more to the coffers of the honorable senator. On occasion, individuals with important requests, yet not high enough on the contributors' list, were accidentally granted a visit with Senator Wright. Once completed, those meetings would end in the firing of a secretary, even if that person wasn't culpable for the transgression. The only time to anyone's memory that this type of mismanagement was not punished was when an appointment was granted one Friday afternoon to a moderate donor from California. Bo came out of hearings to find Jackson in his office. And for a moment, the crusty exterior of the senator was trimmed away and a more vulnerable Bo was in their midst. He was back in high school. Their embrace even brought tears to the senator's secretary. Bo immediately canceled his evening obligations and broke his social activities for the weekend.

This would be the time to reconnect, or at least have the appearance of such an endeavor.

While at dinner, the important conversation began during cocktails and ended with Jackson's query about Slim.

"Do you know where Slim is these days?"

"How would I know. I have more information on Vladimir Putin than I do on Slim."

"No one seems to know where he is. His dad said the last time he saw him was just before Willy's trial."

"Didn't he get married and move to Vegas?"

"I heard that he didn't get married but lived there with a girl for a while. I checked all the real estate sources I had and there was no mention of him owning property in Nevada. No telephone listing. No tax payment of any kind. It's strange."

"Well, he was never very stable," the Senator pontificated.

"He wasn't all that bad. Not enough to drop off the face of the earth."

Dinner commenced and the small talk began but lacked the enthusiasm you might expect from two long-lost pals.

"I have something I need to tell you but we should have that conversation at your place," Jackson said as he picked up the check, which was mandatory these days when dining with the senator.

They retired to Bo's Georgetown apartment for the night. Jackson refused the offer of a drink. He refused the offer of something more significant also while the senator imbibed in both. Jackson quickly and directly told Bo what had been on his mind and what triggered his decision to come clean. He had decided to tell the authorities what actually happened to Valeria on that dark summer night. Bo attempted to show sympathy to his friend's plight but this could not overshadow the threat which now menaced the junior senator from Kansas. As the evening hours disappeared, Bo became angrier at the thought that Jackson was going to turn himself in.

"I can't live with this anymore," Jackson admitted as he slumped forward, resting his elbows on his thighs.

"Sure you can! You've done it for so long, why change now?"

"I was thumbing through one of our albums and came across a picture of Willy. He looked so peaceful, so happy, so innocent … How could I have done this to him. It makes me sick."

"How can you say that. You never paid any attention to him before. You never included him. You thought he was worthless. He is worthless! As far as anyone believes, he did it. He killed Valeria. Hell, I even think he's guilty of something." Bo's words were slurred and the direction of his thoughts didn't always match his words. "Is this about me? You don't have to do this!"

"I've thought about it for a long time and with what just happened … I've made up my mind." And with that, Jackson walked toward his bedroom. Before he entered, Jackson turned and apologized to his friend. "I know how I've treated you as well. Please forgive me."

Bo stayed up the entire night, wired on cocaine and contemplating the potential fallout of Jackson's decision. The senator was used to political turmoil. There was always a solution. It just required time and resources. This could be resolved. He just needed to think it through. When Jackson woke the next morning, Bo was making breakfast—French Toast. It was a favorite of both of them. Bo's mom taught them how to make it on a snowy Saturday morning in high school.

"Do you remember that time when it snowed so hard they canceled practice and you came over in your dad's four-wheel-drive truck," Bo asked as he dipped the bread into the eggs.

Jackson poured himself a cup of coffee before turning to Bo and nodding his head affirmatively. "We were going to go gooling, but Five wouldn't be up for a while so your mom made us French toast. I remember it was the first time I ever had it. My mom was an egg and sausage breakfast burrito gal. Every morning. I got sick of it."

"You liked the French toast so much that you asked her to teach you how to make it."

"I didn't think my mom knew how! I've been single now for … I don't know how long. I live on French toast, all weekend long!" This brought about Jackson's first smile since he arrived in Washington, D.C.

"So that's where the spare tire came from," Bo teased as he threw the first batch into the skillet. "What's that? 'My body has been a good friend …'"

"I won't need it, when I reach the end."

"Yeah. That's it. I miss Cat Stevens," Bo acknowledged.

"Me too."

"I miss gooling! The hanging on to someone's truck bumper and sliding on slick shoes up and down Center Street," Bo enthusiastically offered, as if he were trying to get Jackson to play along with favorite things from the past.

Jackson laughed, another first. "That would probably kill us both now. You know what I really miss? Backpacking. How long has it been?" Bo just shrugged and served up the slices. "I'd like to go again." But a solemn look came over Jackson's face as he stated, "I guess that will never happen."

"Why not? We still have one more left in us."

"I can't. I don't want to take the time. And after ..." Jackson dropped his head. He was looking at his plate without the will to pick up his fork.

"Sure we could. Look, I don't agree with what you say you want to do but I think I understand. The last thing you should do is rush into this decision in your state of mind. I don't know what happened out there in California to bring about this change. I don't know what's troubling you. I do know that you've led a charmed life and what goes up must come down, but that's no reason to throw it all away!" Bo sat down to his own plate and took a bite before continuing. "Look. In five days, we recess for the Fourth of July and I'll have two weeks off to spend with my constituents." Jackson looked up incredulously with a disbelieving smirk. "Yeah, well ... anyway. We could drive out to Colorado and hike up to Long Lake. See if we can find that lost trail. What do you say?"

"I can't."

"Listen. I love you and I'm just trying to help. It would be just the two of us. It probably would be good for me as well. We can talk. We can think things through. If, after the weekend, you still believe as you do now, I won't stand in your way. Please."

Jackson took a bite of his French toast and smiled. "Pretty damn good."

TWENTY-SIX

Locker Mates

(Fall 1970)

Most of us remember milestones in school. Some of which were exciting, others more nerve-racking. The jump from elementary school to junior high is on most people's list for both. Of all the changes and strife that individuals must endure during this intermediate period—including academic, social, mental, and emotional—physical differences are by far the most notable transformation experienced by those entering their first day of seventh grade. Not only is puberty providing uncontrollable modifications within each child's body, the school building itself is an inescapable environment where extreme physical differences are on full display. These images are not just obvious but slap you in the face each time you walk down the hall. Men and boys. Women and girls. Adults and children. There are ninth graders that shave and wear C-cups. There are seventh graders who have yet to experience their first pube or swollen nipple. It's a labyrinth of physical contradictions that is impossible to escape and nearly impossible to comprehend.

Teacher and parental support are obviously needed in order for children to mature emotionally sound. But nothing is more critical than the social stability offered by peers. Those students with siblings present during the transition or those who have close trusted friends experiencing the evolving landscape in lockstep, have a tendency to handle the adjustment much more easily. For some, it's a short-lived discomfort in the midst of great opportunity. For others, it's a living hell for three straight years. It's even possible to experience both. It could be the most torturous period in a person's life and a seedbed of knowledge utilized for the rest of one's days. It depends on how you look at it. Most people consider college or an apprenticeship as the most formative period in a life. But not all.

Junior high school is where you learn how to fight or avoid a fight, to be seen or be invisible, to communicate without saying a word, to lie without flinching, and fear without being discovered. It's when you find out how to dress, talk, hate, cuss, peek, cheat, adapt, and survive. It's during this time that new firsts occur almost daily. First zit. First kiss. First dirty joke. First wet dream. First drink. First drag. First really embarrassing moment. For three years you are educated in social structures, racial barriers, financial influences, educational norms, and physical limitations. You are trained to understand territorial conflicts, to make risk reward calculations, to anticipate action and reaction, to conceptualize time and consequences, and to master probability determinations. And all this learning occurs during the four-minutes between classes and the nineteen minutes at lunch. Come to think of it, some might lay odds that what we learn in junior high tops a bachelor's degree in environmental analysis and social psychology combined.

Most directives of fate are actually just aspects of coincidence really. The circumstances that cause relationships to begin, to linger, to last, may be nothing more than happenstance. Right place. Right time. By chance, Jackson, Bo, and their mothers were enrolling weeks before seventh grade began. They were standing in line together when the locker mates were being assigned. Since Jackson didn't have a partner in mind, his mother suggested Bo. The decision was made without thought of any true consequence to the matter. Neither boy cared one way or the other. However, it would become the most consequential action in each of their young, prospective lives. Bo liked and admired the qualities of his new locker mate. He realized early on that Jackson was impressively popular. He knew that somehow, there would be benefits to an association with such a prominent talent. Bo became more excited each approaching day. Jackson was much more ambivalent about the whole thing. He knew Bo from grade-school athletics but they were from different schools and of different social circles. Jackson thought of himself as independent and not requiring any social support in school. The fact that he had an acquaintance to share a locker was reasonable but not necessary.

The next three years would be much the same. Bo existed in the eyes of Jackson and Jackson was revered by Bo. Both knew of the other's feelings and both were comfortable with that aspect of their accord. Neither was completely satisfied with the reality of junior high (who could be), however, they would come to realize that their friendship created a buffer to many of the more harrowing aspects of the experience. They would use each other in ways that enhanced their status and quickened their advancement beyond their peers who were experiencing the same social dilemmas. They became each other's collateral for the debts that were constant obligations of teenage life. It would be years until either would acknowledge the importance of that one fortunate incident while standing in a pre-enrollment line.

Years later, they would ask each other what they remembered about that three-year period at Sumner Plaine Junior High. Very few events stood out as memorable. Only the ones that made them laugh were on that list. Bo would recall Jackson trying to teach him how to skateboard downhill. Bo, feeling his sprouting oats, didn't need any help. After a major fall where he deposited a large percentage of the skin off his back along the lower half of the hill, Bo remembered an unsympathetic friend standing over him and laughing his ass off. Similarly, Jackson remembered a tennis match where he and Bo were doubles partners and a wayward serve slapped violently into Jackson's bare back. Much of the where and when of the event was lost in his mind. Jackson remembered distinctly being annoyed at Bo rolling around on the ground because the laughter had knocked him off his feet as Jackson squawked around the court like an injured duck. It's such an obvious and annoying characteristic of young teenage boys. All find humor in the pain of their peers. Whether self-inflicted or not, such discomfort always brought about tears, and not the type that come from sympathy.

A notable difference in those two events was the resulting response from the one on the receiving end of the injury and insult. Bo meekly walked away from the laughter and over to Jackson's home where his mother nursed Bo's wounds. Jackson, after receiving the jolt, became angered at the laughter coming from the culprit and proceeded to pound the crap out of his friend—who continued cackling throughout the beating. Bo had come to realize that Jackson's tendencies toward abrupt outrage sharpened his competitive nature. Bo rarely became indignant and then, only toward himself. For Jackson, his anger was motivational. It gave him focus. The best example of this was when Bo, while again sitting on the bench during a high school basketball game against Wichita Heights, noticed how Darnell Valentine was getting the best of Jackson on the court. During a first quarter time-out, Bo lied to Jackson by telling him that Valentine laughed at him after a steal and an easy layup. Over the next three quarters of play, Jackson went off for twenty-four points while being guarded by the future NBA standout. Each time Bo would tell this story, he would quickly be corrected by his friend, twenty-seven points; if you're going to tell the story, get your facts straight.

Junior high was the beginning of real athletic competition in the eyes of each participant. Now, when you observe that level of competition, you are hardly able to stomach the spectacle. But back then, for Jackson and Bo, this felt like preparation for the big leagues. It was also the time when you would learn how to read your teachers and coaches. Junior high is where you determine that the two are polar opposites. Bo, who was always a teacher's pet, thought that when a coach treated him in the same fashion as a teacher, he must, as in the classroom, be talented and a favorite of his coach. They were nice to him. They would encourage him at every step of his development. Jackson, on the other hand, was the constant victim of ridicule and criticism. "Do it again! Don't be so sloppy! If you make that mistake one more time, I swear I'll sit your ass on the bench!" When Jackson would plead as much to his dad, Johnathon would just shake his head and say good, which to Jackson meant that his father didn't really care and masochistically enjoyed hearing about his son's suffering. The truth came at the hands of the sheriff who grabbed his son by the shoulders and said, "If your coaches aren't yelling at you, you're no good." It's true, coaches only rode you if, in their eyes, you had potential. Never once did a coach yell at Bo. Not even in baseball. That was left completely up to the sheriff.

It was a shame that neither could or would recount the more important influences each had on the other during that time. Jackson didn't initially stand up for Bo when he needed help but later came to his aid in a way that Bo always remembered. Thomas Cromwell, the biggest guy in their class, had just thrown Slim out of the locker room and into the crowded hallway, wearing nothing but his jock. Bo was about to share the same fate, but Jackson, although being half the size of Tom, stepped in the way and stared him into submission. Tom challenged Jackson. "I'll meet you at the water tower," which was the local venue for all important fights. But during a shared sixth-hour class, Tom put his arm around the shoulders of Jackson stating, "We're cool." Thus, the event was called off before anyone could find out who was courageous enough to show. From that moment on, Bo was empowered by Jackson's friendship. He also learned the concept that fearlessness is a choice, not a gift.

Jackson, though commanding respect by sporting a seemingly unbreakable shell of confidence, suffered as all did at that age. The common denominator to any junior high existence is insecurity. Bo only noticed it once in his best friend. A freshman nobody, at least neither could remember his name, once made fun of Jackson after a meaningless encounter. Jackson was bothered for days by the embarrassment of being looked down upon. He remembered Bo shutting their locker firmly and saying, "If a blind man says you're ugly, does it matter?" Jackson took those words to heart and credited to that moment a true change in attitude.

Their relationship was proof of social alchemy. Their status grew out of nothing but an elemental bond forged without input or energy. They synergistically became more than individuals. Seventh grade was the inauguration of Whiskey and Wright; a compound that would take six more years to fully amass but one that was incubated within the metal walls of that first hallway locker.

TWENTY-SEVEN

What Do You Remember

(Summer 2010)

A late afternoon flight brought Jackson back to L.A. He loved flying in at night, especially with a full moon illuminating the already gleaming city. A drive along the Southern California coast on a summer evening was usually joyful and relaxing. That night, he would enjoy neither. He didn't want to go back to his drab apartment either but had work to do. Jackson had accepted Bo's invitation and, with his face to Jerusalem, was needing to align all his ducks before leaving in two days. Sleeping had always been difficult for Jackson. Overstimulated minds and bodies create their own cycles. But that night went well and the morning found him alert if not cheerful.

There was much to do and even under the current situation, Jackson found diversion in his to-do list. He had decided to drive home to Sumner Plaine instead of flying. As a retired real estate investor who had divested himself of practically everything, Jackson thought he would enjoy taking the only piece of property he owned home with him. With no job, no property, and no family, his options were open and his prospects were purposely minimized. Besides, as of late, the only joy that Jackson could arouse was driving in his all-time favorite vehicle. An Aston Martin DBS V12 Coupe, high-tech bonded aluminum frame, black interior, Casino Royale Grey. Even in the heart of luxury vehicle heaven, this car turned heads. And to Bo, who had yet to lay eyes on it, he would have given up his desire to have Jackson's looks, his talent, his brains, his body, and his women, just to own this car. Of course, Bo *could* have found the money for the quarter of a million-dollar price tag also but, like dating the same girl, it would never happen.

It would take three full days to properly drive through the desert and across the Rockies before arriving in western Kansas. There were a few loose ends that needed to be burned off before leaving. He met with his attorney. He signed a few severance contracts and made one last trip to the bank. There were goodbyes to be said, fish tacos to be savored, a favorite jazz bar to experience, and one last Dodgers game to be seen. Each activity was consumed in an efficient dispassionate fashion. For his last evening, Jackson had left a message for Crystal. It said that he was going to watch the sunset Monday night and hoped that she would join him before he left for home. It was their favorite beach, the one where they first met.

Ocean breezes have layers and depth. They can be felt. They have an aroma. You can even taste their salty zest. Jackson sat near the water and watched the wave action. It had been years since he had surfed. He wouldn't dare attempt it, not then, not with that body. But nonetheless, he was roused by the desire to attack another wave. The sand filled the gaps between his toes as his memories offered a similar effect to the forgotten images of his years on the West Coast. Beautiful people with beautiful tans walked by but it was the horizon that kept Jackson's attention. His countenance was as light as the dancing sparkles reflecting off the water. This surprised Jackson. Did a beach, surf, and setting sun have this effect on everyone or just depressed has-beens looking to experience one last offering from the great Poseidon. It was so pleasing, that hour on the beach, that Jackson almost changed his mind. "I love this place," he thought. "I could still make a life. I could start again." The thought brought about no obvious physical response but an inner peace was stretching from within, straining to be released from its tightly encased tomb. A great deal within Jackson was wanting to break free, free from expectations, free from the past. His mind was finding a strange balance between the desire to pursue life or give it up. An unusual harmony between aspiration and demise. It was neither appealing or uncomfortable. It simply was present. That balance became intoxicating as Jackson sat watching the diffused solar disc slip cautiously behind the clouds that were muddling a perfect sunset. Darkness soon overcame the residual glow as did Jackson's sullen outlook overwhelm his transitory hope. She wasn't coming. One last look. The beach was empty.

The next day, Jackson drove east, taking the northern route through Las Vegas where he stopped only for gas. The fastest trek home was through Phoenix and Albuquerque, but Jackson was treating this drive as a last opportunity to see parts of the West he had overlooked. As a young man, he had jumped from Sumner Plaine to New York to California without taking an interest in what laid in between. He skipped the Grand Canyon. He and his family had vacationed there thirty-five years ago. It probably hadn't changed much. He wanted to see the otherworldly landscapes of Utah. The first night was spent outside of Zion National Park. Jackson chose to sleep in his car; a mistake he would never make again. Perhaps Daniel Craig could make love in the backseat of an Aston Martin but sleeping was next to impossible.

Jackson had only one wish as his hike progressed from the trailhead of Observation Point. "I wish I were in shape for this shit." After thirty minutes, he turned back. Deciding instead to take in as much of Utah as he could through the driver's side window. He drove through Bryce Canyon then on to Capital Reef. They reminded him of Colorado but without trees. He missed the outdoor lifestyle of his youth. He could have been happy there, he thought. But his desire for a grand existence outshined his need for simple contentment. It was similar to the conflicted feeling he had while sitting alone on the beach two nights earlier. Contentment comes from the choice to attain it. Unlike happiness, which is an uncommon gift and out of one's control. Jackson chose not to backtrack into Canyonlands, assuming it to be the Grand Canyon without the grand. He found a small motel in Moab to rest up for Arches. It was highest on his list. The trailheads were drivable, the paths were short and provided the most unique earth formations on the planet. Arches reminded him of home. Not because of the interesting landscape or the flat terrain. Not the dry climate or the never-ending horizon. It was the wind. Enough to blow holes through bedrock. It was the wind.

Jackson spent the night in Grand Junction before the final journey home. Five lived there for a time after he dropped out of college and gave up his baseball dream. Jackson arbitrarily asked someone at breakfast if they had ever heard of him, something he still was laughing at as he crossed the Kansas border. He pulled in the driveway on Friday. His mom gave him the biggest hug she could and didn't even ask about the car. She was excited to receive the call Thursday night regarding Jackson's arrival. Jackson and his mom had a nice chat before he left to prep for the trip to the mountains. He wanted to get an early start so the packs needed to be prepared. It was a process he had completed dozens of times. Nothing changed for this trip. The backpacks always had to be the same. The only difference for this trip was that they were too old to be packing a lot of alcohol up the mountain. One bottle of Jim Bean would do.

Bo called late that evening after his flight arrived. He was checking to make sure Jackson was there and the trip was still on. The way things had been left, at least in Bo's eyes, it was a fifty-fifty proposition that the backpacking trip would actually occur. He was glad as he hung up the phone. There was a relief to Bo's tone, as Jackson recalled, in the way Bo ended the conversation. He said, "Thank you." Jackson's mom smiled as she had overheard the entire conversation.

"I'm glad you two are still close. I don't think you could find a better friend anywhere else in the world. And that goes for both of you." There are so many things that our parents don't know about our lives but they can see down into our deepest realities and find the truth that we have chosen to bury through time. "It just goes to show that brotherly love does not have to be restricted to family."

Jackson really wasn't looking forward to this trip. He wasn't excited about a long weekend with his best friend. He was, however, totally stoked to see the expression on Bo's face when he first would see the car. He wasn't disappointed. Bo was shocked that they were going to take it to the mountains in the first place. "Why not? It's just a car." They were once again back in high school. Jackson insisted on Bo driving the first leg of the trip and by the time they reached I-70, and the halfway point of the drive, the new had worn off. New day. New car. New conversation. The undesirable time had arrived and after about a half hour of silence, Jackson proffered his question of surrender. "What do you remember?"

They talked and listened and pondered as flashbacks from a summer night in 1992 came in and out of their fleeting memories, like fireflies in the dark. It was an uneventful summer bookended by two very eventful holidays. Everyone was home for the Labor Day weekend. Bo had received a call from Jackson. He wanted to go out that Saturday night to celebrate his recent divorce and Bo's news that he and Nancy had been separated for a while. "Celebrate or commiserate?" Bo remembers asking. The night was hot and loud. Jackson, always a sucker for fast cars, wanted to borrow his brother's new Trans Am. He picked up Bo for a night at Ted's. The wind was howling as it frequently did during summer. It was the type of wind where, if you didn't hold on, the gusts could rip the door off your car. And Ted's was packed, even more than usual for a Saturday night. Loud car. Loud bar. Loud weather.

The drinks kept coming and by the time Carlos arrived, both Jackson and Bo were out of control. This was the first time either of them had been asked to leave their favorite establishment. Management had received complaints from the waitresses. The juices were flowing and both were hitting on the girls pretty hard. They were so drunk, neither one was sure why they had left the building. To them, the night was still young and they were searching for something to do. "Let's go find Valeria."

It had been years since the two had *shared* Valeria on a Saturday night but the intoxicated memories were still fresh. It was an enterprise they honed back in high school and college. Most times Jackson would individually hunt her down, but on occasion they both were involved. Initially, the pickup dates with Valeria were harmless. She enjoyed enticing as much as the two enjoyed the chase. Mostly, they involved Valeria and Jackson making out in the backseat. As they all matured to a more reckless age, the level of sex increased. When Bo heard the rattling of Valeria's belt buckle, he knew the game had changed. It reached the point where the oil farm became the chosen location. That which needed to be done wouldn't work with a third watching in the mirror. At times it would be Bo in the backseat, but those were on single *dates*. When they were together, it was Bo driving and Jackson scoring at the oil farm. On those nights when Bo was driving his sister's car, after Jackson had been dropped off by the two, Bo and Valeria would sit in front of her house and talk. Almost like friends. As with most girls, the talk was usually about Jackson but through the months, Bo would learn more about her and vice versa. She was infatuated with Whiskey but was falling in love with Wright. To her, Bo seemed to sympathetically understand her plight as an immigrant girl chasing an unreachable dream. As a male, middle-class Anglo, Bo couldn't truly fathom Valeria's situation yet sympathy was in his very nature. It was a characteristic, however, that only completely surfaced in the absence of his best friend.

In the summer of '92, Valeria, as she had for years, worked as a waitress at her uncle's Mexican restaurant and would be getting off soon. Bo was aware because he and Valeria had spent some time together the previous May. They talked about her job, amongst other things. She hated it. She felt alone and bored in Sumner Plaine. To her, the feeling of hopelessness was overshadowing her mundane existence. Her parents had gone back to Mexico for good and she had stayed with her uncle, living in the same house the two families had been sharing for decades. Now, she was trying to scrape together some cash to move to El Paso. The Thursday before Memorial Day weekend, Bo was in town for a deposition. He and Nancy had recently separated so he chose to stay through the weekend to see his parents and both sisters who were also home for the holiday. It was to be a mini family reunion but with Bo's recent marital problems, it was kind of a bust.

After being removed from Ted's, Jackson drove to the liquor store then to Valeria's restaurant where they drank and waited in the rear parking lot until her shift was over. They offered her a ride home but she said she didn't want to go home yet. Valeria, bored with her job, her family, her life, was all in. Bo had won the flip and so Jackson chauffeured them around. Valeria grabbed the bottle of whiskey. She wanted to catch up. With Bo in the backseat, Valeria seemed comfortable and more willing than most times, as if it were a real date. Valeria whispered in Bo's ear and reminded him of their Memorial weekend rendezvous. Bo smiled at her suggestions and remembered. With her tongue in his ear, he easily recalled that Saturday afternoon in May. Bo was bored and was driving around town and purposely sauntered through her neighborhood. He found Valeria sitting on her front porch. He stopped. She offered him a beer. He knew it was a mistake when they went inside but his better judgment was overruled by the chub in his pants. There was no stopping the inevitable. Valeria, even though she knew the relationship could go nowhere, was more accepting of their accord. She could, for a time, reach out and touch a dream. Bo hated himself after.

He promised himself that it would never happen again. Not for the infidelity. His split with Nancy was in danger of becoming permanent. It was more for the obvious risks involved. But, just as in May, on that early September night in the backseat with Valeria, the thoughts of risk were completely overwhelmed by the reward foreseen.

Jackson was reading the smoke signals rising in the backseat and drove them to the oil farm. The milo was too tall to drive in to the derrick so Jackson parked beside the field and lit a doobie. Valeria led Bo down the path to their private space. Her shirt came off quickly but as they progressed, she stopped and leaned back against the pumpjack. She had something that needed to be said before they went any further and the whiskey was beginning to provide courage. After Valeria broke the news, she reached for some action between his legs but Bo had gone pale and lost all inclination. Jackson was on his second joint when Bo stumbled back into the car. Jackson assumed that Valeria would be following, but after she didn't show, he asked, "Where's Valeria?" Bo stared off into space with the blankest of expressions and didn't say a word. Bo reopened the door and started to hurl onto the road. Thinking that Bo was too drunk to perform, Jackson went in to the milo field to pick up the slack.

Jackson was gone for about thirty minutes. When he came back, they left. "What about Valeria?"

"She said she wanted to walk home."

When Bo hadn't heard from Valeria over the next few weeks, he assumed that she took his advice and aborted their child. It wasn't until that following Thanksgiving, after he and Nancy reconciled their differences, that he realized the horrid truth of the matter. Or maybe he knew but subconsciously blocked out the possibility that Jackson would actually murder her.

As the Rockies grew larger through the windshield, it became obvious that the actual memories of that August night were pretty hazy. Time can easily dissolve memories that originate in the bottom of a beer glass. Bo pulled over for gas and a bathroom break. It was a truck stop similar to Floyd's Truck Stop on the outskirts of Sumner Plaine. The last time Bo had visited Floyd's was the night Valeria was killed. He didn't throw up in the bathroom as he did that night but the resemblance made Bo sick to his stomach. He asked Jackson to drive the rest of the way.

It didn't take long before the conversation returned to the topic at hand. "How did you ... why did you kill her?" Bo asked.

Jackson drove recklessly through the traffic and didn't answer until he got to the foothills west of Denver. As the overhead sun moved in the direction of afternoon rain clouds, Jackson recalled what for years he had tried to forget. "She was laughing, I think." Jackson hesitated then started over. "When I arrived, she was fully dressed and sitting on the mattress. I asked her what was going on. She looked up and I saw that she was crying. That's when she told me you were the father. She wiped away her tears and leaned back against the pump. After a moment, she became angry. She screamed at you and called you something. But the anger didn't last; she appeared hurt and sad. I didn't know what to think." Bo looked quietly out his window and monitored the clouds on their horizon. "Then she started to cry again as she told me something about wanting a new life, that as a little girl her parents told her not to expect much out of her future. Yet she knew there was more than just poverty and despair. She saw it every time she went to school. S.P. showed her that the dream could come true. She just wanted a chance at happiness. She didn't think that dream was too much to ask. I think she expected you to marry her. I walked around for a while. I don't know how long. Then she said something that stuck in my mind." Jackson stopped talking for a second. Bo slowly turned toward his friend of forty-four years to find he was crying. "She said a child is the result and responsibility of that dream and to abort it would be like killing yourself. And she was right about that at least—it does kill a part of you." Jackson paused; his eyes bright with tears as he struggled to compose himself. "Then, as if she had come to an obvious conclusion she started laughing and said, you both used me. I'm having this baby. It's going to be my ticket out." She was slurring her words but, I knew what that all meant. I just snapped. She turned to walk toward the car. There was a big chunk of concrete that had broken away from the base of the derrick. I hit her on the back of her head. The wind stifled the sound of the impact but I felt the vibration when her skull cracked. I carried her into the milo field and left her there. She wasn't moving. I thought she was dead."

"I still can't believe you killed her."

"She wasn't going to get an abortion. It would have ruined you."

"How do you know?"

"It was obvious."

"What did she call me?"

"Pollo flacido," Jackson said quietly. "I've called you that, and worse, but to hear it from her lips … I couldn't let it go." Jackson seemed to find some clarity in the next few moments. "But I didn't kill her because of what she called you or because she was laughing at us. I killed her to protect you. You are the only friend who ever truly cared about me instead of my reputation." Jackson gathered himself and took a drink from his water bottle. "But she didn't deserve any of this and Willy sure doesn't either. That's why I have to set the record straight."

Bo again added his two cents. "With Willy's conviction, the case is off the books. The evidence has been stored away forever. I've made sure of it. But if you do this, everything will be reviewed. Both DNA kits will move to the front of the line and only one thing will change. The world will know that I am the father of a murdered immigrant's unborn child. Willy will stay in prison, Valeria will still be dead, and you will remain free until the prosecutor decides if there is any new evidence to convict. Since there is no new evidence tied to the murder itself, nothing will change, except I will lose everything."

"I know."

***

Surprisingly, they climbed that mountain and set up base camp before the rain set in. Later that night, while Jackson was slumbering comfortably, Bo heard a thud from just outside the tent's zippered access. Curious, Bo quietly removed himself from his bag and the tent and stepped out under the silhouetted trees surrounding the campsite. Jackson's backpack had slipped from its perch and fell hard onto the exposed roots beneath. A quick glance verified that no intruder from the wild had knocked it from the tree. When Bo picked up the heavy gear, he noticed the outline of "the Judge" as it had shifted in the lower compartment of the pack. Bo stroked the hard lines of the handgun through the thin external casing. He looked back toward the tent where his friend was soundly sleeping. Pausing only a moment, Bo returned the pack to its secure position in the tree.

The next morning, they both rose early and ate packaged grub before heading to Long Lake. Their goal, as has been for each back-packing trip since the first, was to find that lost trail. It was the path they came across on their initial adventure. It was a beautiful trail along a deep natural gorge with breathtaking views of the river below. When they were younger, they loved the precarious nature of the walk. But, if it had rained, as it did last night, it would be easy to slip and fall a hundred and fifty feet to your death. Jackson was sure he knew where the trailhead was and how they went wrong in the past. He also knew why Bo wanted to find it.

There came a fork in their trail. Since the lake was located ahead and to their right, they would presumably take the path on the right. But on that first trip, the immature hikers weren't paying as much atten-tion and went left. Both ways got you to the lake, just from different directions. Jackson led the way toward the hidden trail and onto the edge of the ravine. He kept walking confidently while reminding Bo that the rocks were slick. At the steepest and most narrow part of the trail, Jackson stopped and took off his pack. It was a good time to rest although it wasn't the safest place to do it.

Sliding on the loose footing, Jackson inched closer to the edge of the ravine and peered out over the magnificent vista. "I know why you wanted to find this trail again." Right then, Jackson felt Bo's fingers scrape down his lower back.

"And why's that?" Bo asked in a calm low voice.

Bo's fingers slipped behind Jackson's belt. "I remember the look on your face the first time you saw this view. It was as if you just saw your mom and your best girl in the same moment." Bo grabbed on to the belt and pulled Jackson back from the precipice.

"Let's get to the lake."

They were almost there when up ahead a brown bear appeared. It was too far for it to have noticed them, but Jackson took no chances and grabbed the Judge. He carried it with him until they arrived at the campsite where he replaced it in the bottom compartment of his pack and started gathering wood for that evening's fire.

The next day was usually a day for horsing around and taking a few excursions in the hills above the lake, but at their age, they were content with fishing and a good fire. That night would be their last night on the mountain, ever. The J.B. came out early. It gets dark on the mountain instantaneously. They were both in position when it occurred, Bo sitting against a boulder across from Jackson, who was reclined with his head propped against the trunk of his favorite tree. There wasn't much to talk about. It all had been said a hundred times over. The bottle was nearly empty when Bo reminisced. "I gave her my card."

"What?"

"I told her to get an abortion. I told her I would pay for it and to call me when it was done. It was a force of habit, I suppose, but I pulled out my assistant DA business card and gave it to her. I remember she slipped it deep into her back pocket." Jackson was intensely looking at Bo as the fire glow warmed each of their faces. "It would have been on the body when they found her."

"Didn't your dad work the initial crime scene?"

They both leaned back against their respective supports. Jackson closed his eyes while Bo looked out over the dark and secretive lake.

"You're still going to do it, aren't you?" Bo asked quietly so as not to disturb his friend's rest.

"I have to. I can't live with it if I don't. And I'm too much of a coward to kill myself."

Bo put his gloves on before stretching out in front of the fire. "It's getting cold," Jackson noted. "I forgot to bring mine." And with that, Jackson closed his eyes and tried to fall asleep.

Bo, taking a deep breath as he did just before launching that Mitch Webster pitch deep into center field, walked quietly over to Jackson's backpack. It was hanging up in the tree. Bo removed it from its confinement and unzipped the lower compartment. He walked serenely over to where Jackson was sleeping against his tree. Bo's hand slid into the compartment and grasped the gun handle inside the pack. He squatted down and brought the backpack in line with Jackson's temple. Jackson slowly elevated his eyelids and looked understandingly at his friend of nearly half a century. He closed his eyes as a tear leaked onto his cheek. Without removing the gun, Bo pulled the trigger.

TWENTY-EIGHT

Intertwined Identities

(Summer 2010, continued)

The afternoon was getting late. At first light, Bo had descended the mountain to retrieve the park rangers and report the terrible accident. The rescue team was called in. They knew exactly where the campsite was and left immediately to secure the potential crime scene. The park and county authorities found the site as Bo had left it. The Grand County sheriff followed along with Bo, back up the mountain after he made the essential call. It wasn't to his parents or his ex-wife and kids. Those relationships had been strained to the point of separation for several years now. It wasn't to his chief of staff, although that was clearly going to be the next call. This first call would be to Jackson's mom. The tears seemed honest enough, at least that was what the sheriff surmised.

The scene of the accident and all the evidence was photographed. Jackson's body was bent and slumped to the side just askew from the base of his tree. His backpack and the branch were laying on the rock below another tree. Approximately three feet separated the rock and Jackson's final position on this earth. The backpack had accidently fallen upon the rock after the branch it was hanging from broke. This happened while Bo was fumbling through it for beef jerky. The impact of the pack on the irregular surface of the craggy rock caused the gun to fire. The hole in the bottom compartment created by the discharge was charred on the inside. There were only hints of Jackson's blood on the pack itself. The spray was mostly from the exit wound on the other side of Jackson's head. The tent was still in place and the fire smoldered. The night before, the blaze was big enough to have fully consumed all its contents including wood, paper, gloves, etc. Bo's backpack was still hanging from its tree across from where Bo was sitting the night before. The gun was retrieved from the tightly zipped compartment and packaged appropriately. Fingerprint analysis would later show only Jackson's prints present. When Senator Wright arrived, the deputies photographed the suspect including close-ups of Bo's shirt where traces of Jackson's blood were found. These were apparently deposited when Bo, in his anguish, ran to his friend and held him as he died. The shirt was removed and placed in an evidence bag. After the photos were completed, each additional piece of evidence was packaged for the trip down the mountain. They would be deposited at the coroner's office along with the body for further chemical and ballistic analysis.

Senator Wright was allowed to remain free but was required to stay in Granby while the investigation proceeded. The senator agreed to every demand and was initially questioned without the presence of a lawyer. Innocent people don't require representation, after all—particularly not if they are lawyers. Each of the talking points was as if they had been rehearsed for days. Additional phone interviews were made with the pertinent secondary witnesses. The gun's serial number identified Jackson's father as the lawful owner. In his absence, Jackson's brother was interviewed. He acknowledged all that was known about the gun; that they frequently took it on mountain trips, it was old but functional, and it had a hair trigger. Other family members were interviewed, many of whom didn't know that the trip was taking place. The ownership of the Aston Martin was determined, as it was fully processed for evidence. Nothing significant was found in the car. Associates were called to analyze the relationship between the two campers. When Five hung up the phone, he was sweating, bothered by the event itself and the number of words that were required of him. He sat for hours in his home and retraced every backpacking trip they had taken, including the first trip and the *thing with the Judge*. He remembered thinking at the time that it was a one in a million chance of it occurring again. For it to have occurred with a "perfect" shot to the head, one in a billion. The Sumner County sheriff gave Slim's name to the authorities but they were unable to track him down.

Senator Wright stayed at a local hotel where he stayed isolated and on the phone with his chief of staff and political advisors. They were completely sympathetic to his plight and the loss of his best friend. That was going to be necessary since they were the ones who were going to answer all the media's questions for the foreseeable future. Their tone was important. It would be much easier for the press and the public to buy into the story of the accident if staff felt the senator's pain. When Dick Cheney got away with shooting his friend while they were hunting, the vice president had actually pulled the trigger.

A preliminary hearing for Senator Wright was administered at the courthouse where no initial charges were brought and, after surrendering his passport, he was dismissed on his own recognizance. He would remain a suspect until the investigation was complete. That same day, Jackson's body was released to the family. Bo drove Jackson's car home.

The senator, after receiving advice from his attorney and chief of staff was able to skirt the media for the most part. Months later, a la Dick Cheney, he would grant an interview to Fox News in which he shared with the world his heartbreak and guilt over the chain of events that lead to Jackson's death. By the court's authority, which was clearly deferential to the respected status of the suspect, Senator Wright was allowed free movement within the continental U.S. He chose to remain in Sumner Plaine where he could deal more directly with the pain he had caused. It made him appear and feel more innocent as he continued to claimed responsibility for the "accident." The tears he shed were easy to come by. They were not contrived. The thought of Jackson's permanent absence saddened Bo deeply. Though he lied about everything else, though he was ultimately the cause of his own pain, without bother, Bo was able to coldly isolate his actions from their consequences. He would stay until after the funeral.

Bo visited his parents only once. They were living out their remaining days in a full care facility located only a mile from the family home. Bo's mom was incapable of caring for any of her physical needs and lived in the nursing section while his dad was closed off in the Alzheimer's unit in the next wing. Bo chose to visit without telling his mom of the tragedy. Besides himself, she was the only enduring love in Senator Wright's life. He wanted to at least spare her the anguish. Besides, she wasn't able to talk and couldn't respond well to anything. He assumed that her feelings were paralyzed, just as her limbs. Little did he know that the news had traveled easily to the facility. A couple of male caregivers, who like the senator, didn't understand Karen's mental capabilities, were careless about their conversations while in her room. She overheard their discussion and knew the whole story before Bo arrived. Bo thought the tears on her cheek were a result of dry eyes. She would die later that year.

Bo saw his father during the same visit. He was sitting in front of the TV in his room watching a baseball game. His room was a small and dark place with few items within reach. There was nothing on the walls, no pictures, no mementos from the past to help ease his passing into oblivion. Bo sat for a while before his dad acknowledged his presence.

"Who's winning?"

"Yes."

Bo gave him an update on Karen's condition. He told him what he knew of his grandchildren's lives. He reflected as he realized that he was unaware of the activities of his own children in much the same way his dad was uninterested now. Bo noticed his dad looking at his water container and gave him a drink. After the sheriff put the bottle on the table, he looked straight ahead and said, "Thanks, Bo." Moments later he had lost that fleeting memory. Bo left without saying another word.

The following day was to be the funeral. It was guaranteed to be well attended. Bo wanted to drop by Jackson's home to face the entire family before the funeral itself. He dreaded the visit but it had to be done. One more apology was necessary, to Jackson's brothers. Bo hadn't seen any of them for over a decade and probably wouldn't have recognized them if he had seen them on the street. After the initial uneasiness, and after the fully rehearsed mea culpa, Jackson's mom asked again if Bo would fulfill her son's wish. Before his father's funeral, Jackson had asked Bo to give the eulogy at his own future funeral and Bo had given his word. Neither had thought that it would come so quickly and in such an unusual circumstance. Bo didn't think it was appropriate or that he could actually pull it off and tried to politely demur. But the entire family encouraged him to live up to the wishes of Jackson. Bo smirked at the thought of asking Jackson now if he still had the same feelings toward the proffer of his final tribute. Finally Bo said yes. If he could actually make it through the service, it would go a long way to convincing everyone of his innocence.

Before Bo left for his hotel to prepare some words, Gabby wanted to show him Jackson's old room. There were a few things she thought Bo might like to have. There were walls lined with plaques, shelves crowded with trophies, and drawers stuffed with medals. There was an old high school yearbook and some Cat Stevens CDs. None of which were of interest to Bo. As he looked around, Bo came across a photo framed and sitting alone on the headboard of the bed. It was a picture from their first backpacking trip. Bo remembered a friendly couple taking the snapshot on Jackson's camera but he had never before seen it. He was mesmerized by the image. The four of them were leaning against Bo's family car with backpacks ready to go. Five was in overalls. Slim stooped in the background leaning against his bedroll. Jackson, postured against the car with his legs comfortably and confidently crossed, looked as if he had a wad of Red Man in his left cheek. And Bo, with his lucky Bison baseball hat turned backward, was smiling as if he had just won the big game. In Jackson's room, Bo sat on the bed while Gabby sat next to him.

"Can I keep this?" For a moment there was regret in Bo's heart.

"Of course. It should be with you." Gabby took Bo's hand and looked at him with sad eyes. "I need to confess something to you. I wish I could have done it sooner but you need to know how I feel. I loved how you and Jackson treated each other as brothers. It did my heart good through all the years."

"I always thought of him like a brother," Bo responded as he watched Gabby hesitate. She took a deep breath and then she looked away. "What is it? Mama G, you can tell me anything, if you want."

She looked at Bo's familiar face, the face she had looked upon for more decades than she would like to admit. "You and Jackson *are* brothers." The words were spoken softly but clearly. There was no mistaking what was said.

"I don't understand," Bo remarked, though he wasn't sure he wanted to hear the explanation.

"Your father and I were more than friends in high school. We continued to see each other after we both were married. I ask God for forgiveness every day, especially for the sin against your mother. She was the best woman I ever met. I don't think she knew, nor did my husband. Until now, only your father and I knew that Jackson was his son, and your brother."

Bo got up from the bed, hugged Gabby softly. He took both of her shoulders in his hands and placed his forehead against hers. Without saying a word, he left abruptly. She remained in the room, clutching Jackson's pillow and crying.

***

Bo felt sick as he rose from the pew to make the short walk to the pulpit. He was sitting with all of Jackson's friends on the front row as honorary pallbearers. It was half of the 1976 championship baseball team. Only Slim was missing, though his name appeared in the funeral bulletin. Honorary because the damage to Jackson's skull made cremation the obvious option. His ashes were placed on a pedestal surrounded by flowers and a single picture of Jackson in his KU Jayhawk team jersey, a shiny bat laid over his left shoulder and a smile that went on forever. Only the snapshot of the four boys that she had given to Bo had greater significance to Gabby.

At the top of the stairs, as he approached the pulpit, Bo purposely avoided looking at the family. Yet, like a compass drawn north, his gaze would convey in her direction with each pause of his eulogy. Most who attended the service were unaware of the details of the fabricated story. They knew only of a tragic accident that ended the life of the hometown hero and Bo's best friend. Some attendees, those who took the time to find out the details, were incredulous of the whole thing. A few agreed to be interviewed by the press, but none of them ever thought Bo would have been involved in something unspeakable. A few individuals speculated that Jackson committed suicide and that Bo was helping to cover it up and save his best friend's reputation. All eyes were on the senator. No cameras were allowed but the local, state, and national media were present throughout the back of the church. Bo cleared his throat and looked at Gabby. He became lost in that moment to the point that people were beginning to be uncomfortable with the silence. He took a drink of water and began.

"On behalf of Jackson and his family, I want to thank you all for attending this memorial service. If we all look inward enough, each one could come up with a myriad of reasons for being here. Many of you are close to Gabby and Jackson's brothers. Some of you grew up with Jackson. A few played ball with him. Others attended university and law school with him. One woman, whom I just met, knew him professionally and flew out here from California. Some were Jackson's teachers and coaches. Others were just individuals that filled the stands to admire the talent that comes to a small town like Sumner Plaine once in a lifetime. I probably fit into most of those categories but, as most of you know, am least fit to be offering this eulogy." Bo stopped for a moment and looked at his fingers. They were pale and uncontrollably shaking. He looked again at Gabby, whose eyes were sympathetic and supportive.

"Jackson and I first met as children while playing on the same YMCA basketball team. We have been friends ever since. I'm amazed that we have remained so close for so long. What's more surprising is that we became friends at all. We were so different, especially when we were young. Sports were our common thread but it was one of just a few. He was a young man whose reputation preceded him. I was trying to find my own. He was a natural. I was a work in progress. He kept me in the crowd. I kept him from the crowd. He was humble. I desired anything that would give me a reason to be humble. Jackson never thought he was as good as the world knew him to be. I always thought I was better than everyone knew I was. I loved him like a brother ... But, I didn't always respect him. He respected me like a mentor yet learned to love me. I envied him at first. It took me years to realize that life for Jackson, though appearing so easy, was difficult and trying. Most of us have limited capabilities while maturing and are restricted naturally toward one direction in life. Jackson's numerous abilities were constantly pulling him in multiple directions, often simultaneously. In the battle between the demands of the world, the desires of the heart, and the expectations of both, there are no winners. Only survivors.

"When Jackson moved to Los Angeles and I started a career in Topeka, we lost touch with each other. We had new families, different friends, unique business associates and acquaintances. I would find myself comparing the merits and values of old friends vs. new ones.

Past vs. present. I needed only to hear Jackson's voice or see his smile to know the answer. We had more in common than baseball, more than a school or a hometown, we had a past. Our intertwined identities were steeped in that history. We both are who we are in great part because of each other. We were different links in an unbreakable chain forged by the fire of time, experience, and Sumner Plaine. Such a union could only be shattered by the tragedy of Jackson's death but its existence will be impossible to forget. I thought he was immortal but now, I realize that only feelings are eternal."

Bo sighed and looked up from his prepared words. "I like classical music. A novice, like myself, looks at a music score and see notes. One note equals one pitch, singularly important but singular. An artist looks at the same score and sees something much different. That musician sees association, relationships between individual notes and the relationships of those notes to time. Unison melodies can communicate. They can even move the spirit but they lack the ability to be engaged. When two or three or four different notes are placed in proper time and accord, something magical happens. At times those individual notes, by chance or by choice, can be placed in the wrong position or at an improper time. When that transpires, dissonance occurs. The risk of which drives many back to the security of a unison melody, where there is less risk. From the first clef to the final bar, two or three or four different notes orchestrated in proper time and cohesive relationship create new identities that would never have existed without the presence of the others and without the influence of time; no longer a tone, but music."

"We're born. We die. And in between, we have to find our way. We get to choose when and with whom we share our time. When we are forced to go it alone, we can survive but with limited potential. If we're lucky and others allow us into their space, our capacity changes and a new identity emerges. We're no longer a sound, we're part of a song. Sometimes in strife, sometimes in symphony. Jackson gave me a voice. He allowed me into his life, he offered me an identity I never could have realized on my own. It was a gift I will never …" Bo looked at Gabby and started to cry. He closed by saying, "I'm so sorry."

To all who heard his voice, even the most skeptical of pundits, Bo's sentiments were heartfelt and sincere. Most thought it was the best eulogy they had ever heard. Is it possible that the best way to express a falsehood is to be totally honest in your feelings? At the cemetery, Bo stood alone in the periphery. He left without confronting the family again. Gabby looked for him but Bo clearly didn't want to be seen. He wasn't sure what he would say or how he should react in light of the fact that he killed her son, his brother. He decided in true Scarlett O'Hara fashion to think about that at another time.

About a week after the funeral, Senator Wright was required to appear before a judge in Colorado. The district hearing was in Denver. He would hear the findings of the investigation and the stipulations of the court. It was a formality. The county prosecutor had called the senator earlier and said there was no evidence of foul play and that no charges were to be filed on behalf of the state in the death of Jackson Stillwell. Since no charges were brought, there was always the possibility that they could be instituted at a later date; however, at that time, the senator was not guilty in the eyes of the law of the state of Colorado. Bo left immediately for Washington. For the first time, Bo found safety and solace *away* from Sumner Plaine.

TWENTY-NINE
Twenty Million

(Fall 2013)

I t's difficult to absorb the imprint left over time by Sumner Plaine's
most familiar names. Jackson, for his athletic prowess, and Bo, for
his political accomplishments, became the most famous of all its citizens. If not for Jackson's untimely demise and the suspicious nature
of his death, both would have had signs with their names and plaques
with their accomplishments at every entrance port into Sumner County.
Now knowing our protagonists as they truly were, that obviously would
have been a mistake. It's hard to understand why we as humans do that.
Why is it that we create statues and memorials to people? It doesn't take
long before you realize that they were mortal failures also. Evil, like a
virus, requires a host to exist and we all are equally culpable. None of
us are deserving of adulation. Why not have memorials to ideals, to
principles, to moments in time where good overcame evil, anything but
human beings. As it was, their names are ever present but only in whispered discussions; fleeting memories that whiff through the air without
daring to take hold of anything. To have watched the two as they were
in school and to now visualize their fates, you would not believe that
you were looking at the same individuals. They had started so differently, became so similar, and ended with polar opposite personalities.
Opposite to each other and of their former selves.

Jackson was dead. Slim was AWOL. Five, who did on occasion
hear from Slim but kept it to himself, had turned even more inward
than before. Of their eight core parents, only Gabby was still living,
haunted by her choices and the losses she has had to endure. Senator
Wright, conversely, thrived. The 113th United States Congress found

Senator Wright moving up as a Republican Party leader. Having cajoled his fellow Republicans, the senator was elected as minority whip of the Senate. Having ingratiated himself toward those in the majority, he was made co-chair of the Judiciary Committee. With this position, he began to take on and enjoy a more judicial appearance. Immersion within the law, historical and trending, became his new passion. In it, he developed a newfound deference for the judicial branch. The senator even became acquainted and friendly with one of the currently seated Supreme Court justices.

However, old habits endure. Senator Wright, clearly concerned about his reputation, if not his electability, coveted control of his future. This was especially true with regards to his behavior during the summer of 1992. Most would have thought that Jackson's strange death in 2010 would be more a concern but the issues regarding the accident had faded and were relegated to the back pages of left-wing conspiracy propaganda. It was 1992 that still gave him pause. It had been a long time since he had actually fretted over Jackson's murder. Those were actions of another realm, even another person. That necessary action had been tucked away as if that history belonged to someone else. But he was a practical man, never underestimating risk around his political career. His success was built on his ability to think negatively and plan accordingly.

The federal government continued to receive urgent requests from nearly every state in the union. The need for funding to alleviate the backlog of DNA testing of rape kits and felony evidence was overwhelming. Even Senator Wright, with his newfound *respect* for the judicial system, knew that eventually something would be done. Amendments and earmarks were becoming the norm. The senator found himself back in Topeka mode as he modulated the actions and controlled debate within the Judiciary Committee. Funding would eventually be authorized so he again needed to appear in accord with the wishes of those in need but limit his potential liability by manipulating the final legislative appropriation. He was more determined than ever to eliminate any possibility of DNA testing of the fetal remains of his unwanted child. He was convinced it would be his ultimate downfall if the truth was made known.

Since 2004, small selective grants had been authorized and given to eligible states to be utilized for backlog relief. They didn't make a dent and Kansas, lo and behold, didn't receive a penny. As of 2009, only twenty-six states had appropriated funds for rape kit reform. The sunflower state did not make that list either. A strong lobbying program from state judicial reform advocates and organizations like the Innocence Project placed a great deal of pressure on federal legislators. Regardless, through the Senate and House committees on Judiciary, the U.S. Department of Justice was about to authorize $45 million annually for its community-based sexual assault response initiative.

No matter his personal feelings, the train was leaving the station, again, and Senator Wright knew that if he was to appear responsive to the needs of his constituents, he would have to request a larger portion of these funds be made available to his state. Knowing full well that such a demand would not be acceptable to the Democratic majority of the Senate, Senator Wright pushed hard for five million dollars of those funds to be granted to communities in the state of Kansas. When the final allocation was brought to a more reasonable and representative percentage, two million would be authorized for Kansas. He could claim, almost credibly, that he had tried his hardest but was unable to succeed due to the Republican party's lack of majority in the Senate (a campaign position he exploited during his next re-election campaign).

The final protocol for the statewide distribution of these funds would be determined by state legislators. A level of control from which the senator was unwilling to withdraw. His strong recommendation, which would be tied to any future funding of needed state projects, was to allocate funding based on population and rape statistics. With such, a community like Sumner Plaine which had few people and even fewer rapes than most locations in Kansas, would see minimal if any of those dollars. Once again, the pride of Sumner Plaine, their local boy who became a powerful success, had altered the fate of victims for the benefit of himself. And few were the wiser.

The senator also watched with interest the expanding reach of the Innocence Project. It had opened a branch in Kansas City, Missouri, and taken on a few clients who were behind bars in Kansas. According to their statistics, the project received nearly three thousand requests per year from prisoners and their advocates who claimed wrongful convictions. More specifically, the Midwest Innocence Project had recently taken on the case of Kevin Strickland who apparently had been falsely convicted of a murder in Kansas City back in 1979. That case displayed so many similarities to Willy's conviction that it caused Bo great concern, if not outright fear.

Five, in the midst of his personal breakdown, had fired off a letter to Bo who received it at his residence. It was the only way you could get a letter through to the senator. Only a few select individuals even had that address. Bo had given it to Jackson and Five in hopes that they would one day come visit. The letter stated succinctly the anguish Five was feeling over the incarceration of Willy. It was well written, encouraging action without placing blame— although it was clear to Bo that Five held Jackson and him responsible. Subtle comments were included throughout the body of the letter. Among other things, Bo was reminded of Five's knowledge of the oil farm and its purpose. Five insinuated that somehow DNA evidence that could exonerate Willy had been blocked by political forces. And that there was still a question as to the paternal status of the fetus involved. The senator burned the letter over the stove. He chose not to reach out to his old friend.

Weeks became months. Five received an inquiry response letter from the Midwest Innocence Project. He, with the help of Sheriff Randy Ray, had sent an inquiry and application to the organization. They were evaluating Willy's case. The letter stated unequivocally that the costs of such investigations and the limited resources available should lessen his assumption that Willy's case would be chosen. However, there was a small possibility that it would match their criteria for selection. In that case, Five and Willy would hear from a staff attorney. The timeline could take as much as five years. With that, Five was both elated and dejected, all in the same moment.

Months became years. Bo had forgotten about the letter he received from their team's former third baseman. The lethargic distribution of funds barely kept up with the current criminal caseload of rapes and felony evidence. There wasn't much interest or opportunity for utilizing those limited funds for crimes committed more than ten years ago. The Sumner County murder that was still quietly discussed around restaurant tables was now twenty-three years in their past. Senator Wright had attempted to convince state legislators to limit DNA testing to twenty years or less but failed to conjure enough support to have a bill authored for debate. And so, like Willy, it sat. "It" being the untested rape kit of the Valeria Hernandez's precious unborn child. The result of which would at least add a significant witness to the case if not cast reasonable doubt on Willy's guilt. State statute required the perpetual retention of such pieces of evidence but no similar guidance on its disposition. It made many angry. You have a problem: unsolved crime. You have a new invention to address this problem: DNA testing. You choose, instead of solving the problem with the solution at hand, to live with the problem instead. Solving problems is clearly not the design of the modern political machine.

What is the design of the current political apparatus? It is the perpetual pursuit of money. Perhaps it's too cynical to state that all elected authorities are concerned with money more than service. It's possible that some public servants begin altruistically but find that the system itself is the restraining factor. One that is impossible to overcome because of its inability to function on behalf of anything other than itself. The senator allowed himself to be seduced by the power without the need for purpose. It had become easy for him to exist and thrive without doing anything of importance. His primary concern then, as every year, was raising funds for the next campaign.

The 2012 election had depleted his accounts even though his feckless opponent was no match at all. Prior to that election, Senator Wright was concerned and, in his mind, needing to rehabilitate his image. After the accidental yet suspicious death of his friend two years earlier, he couldn't be too cautious. Taking direction from the Chappaquiddick playbook, Senator Wright decided to play the sympathy card and place himself in the public eye as someone who suffered as much as his victim. Needless to say, this took a lot of effort and money but, in the end, led him to an easy victory and an increased approval rating. Or it could be that killing someone isn't enough to unseat a Republican incumbent in Kansas.

Even with the need for campaign funds, the senator restricted his position and only allowed high-flying donors time with him on Friday afternoons. There could be exceptions but, as we all know, this was quite rare. One Friday his secretary added a name unfamiliar to the senator. "It's a woman. She says the two of you have met. And it would potentially be a large campaign donation." First of all, at his age, gender no longer held the allure it once did. Also, everyone said they know the senator and were interested in making a donation. He had met tens of thousands of individuals over the years. He shook off the request but his secretary pushed back. "I think you should consider this one." Her eyes and tone were convincing.

"Okay, show her in."

"She's not here anymore. She wants to have lunch with you tomorrow."

"That I will not do."

"Are you sure?" she queried, placing a note in front of the senator. In unfamiliar handwriting, it read "20 million" and was signed "Ms. Evans."

"Set it up."

A humble Georgetown deli that was chosen as the semi-clandestine spot. Bo still didn't recognize her until she mentioned the occasion of their one and only introduction. "We met at Jackson's funeral." He struggled to recall as most of that day was hazy at best.

"You were the one who flew in from California, weren't you Ms. ..."

"You can call me Crystal."

Bo stopped cold as he walked around to his side of the table. As he turned and looked into those sad yet attractive eyes, he recognized the name. "I'm so sorry. I wish I would have asked your name at the funeral. We could have spent some time together." The senator knew that wasn't true but thought it was what a normally sensitive individual would have said. He sat down without taking his eyes off her. "So, you're the first one to steal Jackson's selfish heart."

"He wasn't all that bad."

"Hell he wasn't. I grew up with him," Bo said half-jokingly.

"I wasn't sure that I should or even wanted to go to the funeral, but I'm glad I did. Your words, they meant something to me. Afterward, I somehow felt more accepting of his death, my life, everything."

"Thank you. But you could have put all that in a note. Why come here?"

"Two reasons. You were all he talked about anytime Sumner Plaine was the topic of conversation. I wanted to meet you more socially. The other, you already know, or you wouldn't be here."

"Ouch."

"About a year after Jackson's death I received a phone call followed by a letter. They were both from a lawyer with one of the biggest firms in Los Angeles. Jackson had left me his entire estate. If my son was still alive, I would have kept it all for his sake but now, the money just brings up memories of a dream that turned into a full-fledged horror show."

"I'm sorry about your son. Can I ask what happened?"

"Thank you. He came along after Jackson. He committed suicide." Her words were somber and with little emotion. With practice, she had grown to accept all that fate had to offer. Jake's suicide occurred three months after Jackson was murdered.

"I knew he was successful, but twenty million!"

"I lied. It's actually more. I used some to pay off the mortgage on my dad's house. He left it to us after he passed. I took about 150 thousand to shore up my 401K, and I kept the one thousand shares of stock left in Jackson's portfolio. That left about twenty-two million dollars. You were his best friend. He loved you. He believed in you. He would have wanted you to have it."

"I don't know what to say. Thank you."

After lunch, they walked through the parking lot and stopped at Bo's car. She smiled. "I remember this. Jackson used to drive it when we would meet for coffee. Casino Royale Grey. Funny name for a color." She walked away without saying goodbye. When Bo asked her what stock was left in Jackson's portfolio, she said. "Tesla. I think they make batteries."

Now the senator was smiling. It's hard to say if it was because she didn't know much about the stock she owned or the fact that he just made a killing on a killing. That last thought, however, didn't hang around long. It had become part of Bo's internal defense mechanism. Any notion that brought attention to his unprincipled actions was quickly eliminated from his daily cognition and sequestered to the hidden part of the brain where no illumination could reach.

THIRTY

It's the President

(Summer 2016)

While still physically and spiritually acute, Bo found the mental aspect of the day in and day out of his senatorial life taxing. Each step into the arena required more preparation than the day before. Always needing the right answer, remembering what lies he had told, how each related to reality, you could see the mental garnishment that this game was demanding from the wages of his success. It was the in-between moments when it was most noticeable. He was frequently caught staring out the window while losing his focus on an issue at hand. He would retreat whenever possible. Phone conferences in his office. Coffee breaks in lonely unused lounges. Working lunches while sitting alone on a bench across the street in Senate Park. Always loving the drama of the Senate floor, he began watching debates on a monitor instead of in person. Some would claim he was reflecting on the personal hardship the last few years had created for him. But for Bo, he was again becoming bored with the mundane aspect of his existence.

The year 2016 saw an unusual alteration in the political landscape, especially within conservative movements. It was as if colliding black holes warped a wrinkle in the dark matter of space and the effects of the waves created some type of invisible social variation on earth. And it was all over the globe. The balanced and minimally oscillating political pendulum was beginning to swing hard to the right. In the United States, it was more than just a conservative shift. The reality TV society had nominated one of its own. And things were about to change. Most didn't see it coming, but those who did found new strength in old political positions. Senator Wright, although not the first to grab a seat on the Trump election bandwagon, held quietly in the shadows only until the path of the chosen was cleared. Prior to the official nomination, the senator became one of the new Republican presidential nominee's fiercest supporters, and as such, a recipient of the President's favor.

The fervor created by the Republican Senate months prior to this presidential election clarified where the political priorities of the party abided. The extraordinary move to disregard a Supreme Court nomination offered nearly an entire year before an election simply because you have the power to do so spoke to their absolute compulsion in dictating the makeup of the third branch of government. In a way, nothing else mattered. It was more important than gun rights and pro-life positions put together. The Senate put their faith and no small amount of political capital on the line by doing so. An act that all party members were in favor of. Senator Wright led the way. The hope that Donald Trump would be able to nominate one or maybe two justices to the Supreme Court became the dream of all political dreams. The Democrats refused to believe it possible and the Republicans refused to wake up. As the Democratic nominee for the Supreme Court became an afterthought, whispers about his replacement were rampant.

Rumors are the street drugs of Washington, D.C. Their existence is acknowledged and despised, yet once exposed, their addictive bond becomes difficult to sever. If Trump could get elected and the Senate remain in Republican hands, the process of choosing a replacement for Justice Scalia would shift toward a new conservative nomination. The rumored list of possible choices was long in the beginning. So, when Senator, and former judge, Wright's name was mentioned, most in the press and the Senate ignored the implications. Senator Wright himself dismissed it as hearsay or background media noise. It did, however, cause him to reminisce. He recalled with contentment his years as district judge. Each memory piqued emotions to the point that he had completely forgotten, or at least easily ignored, the more corrupt aspect of his term. Like the murder of his best friend, something in Bo's core had been altered to the point that his memories of past sins were easily abandoned. Character flaws that would harbor just below the surface and torment the mind of the most heinous of criminals could, for Bo, be erased as if they had been reassigned to someone else.

A lifetime appointment to the Supreme Court was as unfathomable now as it would have been back then. Still, he had to realize that it wasn't completely out of the realm of possibilities, and so, he created a task force within his staff to covertly research the potential and poll members of the public and Senate Judiciary to see what direction the winds were blowing.

Over the next few weeks, still months prior to the November election, nothing negative had arisen with regards to the senator. It became clear that his past issues surrounding Jackson's death had not affected his favorability; he quite possibly could make the short list of nominees. The thought thrilled the senator. In fact, he had discovered a new obsession. All actions from this point forward, every speech, every appearance, each bill sponsored, had to propel his image as a solid conservative legal authority with great expertise and wisdom. The senator directed his chief of staff to double the number of members on the payroll. They were to implement a campaign-like strategy with the intent of placing his name on that short list. But by this time, everyone realized that the decision could not be wrestled out of the hands of Mr. Trump. Senator Wright was completely aware of this also. He had spent enough time with the man to realize how unconventional his decision-making was. This worked in the senator's benefit. He had spent a lifetime making people believe what he wanted them to believe. Those with the greatest ego and lowest IQ were the easiest to sway. He had three months to mold the thoughts and impress the sensibilities of the Republican presidential nominee.

The day of the election arrived. Late that evening, after the stunning results were official, the Senate majority leader was on the phone congratulating President-elect Trump and offering his assistance in all transitional requirements. The first of which were the motions needed to create a quick and efficient vote within the Senate for a new Supreme Court justice. The leader was surprised at how quickly the list was made available to those who would be involved in the vetting of each name. Only a few individuals outside of the President-elect himself were knowledgeable of the list's content, but as interviews were held and background checks were made, there were five good guesses as to the actual names being considered. Amongst those names was that of the boy from Sumner Plaine. The office of Senator Wright had no comment when approached by the press and in an interview with Fox News, the senator was respectful of the process and coy as to his potential. He skillfully dodged questions and properly deflected insinuations as to his candidacy. All the while, his campaign machine was in full-court press mode. They were now specifically charged with engaging each member of the Senate Judiciary committee responsible for placing the President's choice for the Supreme Court vacancy before the full Senate.

It didn't take long for individuals in Sumner County to receive phone calls from the FBI and Senate Judiciary staff members. They were requesting background information on Bo. Some thought it was another investigation into Jackson's death. Others knew it was regarding a possible Supreme Court nomination. People began to feel left out if they didn't receive a call or email requesting information. At the coffee shop, some would make up stories or aggrandize their experiences with the investigators. Others would fabricate a nonexistent call completely. It was at least another opportunity for the small community in southwest Kansas to feel important in a world that didn't know it existed.

Only strongly bipartisan motions of truly important issues move along quickly within the halls of Congress. The only other action that rivals this level of impatient efficiency is the act of filling vacant seats to influential positions orchestrated by a single party in the midst of a unique power-grabbing opportunity. The nomination was to move to a full floor vote within two weeks of the President's inauguration. The President's staffers, along with the FBI and Judiciary Committee, needed to quickly finalize their background checks before making their final recommendation. And, they were down to two names.

Three days before the nomination was to be announced, there were two individuals brought to D.C. for closed-door interviews with high-ranking members of all three investigating entities. These were secret meetings for the most part and the identities of the witnesses were known only to those in the loop. Senator Wright, although he was one of the last names on this shortest of lists, was definitely in the loop. Only he would recognize and understand the importance of one of the witness's name, Brad Andrews. Five had received emails from the FBI to which he did not respond. We all can imagine how the phone interview went. He received a hand-delivered subpoena the following day.

In a perfect world, where good people get recognized and awarded for their selfless accomplishments, Five would have called Bo and the two would have shared a good laugh over dinner following Five's interview with the committee. He was in and out of the city the same day. But he didn't come alone. A friend, who wanted to stay for a while, joined him for the jaunt. Five's companion had never been to Washington, D.C. There's a lot to take in.

Senator Wright waited out the verdict in his office, even refusing to take part in the normal obligations of his position. He sat at the window and looked out onto his world. Once again, he had withdrawn to somewhere deep within. He had been told to expect a call from the President sometime that afternoon and the senator wasn't going to move until that call came. Each time one of the lines on his phone would blink, he would casually stare at it until it stopped and disappeared. His heart jumped when a line remained lit for some time and the door to his office opened. It was his secretary.

"It's the President."

THIRTY-ONE
Are You in Need of Confession?

(Spring 2017)

The call was cordial and complete. The two knew each other well enough that the conversation didn't require a professional foundation. The President acted as if the choice was inevitable. The senator performed as if the decision was astonishing. Neither sentiment was credibly true. They would both feel satisfaction at the conclusion of the call. One would think that of the President. But to be informed that you had just been nominated for the highest judicial position in the land, in the most judicially regulated country since the beginning of time, more excitement would have been expected. People started to notice this with Bo. Colleagues and co-workers alike saw this change. The calm demeanor he presented bordered on arrogance. As if all aspects to his life were destined for greatness. He might not have known it from the beginning, however in Bo's mind, every success in his life had been patterned through time. Each accomplishment was less a personal achievement and more fulfilling providence.

Senator Wright was left alone to contemplate the fortunate status in which he found himself. He thought momentarily about the preparations necessary for his testimony before the Senate Committee on the Judiciary, but what would have stirred caution no longer burdened him. There would be the standard partisan vitriol presented by the Democratic minority yet the votes had already been tabulated or he would not have received the nomination. No, he had only one real desire though it was almost as fleeting as his concern for the Judiciary hearing. He actually wished for a moment he could call Jackson. Bo hustled that sensation away as quickly as possible. Even he couldn't tolerate such hypocrisy.

The senator remained in his office for the rest of the afternoon accepting calls of congratulations and well wishes. He was just about to leave when his secretary entered the office.

"Do you know a Father Batchelder?" The senator's expression confirmed that he did not. "He didn't think you would. It's a new occupation, apparently. He said to tell you it's Slim." Bo just stared at her. "He's here. He's wearing a cassock and a clerical collar. He seems legit." Then she smiled. "Do you want me to get rid of him or are you in need of confession?"

"I don't know who he is. Tell him I'm not available."

It would take about three weeks to go through the formality of Senate approval before Bo would be sworn in and be seated on the court. He had plenty of time to think about how this happened. He stopped all of his senatorial actions and left any responsibilities to his staff. A new appointment for the senator's seat in Congress would not come from the governor for another month. Bo didn't care. This was a coronation. He deserved to relax his way in preparation for his duties as one of the most powerful persons in the country. He used to think being a United States senator was just about as powerful as you could get, yet there, he was still only one in one hundred. In reality, only one in five hundred thirty-five. In comparison, one in nine! Pretty impressive. Who would have thought? Not Jackson, not Bo, not S.P. If it wasn't such a travesty of justice, all would have considered it a dream come true. Yet, would you actually consider it as such? While in high school, Bo would have been satisfied becoming a teacher and coach, with a family and a home in Sumner Plaine. After law school, he would have loved being a respected attorney in the state capital. Or even a local politician with the esteem and dignity his wife and children knew him to possess. Does it count as a dream come true if it never was a dream? Little did he know that the dream was about to be permanently altered.

Philosophers and spiritualists throughout history have noted that for those persons who claim worldly accomplishments per their own honorable merits, when in reality, those achievements had been purchased by unscrupulous resources, a rectifying response is provoked within the cosmos to keep that person's destiny appropriately muted. And in this case, the counterbalancing reaction to Justice Wright's illegitimate success was occurring in a KBI warehouse in Topeka, Kansas. Stock container #LB-1201960, a medium-sized waterproof vessel consisting of ten similarly dated packages of biological evidence, was being removed from its elevated perch. Amongst those ten kits was Evidence SC1992.2, which held samples of the fetal remains of Valeria Hernandez's unborn child. It would take three months for the testing results to be made available for investigative purposes.

In June of 2017, a certified document landed on the desk of County Prosecutor North. It contained the information he had been waiting for since his motion for a second murder trial nearly ten years ago. Even before opening the parcel, he called into his office one assistant attorney and two paralegals to discuss the preparations needed to refile the motion against Willy Harper. Prosecutor North started giving out instructions as he opened the parcel. He was in mid-sentence when the actual results became known to him. He stopped. He looked out the window as if he was looking for help understanding what had just passed before his eyes. He re-read the document a second time while those in the room stared in perplexed deliberation at their boss. North quickly shoved the information back into the envelope and quietly dismissed his co-workers. The door was shut and the ambitious prosecutor remained at his desk for the next four hours trying to get his head around this shocking change in the status of this case. Was this just a coincidence? A justice on the Supreme Court, in an earlier life, was about to have a child out of wedlock and an acquaintance of his just happened to kill the child's mother for some unrelated reason? Not likely. Was her and the unborn child's deaths a murder for hire? Possibly, but why wouldn't Willy turn on his accomplice to cut a better deal? With Senator Wright's conspicuous attempts to impede the DNA testing of the fetus, it would appear that he had reason and intent to interfere with the investigation. Was it possible that Willy was an innocent victim and that someone else killed Valeria? Perhaps. Could it have been someone more closely associated with the senator? Maybe, but there's no evidence toward any of those ends. Could it be that a sitting justice on the Supreme Court of the United States of America was a murderer? And how did this all relate to the peculiar circumstances surrounding the death of Jackson Stillwell?

In all his deliberations, Prosecutor North came to an unsettling conclusion. Regardless of what course he was to take, he was going to have to admit error, egregious error, in the conviction of Willy Harper. For someone with ambitions of political successes, that so far have been unrealized, this marring of his record would surely end his political career. Even if he was able to somehow get an arrest warrant for Justice Wright, the case would immediately be snapped up by officials in the Kansas or U.S. Department of Justice. Perhaps this information was best kept below the radar of other entities. Because if this evidence wasn't exculpatory, at the very least it created reasonable doubt in the conviction of Willy. North didn't know what to do. He was going to have to get an additional legal opinion as to his obligations regarding this information, but who could he trust not to run with such scandalous information?

At the offices of the KBI, a thorough yet discreet investigation had actually been in the works while North sat on his hands and hoped the problem would simply go away. Only after this investigation concluded and the decision was taken to charge Justice Wright with double homicide did the director inform Mr. North. The agreement between the two would be that the KBI would not find fault in the prosecution of Willy Harper if Prosecutor North would agree to cooperate with the decisions of the Bureau. He was also to provide supportive documentation and evidence needed to connect past trial information with that of a new and, as of yet, undisclosed witness's testimony. There was really no choice in the matter.

The investigative conclusions were as follows: Justice William B. Wright, in the spring of 1992, did create an unwanted pregnancy with Valeria Hernandez. Approximately three months later, in a location frequented by the victim, the accused, and his friends, Mr. Wright did purposely and willfully commit a fatal assault on Miss Hernandez and attempted to cover up the crime by hiding the corpse in the milo field south of Sumner Plaine. In order to further conceal his actions, Justice Wright withheld evidence during the trial of Willy Harper and created barriers to the procurement of DNA testing during and subsequent to that investigation. In addition, the death of Jackson Stillwell, a close and long-standing acquaintance of Justice Wright, was now considered suspicious and not coincidental. Though difficult to prove, newly obtained testimony made Justice Wright a strong suspect in the murder of perhaps the only individual with knowledge of the crime, Mr. Stillwell. When called upon, Prosecutor North would corroborate the findings and admit that evidence provided for the conviction of Willy Harper was completely circumstantial.

The pieces were in place. Something this explosive had to be handled delicately. It would clearly be best if Justice Wright would turn himself in voluntarily without incident. Utilizing FBI officers, a warrant was delivered to Justice Wright as well as his attorney explaining the charges in detail and that he would have thirty hours to turn himself in to authorities within the District of Columbia. The documents were delivered simultaneously on Friday, September 8, 2017, at eleven a.m. Bo's attorney couldn't believe it. He made numerous calls to the newest justice on the Supreme Court but none were returned. Bo spent the afternoon shuttered in his office making the mental calculations needed to ascertain his options. He would, as he had done so many times before, take the lead in determining his defense strategy and media presentation. His talking points were quickly manufactured and points of evidence were written as if he were going to represent himself in court. The smug son of a bitch thought this was just another bump in the road. The fact that he had killed the only person who would be able to verify his innocence; the consideration that his entire political career had been used to obfuscate evidence that would now become obvious to the entire world; the understanding that his year-long dream of being a Supreme Court justice just went out the window even if he were to be found innocent of these murders, didn't cross his mind as he prepared for his next *political* challenge.

Bo left the office at his usual time for a Friday, allowed his staff to go home early, and made his way to his favorite bistro for dinner. As a justice, he had made it a point not to associate with many of the questionable individuals that were common companions when he was a sitting U.S. senator. Having no other friendly acquaintances, eating alone became the norm. This quiet, solitary Friday evening dinner in a back corner of a small restaurant near his Georgetown condominium was no different than any other evening. Small ribeye, au gratin potatoes, asparagus, and a glass of wine would be the fare. The only thing different on this evening would be that Justice Wright would spring for a much more expensive bottle of wine, the one he had been eyeing for some time yet unwilling to lever his wallet that far open. He took the remaining contents of the Chateau Lafite Rothschild and a serving of peach and pistachio tart on his walk back to his home. The lingering aspects of his evening would be spent consuming the remainder of his meal, catching up on the news, and a quiet read before going to bed.

***

The following day, Justice Wright arrived at the Supreme Court office complex to tidy his desk, read a few emails, listened to his lone voice message, and finalize an opinion he had started three days prior. It was his habitual Saturday practice, never liking to leave things unattended prior to a busy Monday's work schedule. He went through the motions of the morning, gathered his belongings, and took lunch to his favorite bench in Senate Park not two blocks away. He carried his heavy briefcase and the sandwich purchased from the basement cafeteria. The briefcase was heavier than normal because, in addition to the standard number of correspondences he would review over his lunch break, he brought along the handgun that he'd bought for protection over a decade ago.

After he finished his meal, he reread the transcript from Five's testimony before the Judiciary Committee. The testimony of the closed hearing was made available to Bo after he received the nomination. There were eighty-seven questions asked of Five. Each was summarily answered "yes," "no," or "I can't answer that." Bo almost laughed as he envisioned the impotence of the committee in the presence of such an unshakable entity. Yet the voice message he listened to that morning was from Five. Something in that cryptic recording troubled Bo. He again read the arrest warrant from the KBI, which he received the day before. He had till five o'clock to surrender or be subject to public arrest. He couldn't be quite sure but Bo assumed he was being trailed by the FBI and that an arrest would be made eminently if he failed to appear. He looked across the vast park and was mesmerized by the sight of a father and son playing catch.

THIRTY-TWO
Mom Says I Have To

(Fall 1966)

The soul of a community lies within its children. Though a soul is immeasurable, a community's support of those most in need is part of the natural warmth that incubates the proper development of that spirit. A community's hope for its children is only overshadowed by its obligation to them. Sumner Plaine was such a community. It operated on the premise that all bad people were once good kids. And in that community, all its citizens took pride.

Most small communities are similar. They are good at providing resources for families and children. Sumner Plaine school district, city recreation department, YMCA, even private organizations, found satisfaction in the fact that the youth of the community were always given what they needed in order to enjoy a happy and productive childhood. The education was always exceptional with curriculums that offered a balance of learning and activities. Most of those social programs, like music and athletics, didn't kick in until junior high. The city rec and YMCA were created for just such a gap. They provided summer and after-school activities as well as individual and team sports for kids to enjoy. In Sumner Plaine, these started in third grade. They were vital programs, especially for single-parent families where time was limited and support was inadequate. Not so for Jackson and Bo. Especially at this young age where paternal dreams were at their peak and any extra attention was welcomed by eager children. Jackson's older brothers and their dad had him involved at the earliest possible date. No matter what the sport, Jackson was in the middle of all family training. Bo's earliest and most fond memories were of him and his dad in the backyard playing catch. It was an activity that ceased abruptly when the sheriff realized the limitation of his son's athletic talent—long before Bo wished it would have.

This was the beginning of Jackson and Bo's journey. They played on different teams during flag football that year but were coincidentally teamed up in the winter basketball program. If you think that junior high basketball is a joke, third grade is a complete riot. Most kids show up with a tacit understanding of the shape of the ball and that's about it. All, that is, except little Jackson Daniel Stillwell. In an attempt to give all children a chance to learn the game, their coach had to make a rule change. Jackson was not allowed to steal the ball until at least one shot had been attempted by the other squad. He had already learned the art of timing up the opponent's dribble in order to snatch the ball without fouling the player. He would then easily drive the length of the floor to score an easy layup. Once the rule was in force, at least a few kids were actually able to get a shot off.

The practices and games, for the most part, were unremarkable. Once in high school, if you would have asked Jackson or any other participant on their third-grade team what they remembered about that season, the answer would be nothing. Bo, however, was different. There were a couple of instances that he would recall many years later.

He remembered his first introduction to Jackson and thought it was weird, even for third graders. Bo actually recalled their first practice and the excitement of another team sport. His mom and Jackson's mom were sitting together and watching the kids run through their drills and work on their technique. At the end of the practice, Jackson went up to Bo and asked him his name.

"William but my family calls me Bo."

"Well, which is it?"

"Bo. What's your name?"

"Jackson. My mom says I have to be your friend."

"Okay." And with that Jackson turned and ran toward his mother.

Competition at that age was limited and a team was only as good as its best player. Jackson made their team unbeatable. The scores were always 22–4 or some such spread. Jackson would always score sixteen points, Bo would score four, and some other lucky boy would throw up a prayer that would find its way through the hoop. It was the same for each game. No one knew how, it just played out that way.

At that age, the dads rarely came to the games and never to a practice. Another of Bo's memories, one that for some reason he hung on to for years, was the first game his dad came to. His bark was quite noticeable in the mostly empty gymnasium and easily discerned from the floor. His dad would applaud when Bo made a basket or stole the ball but the constant coaching from the stands bothered Bo. Not for what you might consider, that of a child being embarrassed by a loud and obnoxious parent living his dream of basketball greatness vicariously through his eight-year-old son. The coaching his dad was offering seemed to be directed at Jackson, instead of Bo. Bo would hear "drive" when Jackson had the ball or "stay low, Jackson" when he was on defense. After the game Bo's dad even pulled Jackson back on the court to offer a pointer on free throws.

Bo's dad showed for only one other game but, apparently, had gotten the message somehow. It was the season-ending championship game. He sat next to Jackson's dad and didn't say a word. The team won, 22–6.

By that time, all the teammates were familiar enough that friendships were forming. Jackson and Bo were frequently brought together, even after the season was over. Their parents were old acquaintances from high school, and each liked the idea of their son being an influential part of the other boy's life. They would schedule family gatherings together. They would alternate the responsibility of carpooling to practices and providing snacks for games. The time spent in their vehicles became yet another opportunity to become better acquainted. Similarly, the two homes became as familiar to one child as the other.

Jackson and Bo weren't always on the same team but if strings could be pulled or favors offered, during the next season they would be teamed up again. These grade-school sporting programs were the only time Jackson and Bo were together. They went to different elementary schools and different churches. Which was probably a good thing for Bo. Jackson, though constantly encouraged by his mother, didn't seem to think much of Bo. And if Bo would have been shown up by Jackson any other place besides the basketball court or the baseball field, his parents didn't think his little insecure heart could have taken it.

The friendship finally started to warm when Bo was invited to stay the night at Jackson's house. It would be the first of many sleepovers for the two. Away from the sporting arena, Bo could hold his own and Jackson found an acceptance of his friend, if not complete respect. Both mothers doted on the pair. Jackson and Bo would soon consider their "second mother" as lovingly and respectfully as their first. The boys would be the connecting point of two families. Families linked by community, by school, and by blood. For what could be more unifying than two young friends who treated each other like brothers.

Epilogue

Who are those boys?

Bo, satisfied by his sandwich, continue to enjoy the sight of the father-and-son activity on the expansive green lawn. As I watched Bo on that bench, I couldn't quite tell if he was dejected by his failure to ultimately fool the system, or the realization that he finally had found something in which he could truly find pride, yet now, it would become a destiny unfulfilled. I wasn't sure if his somber disposition was from realizing that he risked everything just to cover up an illicit affair and unwanted pregnancy. Something that, though immoral, legally occurs on a daily basis within our current state and federal governments. My guess was that his sullen demeanor was caused from the thought that by killing his best friend and brother, he had inadvertently stymied his only defense against murder charges and subsequently ended his own life. But he seemed more interested in the game of catch than his current state of being. I'm finding that as Bo's life comes to its climactic end, I'm losing some of my abilities of discernment. They told me that would happen.

My memory is starting to fade also. They don't encourage reminiscence up here. "The past is meaningless," they have said many times. "And there is no future. Time simply is." Still, I like to sneak in a recollection or two. My most interesting one was watching Five during his interview with the Sumner County sheriff. Randy, more so than Sheriff Wright, was a respected Sumner County officer and considered a friend of Bo's and Five's families. He was asked by the FBI to have a go at the cloistered friend of Justice Wright. It was clearly a different atmosphere to the FBI phone interview and the Senate committee hearing. I don't know if it was the friendly request of a respected member of the community. I'm not sure if it was the fact that Five was angry that Bo failed to reply to any of his and Slim's requests for communication. I'm not sure if it was simply that he was so bothered by Bo's callous disregard of the plight of Willy. But for whatever reason, Five opened up completely to Randy regarding everything Five knew about Bo's relationship with Valeria, his frequent usage of the oil farm, the likelihood that Jackson would have been aware of the pregnancy, and the information about "the thing with the Judge" that occurred on their first backpacking trip. In that moment, Five decided to contribute all that pent-up verbal capital for the benefit of Willy, the memory of Valeria and Jackson, and the soul of Sumner Plaine. When he was finished, a relief came over his face as if the worst was over and that even if it shortened his life, Sumner Plaine was worth it.

One of my earliest recollections on earth was being in a large gymnasium and playing on tall bleachers while my brother played basketball. Eventually I would sit with mom because she wanted me to watch.

"Who are those boys?" I asked.

"The one who just shot the ball, his name is Jackson. I don't know his last name. The other, the one who just passed Jackson the ball, he's William Wright. He's in your brother's class. Come to think of it, he'll be in your class too, next year."

I loved my mother. She always said that I had a gift; I could learn so quickly. By the time I was a second grader, my English skills were already better than anyone in my first-generation immigrant family. And with reading and math scores that were off the charts, the school administrators were going to move me up a grade next year. I skipped an entire year and went from second to fourth grade.

I watched the rest of the basketball game knowing I would be with those boys next fall. I became hooked. It seems far too young now, but they were my first two infatuations. At different points in time, they were my first loves. Of that, I had and have no doubt.

Of course, all it would get me was an unwanted pregnancy from one and a crushed skull from the other. I don't recall much other than how, from such an early point in my life, I wanted to be a part of theirs. Like I said, they don't encourage recollections up here. In fact, they don't let you come back at all except in extreme circumstances. My freedom to view the progress of my former existence was allowed due to my "unforeseen" death. It granted me an exemption from the *no going back* regulation. No interference mind you. That is strictly prohibited. But I was allowed to watch those who were closest to me as their lives proceeded. Once the last one was gone, I have to return.

As I continued watching Bo, the last thing I heard was "to S.P." then the sharp crack of a gunshot. I feel my vision fading.

THE END

CPSIA information can be obtained
at www.ICGtesting.com
Printed in the USA
LVHW041931170322
713623LV00005B/130